PLAYING DIRTY

A gripping crime thriller you won't want to put down

DAN LATUS

Frank Doy Book 11

Joffe Books, London
www.joffebooks.com

First published in Great Britain in 2023

Cover art by Jarmila Takač

ISBN: 978-1-80405-935-7

CHAPTER ONE

'And that's it?' George Reagan said. 'That's all you can tell me?'

The other man nodded and looked away. He was afraid to say anything more. The consequences of doing so were unpredictable, life-threatening even. He had a fervent wish not to spark an outburst of the terrible temper he had seen on so many occasions.

George Reagan stood at the window, looking out across the city to the place where the cranes were working on his new high-rise hotel. When work had first started, the groundwork that is, it hadn't been possible to see anything at all from here. How he had longed to see the structure rising, and when growth finally had got going visibly, he had watched closely and ached to see the building tower over the neighbouring apartment blocks. Now it did.

All these many months later, the hotel dominated the skyline and, from a distance at least, the building looked to be complete. It was the one physical, coherent thing he could claim to have created in his life, and would prove to be a permanent testimony to his career and life as head of the family business. No one would ever be able to take that away from him. Certainly not Oscar!

Thought of his bloody nuisance of a brother made him scowl for a moment. Oscar agreed with nothing he did or proposed, including the hotel project, which he wanted stopped. Oscar always wanted things done differently, as if on principle. He had come to be a real Trojan horse, the enemy within. George knew that fundamentally Oscar wanted to be in charge of the family business, and had long believed that he should be. Well, that was not going to happen. Not on his watch! Kid brothers, eh? Who needed 'em?

The new hotel came back into focus. Just look at it now! It had a roof and walls, sunshine was reflecting off a thousand glazed windows, and at the edge of the area where he knew the car park to be, he could even see the newly installed flag poles. Six of them, in a row. How he looked forward to seeing flags on them, all flapping in the breeze from the ocean.

He knew what flags would fly there, too. One for Reagan Enterprises, the Reagan family business empire. Then one each for the city of Puerto de la Cruz, the island of Tenerife, the Kingdom of Spain, the European Union, and even the dear old United Kingdom of Great Britain and Northern Ireland. Perfect. Everywhere that mattered to him covered.

* * *

But it wouldn't be for a little while yet, he thought with a sigh — if ever, if what he'd just been told was to be believed. The way things were going, Oscar might well get his dearest wish, and see the hotel stopped and abandoned. *Well, to hell with him! Over my dead body will that happen.*

He turned and moved away from the window, to glower at the man on the sofa on the far side of the room.

'So what you're telling me,' he snapped, his anger mounting, 'is that we're fucking bust! That it, Ed? That what you're telling me? That my brother is right, and has been all along?'

Ed Davy, accountant for Reagan Enterprises, shook his head. 'I never said that, George.'

'You might as well have done.'

'George, calm down. Please! Remember, I'm just the messenger. I can't help it if you don't like the message.'

'Yeah, yeah!'

Reagan turned back round, to look at the view from the window again.

'These are facts, George,' Davey added. 'I'm afraid you need to face them.'

'And so do you, Ed. So do you. It's your wealth and happy home life at stake here, as well as mine, remember?'

Ed Davey lifted a hand to acknowledge the point. They were in it together. He knew that. If the Reagans went down, so would he.

Nothing else was said for a minute or two. Then, with a weary sigh, George said, 'So how bad is it, really?'

'Bad enough, George. I can tell you that. We have two weeks, at most, to find the money we need. Otherwise, Oscar will be proven to have been right all along.'

CHAPTER TWO

'Rosedale,' Jimmy Mack said. 'Just for a while.'

'Rosedale?'

Looking defiant, Jimmy said it again.

'What are you going there for?'

I might as well have asked why he wanted to go any-where at all. Holidays, even short breaks, are not part of Jimmy Mack's lifestyle. He's a virtually retired fisherman, and a real home bird now. Going to the Co-op in nearby Loftus is about as far as he gets these days.

'There's a problem I need to sort out,' he said mysteriously.

'Oh? Can I help?'

He shook his head, turned and walked away.

All I could do was shrug and feel baffled. It wasn't like him to be so laconic. A problem? The only problems I could recall him ever having had all been brought to his door by me, or by my activities, and I was pretty sure I hadn't caused him any new ones recently.

I watched for a moment as Jimmy returned to his cot-tage, and then I went back inside mine, with another meta-phoric shake of my head. Something was up. I didn't know what it was, but something had got into him.

As the only two remaining residents of Risky Point, our perilous refuge on the Cleveland coast, we're good pals as well as neighbours. We're used to sharing things, including the things sent to try us, such as coastal erosion and the danger to our cottages, the last ones still standing at Risky Point. Jimmy doesn't have too many problems of his own now, but mine bring a lot of interest and engagement into his life. He complains plenty about that, when it suits him, but I believe he actually enjoys it. His life would be a bit dull without me as his neighbour.

I'm a freelance Jack-of-all-sorts when it comes to making a living: security consultant, occasional bodyguard and sometime private investigator — when someone wants a missing dog or husband found. So I generate and receive plenty of problems — far more than enough for any one person, actually. Jimmy Mack is my back-up man and confidante, and the guy who looks after the shop when I'm away from home. In return, he gets . . . Well, not very much in material terms, it must be said, but he does have a lot more eventful life.

On this occasion, I had been about to tell him that I would be away myself for a little while, but he'd beaten me to it. Leon Podolsky, my long-standing Russian pal and occasional collaborator in Prague, had called. He could use my services again, apparently, which was fine by me. It was always good to see him, and he was a generous client if and when it came to payment.

There was something else on my mind, as well. I needed a change of scene. So much had been happening here lately that Risky Point no longer felt like a safe retreat. It had just been one damn thing after another. Too many people, good as well as bad, knew where I lived, and I had become too accessible. It was time to close things down and get away for a while.

But Jim had got in first, with his announcement about going to Rosedale, a valley just a few miles away in the North York Moors. I had been so stunned that I hadn't told him I would be away as well. Not that it mattered. It was as much a courtesy as anything else. I would catch up with him again later, and let him know what I was doing before I left for Prague.

So I sorted out a few things I needed to do. Packed what I needed to take with me, sent a few emails, made sure I wouldn't be leaving any unpaid bills behind, and . . . and then lost interest and decided I'd better talk to Jimmy again immediately. I couldn't leave him wrestling with a troublesome situation that I knew nothing about. It might ruin my trip to Prague.

* * *

'It's the nephew, actually,' Jimmy said, a little more forthcoming now. 'He's got the problem.'

'In Rosedale?'

'Yes. That's where he lives.'

'What kind of problem?'

'A big one, and I told my sister I'd look out for him. So I'll have to go.'

'The sister in Whitby?'

He shook his head. 'The other one. She's dead now, bless her, but I told her before she passed away.'

Family problems, then. I decided I'd better leave him to them. I couldn't help with that kind of thing.

Just then, a young woman I didn't know came out of Jimmy's cottage and peered around, seemingly looking for him.

'Fine company you're keeping, Jim,' I suggested with a smile I couldn't hold back.

He looked round and tried to smile himself. 'It's not what you're thinking,' he said.

'No? It never is, Jim! Not where you're concerned.'

He snorted and looked both indignant and pleased at the same time.

I'll admit that by then I was quite intrigued. Jimmy didn't have many visitors, especially young women. Offhand, I couldn't remember him ever having had any of the latter that hadn't visited me first, not that I want to sound like

I'm boasting about it. I'm no ladies' man either. But I do occasionally have female clients and friends on the premises.

'Everything all right, Uncle Jim?' she called. 'We'll have to be going soon, you know.'

Ah! So that was the explanation.

Jimmy acknowledged her with a raised palm. I looked at him with fresh interest.

'Amy, my sister's girl. It's her brother, Jason, that's in trouble.'

So they were both heading for Rosedale. That sounded better. He wasn't going alone. I felt reassured.

'I'll just leave you to it,' I said, ready to turn away.

He sighed, thought for a moment and then shook his head. 'No. You'd better come in and hear about it, Frank. Maybe you can help. More than I can, anyway. It's more in your line of work than mine.'

CHAPTER THREE

'Who are you?' Jimmy's niece asked, looking at me as if I was something unpleasant the cat had brought in.

'The next-door neighbour. Frank Doy.'

She didn't look impressed. Turning to Jimmy, she said, 'Are you ready?'

'Amy, love,' he said wearily. 'I'm not really what you and Jason need. I'll do my best, but . . .'

'Come on! Let's get going,' she snapped.

'Frank, here, would be a far better fit, if I'm being honest,' Jimmy said, persevering. 'He's been a good friend for a long time, and a lot of help to me. I think we should bring him in.'

'No way!' Amy said, shaking her head violently. 'We don't need any next-door-neighbour involvement, thank you very much.'

'On that note,' I intervened quickly, 'I'm out of here. See you, Jim!'

I made my way out fast. As I said before, domestic problems are not my territory, and that was what Jimmy seemed to have right now. I wanted no part of it, or of them. It was time to get back to my own affairs.

* * *

Later, the phone rang. The landline phone. I grimaced and hesitated, my mind on how I wanted to be out of the house in the next few minutes and on my way to the airport. But the phone kept on ringing and old habits die hard. So I picked the damned thing up.

'Mr Doy? This is Amy, Jimmy Mack's niece. We met . . .'

'Hello again.'

'Hi. My uncle asked me to call you. Could you possibly come over to Rosedale to join us?'

I closed my eyes for a moment, surprised, and no little exasperated.

'It's actually a bad time, Amy. I'm just about to set off for the airport.'

'I know. My uncle told me you were going to Prague. I'm really sorry about this, Mr Doy, but Uncle Jimmy would appreciate it if you could come. And so would I. It's very important. We wouldn't be asking for your help if it wasn't.'

I smiled reluctantly at the change of tone, already seeing what was probably going to happen, and knowing I couldn't avoid it. Jimmy — the sly old fox! — would have thought Amy would have a better chance of changing my mind than he would himself. He wasn't right about that, but there we were.

'Please,' she added. 'I'm afraid I was wrong about you. I want to apologize.'

'Oh?'

'Now I know what you do for a living, I can see Uncle Jimmy was right. We do need you, or someone like you. We would pay you, by the way. Don't worry about that.'

That made me wince.

'Look, Amy, I would help if I could. I really would, believe me. And there wouldn't be any question of paying me. Your uncle means a lot to me. We're good friends. But I can't get involved in domestic or family problems. I don't do that sort of thing, and I'd be no good at it.'

'It's not what you think. The problem, I mean.'

'Isn't it? So what is it?'

9

'My brother's missing. Jason, that is. We came to help him, as arranged, but he's gone. He's just not here. And we're really afraid they've got him.'

'Who has?'

'If they have,' she said, bypassing my question, her voice wavering, 'I don't think we'll see him again. He'll be dead.'

CHAPTER FOUR

'So we're fucked? Oscar's right? Is that what you've come to tell me, Ed?'

'Not quite, George. But, as I told you, it is a difficult situation.'

'Tell me about it,' Reagan grunted.

'Long term, we should be OK. Get the hotel and casino complex up and running, and we'll have an income stream from it that will enable us to borrow more money. Short term is the problem. Default on the payment to the Italians, and they get the hotel.'

'The fucking Mafia, you mean.'

'Yes. Well, either them or the Arabs,' Davey added with a frown, reconsidering. 'They'll have to go to court to sort that out.'

'Or sort it out on the street, more likely,' Reagan pointed out.

'Probably. Anyway, the point is we signed up legally with the Italians for the default situation.'

'Only because we thought it wouldn't be a problem,' Reagan snapped.

'Agreed. And it shouldn't have been a problem. It's Covid that's done for us, us and a lot of other businesses.'

'Yeah, yeah.'

Reagan scowled as he thought about all the empty beaches and clubs, and the way their cash reserves had evaporated through loss of income as the tourists stayed at home in droves for all those months of panics and lockdowns. A couple of years even. Nobody to buy drugs any more, never mind hotel rooms.

It was too depressing to think about. He knew he'd better change the subject, for the sake of his mental health. What was gone was gone. No point worrying about it, or thinking about what might have been different. Got to just get on, and deal with the here and now. That was something he'd learned early in life. It was a lesson that had stood him well in business, as well as in other areas of life.

'So how much do we need, Ed, and when is the next payment due?'

'The due date is noon a week next Monday. By then, we need to pay ten million sterling, mostly to the Italians. That would put us in the clear for the next six months.'

'But we don't have it?'

'Nothing like it.'

'And can't borrow it?'

Ed Davey, wearing his accountant's hat, shook his head. 'The only banks and people we haven't borrowed from so far are the ones that refuse to do business with us. There might be investors somewhere in China, I suppose, but I have no idea who they would be. And looking there for funds might get us into more trouble than we're in already.'

In the uneasy silence that followed, Reagan refrained from saying it again but it was what he was thinking. They really were fucked this time. And, for once, he had no idea what to do about it.

CHAPTER FIVE

So I went to Rosedale. I had no option after Amy's phone call. She had told me they were at Jason's house, and where that was. I collected my travel bag — in the forlorn hope that I might still be able to go to Prague, maybe on a morning flight — and slung that and my emergency kit bag in the Land Rover. Then I set off.

It was close to the end of October now. The weather was chilly and damp, beneath a ceiling of thick, heavy cloud that was shortening the day. Six in the evening when I left Risky Point. Another hour or so, and it would be black dark.

Maybe I would still make it to Prague, but I wasn't counting on it. It looked like Leon would just have to manage without me for a bit longer. Whatever had happened to Jason in Rosedale, it was probably going to take more than a couple of hours to sort it out.

At that moment, I still knew very little. It was easy to sum up what I did know. Namely, Jimmy Mack's nephew was in trouble, seemingly under duress, and had now vanished. It appeared that bad people were involved. Jimmy and his niece, Jason's sister, were upset and feared the worst. They wanted my help. That was it. All I knew.

Amy had been too distraught to tell me more, except that they couldn't call the police. They didn't dare, for fear of making things worse. I hadn't pressed her. I had just said I would come at once, and do what I could. There was no way I could have done anything else. I didn't owe Amy a thing, but I owed Jimmy Mack plenty. And it wasn't like him to ask for help from anyone.

* * *

Rosedale is one of several valleys in the North York Moors that run north-south, to the south of the much bigger Esk Valley, which stretches west from the coast. The latter I regard as the dividing line between Cleveland, where I live, and the North York Moors. I don't know if the geographers would agree, but it's a definition that has always served me well.

From my base at Risky Point, the northern end of Rosedale is only twenty miles away. But Rosedale Abbey, the village where Jason lived, is at the southern end of the valley, nearly another ten miles further. That's as the traditional crow flies. The road distance is quite a bit more than that, on slow little roads, and it took me a good hour to get to Jason's place.

The cottage was halfway along a short stone terrace. I parked out the front, at one end of the terrace. Amy's car, which I recognized from seeing it at Risky Point, was towards the other end. Amy herself must have been watching for my arrival, and she rushed out to meet me.

'Has he turned up yet?' I asked.

She shook her head and led the way inside.

* * *

Rosedale was a centre of ironstone mining in Victorian times, like the part of Cleveland where I live, and the house was a typical miner's cottage from that period. It had the ubiquitous design: two rooms down, and two rooms up originally. To that, had been added in the twentieth century an extension housing a kitchen downstairs and a bathroom upstairs. As such cottages generally are, it was modest but comfortable, so long as you didn't have a big family — and perhaps even then for folk used to traditional space standards.

The front door gave immediate access to the living room, where I found Jimmy Mack sitting in a small armchair, looking thoroughly miserable.

'Thank God you've come, Frank,' were his opening words.

'Jimmy.'

I nodded and gave him a grin. Then I turned back to Amy, who seemed to be in a lot better state than her uncle.

'So what's going on?' I asked. 'Give me a quick summary.'

Without sitting down herself, she waved me to a chair and said again, 'I owe you an apology, Mr Doy. I didn't know who or what you were until Uncle Jimmy told me. I had no idea that he lived next door to a man like you.'

'You should feel sorry for him,' I told her with what I hoped was a reassuring smile. 'He's very unfortunate. Just call me Frank, by the way.'

Perched on the kitchen chair she had directed me to, I said again, 'Give me a rough idea what the problem is, Amy. Jason's missing, you said. Why, and why is that so worrying?'

'He's scared to death, and he's running.'

'What, or who, from?'

'His wife's family.'

Uh!

'Go on,' I urged. 'You expected Jason to be here?'

'Yes. He said he would be. That's why we came.'

'You spoke to him?'

She shook her head. 'No. Uncle Jimmy did.'

I glanced at Jim, who nodded agreement. He looked out of it, too stressed to cope with whatever was going on.

'Take it easy, Jim,' I told him gently. 'We'll get it sorted.'

Turning back to Amy, I said, 'So what's this about his wife's family? And what do you think has happened?'

15

She sighed and said, 'I'd better start at the beginning.'

I nodded and waited for her to get started.

'Jason is my brother, three years younger than me. He's lived in Rosedale for a long time, and he manages the local nature reserve. A couple of years ago he made a big mistake. He got married.'

'Lots of people do that,' I pointed out.

'Yes, of course they do, and for most of them it's probably a success. What I meant was that Jason's marriage was a big mistake. It didn't last five minutes, and the consequences have been dreadful.

'After a ridiculously short time, just two or three weeks, Francine decided Jason and rural life weren't for her, and off she went back home to her family. Jason was disappointed but he picked up and carried on, trying to put it behind him and just doing what he was used to doing.

'Everything settled back down again in time, and his life was OK again until recently. Then he won a lot of money on the Lottery. That was the start of it, the trouble.'

Amy paused, sighed and added, 'When I say a lot, I mean a lot! He literally won millions — ten, actually. And that was when the trouble started. Francine reappeared in his life and demanded a share of the money.'

'Jason won ten million quid?'

Amy nodded.

I shook my head in awe. I could hardly believe it. That sort of thing didn't happen to people I knew. Not in real life, it didn't.

'By then they were divorced, presumably?'

Amy shook her head this time. 'No. I don't know what Francine had had in mind, but Jason had never got round to doing anything about a divorce. That was his second mistake. The first, of course, had been marrying Francine.'

CHAPTER SIX

'Daddy. Can I . . .'

'Not now, darling. I'm busy.'

'You never have time for me any more,' Francine said, pouting.

'We've got a problem I'm trying to sort out. I was just going to phone . . .'

'When was the last time you talked to me, Daddy? Why do I always come second, or last, on your to-do list? Tell me that!'

Exasperated, George Reagan pushed the phone aside. Francine came further into the room and, like a vulture inspecting its find, perched on the chair on the other side of his desk.

'It was different when Mum was alive,' she resumed. 'I had someone to share things with, and to ask for advice. Now I only have you — when you're not busy, that is.'

'Francine! Don't exaggerate.'

'It's true.'

Reagan admitted to himself that it probably was true. It had been different when Olivia was alive, before she ate her health away with all the coke she got addicted to. And all the other stuff that he didn't even know she was using until it was too late, even though it was supplied by his own dealers.

Not that he'd minded all that much until she hit the home straight and left him with an un-mothered teenage daughter. It had been a long time since he and Olivia had hit it off together. And he'd always had Linda to console him. But Olivia had been very good with Francine. He couldn't deny it. Now, though, he was having to do more sole parenting than he had ever envisaged, or could ever have wanted to do.

Luckily for him, Linda didn't complain or demand his constant presence. She knew the business he was in. She was happy to stay out of the picture herself, and just see him when he had the time.

After all, she knew what it was like. Linda's background was much the same as his. They were both from East End families that had learned how to survive and prosper any way they could. And her father had been much the same as he was himself. She had even said so, but not as a complaint. That was one of the many good things about Linda. She never complained, not about anything.

'What do you want to talk about, Fran?' he asked now, with a weary sigh.

'My husband,' Francine said plaintively.

For a moment Reagan was puzzled. Then he remembered. 'Oh, you mean what's-'is-name! That kid from England you met here the other year. Jason, wasn't it?'

'Jason, yes.'

'It's a long time since I heard that name mentioned.'

Reagan sighed. 'What about him anyway? You dumped him didn't you? Walked out on him, and came back home?'

'He's still my husband, though,' Francine said even more plaintively.

Uh! Reagan thought. *That sounds like trouble.*

It was a long time since the name "Jason" had been mentioned in this house. His women folk had virtually banned it after Francine came home.

Husband, though? Was that what he still was after all this time apart? And was Francine really a married woman? Not for long, she hadn't been. That must count for something, surely?

It all seemed so long ago now anyway. He'd almost for-gotten about the so-called marriage on a beach, which had annoyed him no end, and which he'd never had anything to do with anyway. He'd just been informed by Olivia that it had happened, that his daughter had got married. Francine had got a feller.

Not much ceremony about it. Not that he'd minded very much. He'd been perfectly happy to leave such matters to his wife and daughter. There were enough demands on his time just running the family business. And if his daughter had insisted on a no-frills wedding, well, that had been entirely up to her. And she'd certainly had one! At the time, he hadn't been able to believe what she'd just gone and done. At least it hadn't cost him a fortune. The petty cash had taken care of the bills.

'Jason has won a lot of money on the Lottery in England, Daddy, and he won't give me my share.'

'Oh?'

'He offered me only half a million pounds, the miserable little bastard!'

'Hey! Language, Francine. Language.'

Francine pulled a face.

'What did you just say?' Reagan said, tracking back. 'Are you serious? He wants to give you half a million quid? Hell, girl, you should grab his hand off!'

'But it's not good enough, is it? I'm his wife, after all. I should get half what he won. I'm entitled to it by the law of the land.'

Which land?

Reagan, not sure what he was hearing, or whether to believe it anyway, paused to think for a moment and then said, 'So how much did he win?'

'Ten million pounds, sterling.'

'Jeez!'

Shocked, Reagan pushed his chair back heavily and stared at his daughter with renewed interest.

'Ten million quid?' he said thoughtfully, as pieces of the puzzle challenging him began to click into place.

CHAPTER SEVEN

It wasn't hard now to see where Jason's trouble had come from.

'So what did he tell Francine?'

Looking disdainful, Amy sighed and said, 'Jason did offer her some money.'

'Half?'

'No. He couldn't do that. He'd already made plans for most of what he'd won. But he offered her quite a lot anyway. Well, most people would consider half a million pounds a lot of money, wouldn't they?'

All I could do was nod agreement. I tried hard not to think about what I could do with half a million pounds.

'And she said?'

'Well, I won't tell you what she said initially,' Amy said with a shudder. 'That woman has a far bigger vocabulary of four-letter words than I have. But she had her tantrum. Then she departed, saying she would see what her family had to say about it.'

'Who are they? Royalty?'

Amy shook her head. 'But they are big hitters — literally. They're a criminal Essex family based in Tenerife. Jason says they've killed people, and two members of the family are in prison for murder. That's why he's so scared.'

'Actually,' she amended, 'he's bloody terrified — and with very good reason!'

It was time for us all to draw breath. Amy turned away for a moment. Jimmy was muttering in the background. As for me, well, I knew for sure now that I wasn't going to make the flight to Prague in the morning.

'What's Francine's family name?' I asked Amy.

'Reagan.'

I decided to make a quick call to my research department — that is, Henry Bolckow, of Middlesbrough. I needed to know more, a lot more, about the Reagans.

Then I found I couldn't, not on my mobile, at least.

'No server coverage,' I said, grimacing with frustration.

'There isn't in Rosedale,' Amy told me. 'None at all. You'll have to use the old landline phone.'

'May I?'

'Who do you want to call?' she asked, sounding suspicious.

'A consultant I know. I want him to see what he can find out about Francine's family.'

'Does that really matter at a time like this?'

'Yes, it does. To me, at least. I need to know what we're up against.'

She shrugged, as if to say she differed and objected to me wasting time, but she pointed me towards the phone in a corner of the room.

I made the call but failed to reach Henry. He wasn't there, in his office, and I didn't leave a message because I couldn't be confident it would be him that picked it up. Henry's lifestyle was a bit rackety.

'I'll have to try again later,' I told Amy. 'He's not there at the moment. Not answering, at least.'

'And he's a consultant?' she asked, eyebrows raised. 'Funny way to run his business.'

I didn't rise to the bait. It wasn't worth it. Already I'd gathered Amy was by nature impatient and a bit provocative. There was no point debating anything with someone like that, I've found from long experience. You might win one argument, but then they just look for another battlefield. It's in their blood.

'Now, where were we?' I said instead. 'Tenerife, eh? Is that where Jason met Francine?'

Amy nodded. 'Briefly. He was on holiday. He was only there a bloody week!'

I couldn't help thinking if Jason had gone to Greece, or even Blackpool or Skegness, none of this would have happened.

'What did her family say after Francine told them he would only give her half a million quid?'

'To summarize, they said they didn't want half the money. They wanted all of it. Half for Francine, as was her due as Jason's wife, and half for some construction project they require him to invest in that they've got going in Tenerife.'

'And Jason said?'

'Get stuffed!'

'To which they replied?'

'They laughed in his face and pointed out that in the event of his death, his widow would get all the money. They advised him to think about it sensibly.'

'Nice of them.'

'Very.'

So Jason's options were to live or not to live? Either way, Francine and her family would get the money. Mmm, I thought. The young man really was in trouble.

'I'm guessing Jason still said no?'

'He did. As I said, he has plans for it. His idea is to buy a farm, an estate actually, and rewild it. He's even identified a suitable estate and made a bid for it.'

'Because nature and wildlife are his passion, presumably?'

'Exactly. They have been ever since he was a little boy. They're his job, too, of course, his career. So far as I can see, the estate would just be a nature reserve on a bigger scale.'

'And Francine didn't fancy that, presumably. What did she want to do with the money? Any idea?'

'Oh, yes! Francine wants one of those posh houses in southern California where celebrities, and people like the Sussexes, live. Beverly Hills, or wherever it is.'

'The Sussexes?' I asked mischievously. 'Aren't they celebrities, too?'

Amy snorted with derision. 'Celebrities? They're a joke! That's what they are. Childlike narcissists, both of them. California is the right place for the pair of them.'

I had to grin. Amy was like the ball that thunders down the bowling alley to despatch all the skittles in one go.

'Right. I understand the situation. But something else must have happened now, if Jason has gone missing. You think the family have abducted him?'

She shrugged. 'I don't know. Perhaps not. He may just have decided to make himself scarce. I know there's a deadline next week for his bid for the estate. He won't want to miss that.'

He won't want to be dead either, I was thinking. That could be why he'd gone missing. Threats like the one he was facing have a way of preying on your mind. I know. I've been there.

CHAPTER EIGHT

The idea hit George Reagan like a tsunami. It came out of nowhere and simply engulfed him. He knew he had to do something about it immediately.

First, he sought Francine and put a proposal to her.

'Darling, I realize how disappointed you are about not getting your share of the money your husband won, but unfortunately there's not much to be done about it now. You left Jason a long time ago, after all, and you hadn't been with him for very long anyway. So you can't really claim to still be his wife, can you?'

'Legally, I can,' Francine said with a pout.

'Well, maybe. But I'm not too sure about that, to be honest. Marriage law isn't my thing. Anyway, there are other things in life beside money, aren't there?'

'Really, Dad? When did you discover that?'

'Since your mother passed away, I suppose. Look, I know how much you've long fancied living in America, California even. How would you like to spend some serious time over there, looking around and working out if that's where you would really prefer to be?'

Francine snorted with derision and said, 'What with Daddy? I can't afford it — not on the allowance you pay me!'

'Oh, don't worry about that, Darling. I'll pay for it. Spend a few months over there and see how much you like it. I just don't like seeing you hanging around here, looking so unhappy.'

Francine weighed up what she was hearing, wondering if it was a serious offer or a joke at her expense. 'Would you do that, Daddy?' she asked, when she couldn't see any obvious flaws — apart from the obvious ones! 'Would you? Really?'

He nodded. 'Everyone deserves the chance to follow their dream, Francine. I've always believed that.'

'Oh, Daddy! How wonderful.' She threw her arms around him and gave him a great big kiss. 'I love you so much.'

George Reagan smiled with contentment, and not only because his daughter seemed to appreciate him for once.

* * *

So that was the first part of what needed doing sorted, George thought afterwards. He could get Francine out of the way. Now he had to focus on her former husband, or whatever he was. The lad's winnings would solve Reagan Enterprises' problem very nicely.

Even if the guy refused to see sense, it wouldn't matter. With him dead, the money would come to his widow — and hence the family — anyway. Perhaps not soon, or quickly enough, but come it would eventually. And in the meantime, the assurance that inheritance would happen meant they ought to be able to borrow money from somewhere to meet the deadline.

He smiled with satisfaction. Why did he need an account-ant? He'd solved the problem himself, no thanks to Ed Davey.

* * *

Next, he brought in George Reagan Jr, who was just "Junior" to most people in the family. Junior was the second oldest of his children, born when Reagan was married to his first wife. Now in his mid-thirties, Junior was loyal and capable enough, if a bit lacking in the brains department, and George had long been grooming him to take the helm of the family business eventually. He had even been given the title Deputy Chairman already, if only to put a spoke in Oscar's wheel.

Junior was a hard young man, a quality George valued and had seen in him at a very early age. He could be trusted to do whatever needed doing without question. Unlike Oscar, that bloody brother of his! Oscar had a different opinion about everything, and seemed to be getting worse as he got older.

I'll be damned if I'll ever let Oscar take over, George thought once again, with a ferocious glare. *To hell with him! No, it's going to be Junior who steps up to the plate, when the time comes. I'll make bloody sure of that, if it's the last thing I ever do.*

This back story was why George Reagan had always encouraged Junior to call him "George", not "Dad". Fears or even thoughts of nepotism were not going to be allowed to hinder the succession plan. To George's mind, the family business was a meritocracy, not a royal aristocracy, and no way in the world would he ever let his younger brother take charge of it.

* * *

'Got a job for you, Junior,' George said when he called his son on the phone. 'Two jobs, actually. Can you make time to be away from home for a couple of weeks?'

'No problem, George. What's on your mind?'

'Come and see me. We need to talk face to face.'

CHAPTER NINE

'Any idea where Jason might have gone, if he has just taken himself off somewhere?' I asked Amy.

'I've been thinking about that. The obvious place, and the only one I can think of, is the nature reserve. He's really into the job, and he has an office there where he spends a lot of his time, even when he's off-duty. It's virtually home-from-home for him.'

'Have you tried calling him there?'

'No. I didn't think of that. Let me find the number for the reserve.'

While Amy was doing that, I did some quick thinking. She could well be right. The nature reserve seemed a pretty good guess to me. Jason had probably wanted somewhere quiet and familiar, and safe, psychologically at least, where he could sit and think. He would be trying to work out what to do for the best, and maybe worrying about how he was going to survive. Where better to do that than the place where he spent so much of his life?

An ordinary, innocent citizen might well wonder why Jason hadn't simply contacted the police about the threats he had received. If he hadn't, as seemed to be the case, I could understand it. Bringing in the police might well have expedited the process leading to Francine becoming a widow, or leading someone close to him becoming a fatality. So perhaps Jason was more worldly than I'd been thinking.

Amy came up with a number for the reserve and made the call, handling the unfamiliar old landline phone reverently, as if it were an artefact from an archaeological dig.

The phone rang for a minute or two before it was answered.

'Jason? Is that you? It's Amy. How are you?'

She listened to the brief reply, and then said, 'We've been worried about you, Jason. Uncle Jimmy and me. We're at your house. We expected to find you here.'

Some sort of explanation was given. I couldn't hear what was said. My eyes were on Amy, trying to interpret her body language as well as listening to what she said.

'Jason, we want to help. We can't do much in a practical sense ourselves, but we've brought in a friend of Uncle Jimmy's who might be able to. He does security and personal protection — stuff like that — for a living.

'No, Jason! Not at all. He's a good man. He lives right next door to Uncle Jimmy at Risky Point, and Uncle Jimmy swears by him.

'Who is he? Frank Doy. That's his name. He's here with us now and he wants to see you. He can be with you in the next half hour. Is that OK?'

A bit more was said. Then the conversation ended and Amy put down the phone.

'Can you go?' she asked, turning to me.

'Of course.'

'Good. Jason said he'd had to get out of the house because men sent by Francine's father are here.'

'Where? In the village?'

'That's what he said.'

I grimaced and got to my feet. 'They're very close, then. I'd better be on my way.'

CHAPTER TEN

'Where's the reserve?' I asked Amy. 'Do you know?'

She nodded. 'It's near the head of the valley, just off the road on the east side. Five or six miles from here.'

'Can you show me on a map?'

'Of course.'

I brought out my phone but Amy had already reached for an OS map on a nearby shelf. It didn't take more than a minute or two for her to show me where the reserve was. Looking at the map refreshed my memory of the area, and reminded me there was no road out of the valley at the north end. It also gave me the germ of an idea for getting round that problem, if it became necessary.

'Right,' I said, straightening up. 'I'll get moving.'

'I'll come with you.'

'No.' I shook my head. 'I'd rather just go myself.'

'Why?'

'If the Reagans do have men here, they'll be keeping an eye on the house and they'll probably know you and your uncle are family. So if you leave the house, they'll want to follow you and see where you go. Me, I'm just a stranger who called in for a few minutes. I won't be of much interest to them.

'Besides,' I added quietly, 'I don't think we should leave your uncle alone, here or anywhere else. He's very stressed. And I don't want him with me. He's not well enough. I want you to take him back home and look after him there until I get back to you. He'll be better there.'

Safer, I meant, but didn't want to say in case Jimmy heard me. I didn't want him rallying and trying to force himself to come with me. He wasn't up to what I might have to do. I wanted him out of the way, and safe.

'I'll be in touch,' I added. 'And, if necessary, I can arrange police protection for you both.'

'What are you going to do in the meantime?'

'First, talk to Jason. Then move him somewhere safe, if he'll agree to it.'

'Where, though?'

'I won't go into that now, Amy. It's a bit complicated, and I want to get moving.'

* * *

It was a truly black night when the three of us left Jason's cottage. It was that much later, of course, but there had been a dramatic change in the weather as well. Heavy cloud and torrential rain together with a fierce wind had moved in, making it even darker and colder than it would have been anyway. The conditions suited me. Anything that made life more difficult for people who might be keeping watch was fine by me.

I went first, slipping out of the back door and into the small garden behind the house, leaving Amy and Jimmy to lock up and exit via the front door. They did so in the glare of the light over the front porch, which I'd told them to leave on for a couple of minutes and then come back to switch off. I wanted them to be seen going about their life in the normal way.

While that performance was going on, I climbed over a low, shaky, wooden garden fence, manoeuvred around a thick, old hedge and made my way to the Land Rover parked at the far end of the terrace. I got in, started up and left, following a late-working farm tractor as it headed out of the village. Amy and Jim would be leaving a few minutes after me.

The road I took was narrow, mostly a single lane, but the surface was good and there was no traffic once the tractor turned off at the first farm it reached.

My wipers were soon going mad, squeaking and thudding, as they tried to keep pace with the rain, but I didn't have far to go before they could have a rest. The journey took me twenty minutes, longer than I'd anticipated, and gave me time to work out how best to approach Jason and what to say to him.

I would keep it very simple and straightforward, I decided. My involvement was because I had been asked to help, and I would help if I could. But it would be up to him how much involvement he wanted from me. It was entirely possible that he would reject my offer and show me the door, in which case I might still be on the plane to Prague in the morning.

That seemed an unlikely scenario, though. Jason was in big trouble. He would have to be uncommonly stubborn or an idiot to reject my help.

I reached the reserve without being able to see much of it. It was cloaked in a heavy blanket of cloud, rain and utter blackness. In daylight I might well have seen a small lake, a few streams and a lot of boggy grassland with clumps of reed. Plus ducks and geese, and other things with wings. Swans, maybe. That night, I didn't see anything at all on the approach until I reached the actual entrance to the reserve, apart from sheets of rain hammering at the windscreen. Then, my main beams picked up the name board: *The East Rosedale Nature Reserve*.

I drove in between two massive timber pillars and under another name board stretched overhead between them. A light, probably triggered by a motion detector, came on a little way ahead. It was a security light over the main door to a timber building that looked like the HQ of the reserve.

I had arrived.

CHAPTER ELEVEN

'Two things, Junior,' George Reagan said. 'I want you to see to them both.'

Junior nodded and waited expectantly.

'I've decided we need a new accountant. Davey has outlived his usefulness. All I get from him is problems, when what I want is solutions. He's not gonna change. I know that. He's not capable of it. So he's gotta go.'

'He's been with us a long time,' Junior said after a moment's reflection.

'Yeah. You're right. But his advice lately has been crap. To be honest with you, Junior, I believe he's in bed with Oscar.'

Junior thought about that a moment, nodded and said, 'You could be right, George. Have you got somebody in mind to take over from him?'

'Not right now, no. The problem has come to a head suddenly. The business has a liquidity problem that I didn't know we had until yesterday. Then Davey came in here and told me we're damn nearly bust.'

'That can't be true, surely?'

'I think it's probably close to it. The hotel project has been soaking up reserves at a time when our income stream has been almost non-existent. That's meant we've been struggling to pay back money we've had to borrow. If we don't come up with ten million quid by a week on Monday, we'll be bust.'

'Jesus!'

George confirmed that there was a problem, and talked about it in more detail.

'So it's the hotel?' Junior said at length.

George nodded.

'And we can't just pause work on it?'

'We could, but if we can't repay the ten million by the due date, the project will no longer be ours anyway. Legal ownership will pass to the Italians. Maybe the Arabs will come into it, as well. Davey wasn't quite sure.'

Junior thought about it. The news was shocking. It kind of took your feet away. He would never have thought something like this could happen to them. But he could also see that the problem had to be faced. It wasn't going to go away by itself.

'What about the rest of the business, George?'

'That's fine, or it will be. We still own plenty of property. Our tenants pay their bills. Holiday lets are down, of course, like the coke trade, but they'll soon pick up now the pandemic is mostly behind us. No problems with the time-share either, or the rest of it.'

'So it's just the hotel and casino complex?'

George nodded.

The solution seemed obvious to Junior. He couldn't really understand why it wasn't to his father, as well. There must be something he wasn't seeing.

'Why not just walk away from the hotel?' he said quietly. 'Let the Italians have it. Save the rest of the business. Why not?'

'No way!' George said angrily. 'That's what Oscar has wanted to do all along, but it ain't going to happen. Not on my watch!

'We'll get through this, Junior. We'll finish the hotel, and get it open — the casino as well — and all our problems will be a thing of the past. Mark my words!'

Junior nodded. It wasn't a statement that entirely persuaded him, but George had always been right in the past. Hopefully, he would be again.

'Davey should have told me things were going wrong sooner,' George resumed. 'He should have given me more time to work something out.'

'You're right about that.' Junior shook his head. 'Just yesterday, for God's sake!'

'But he didn't,' George said grimly. 'And here we are. As it happens, though, there is something we can do. I've discovered an answer to the problem, no thanks to Ed.'

Junior perked up. He should have known George would come up with something. He wouldn't be head of the family if he didn't have a reputation for getting them out of tight corners.

'Your sister's husband, or ex-husband or whatever the hell he is now, has ten million quid that he's just won on the Lottery.'

Junior frowned. 'Her husband?'

'That Jason bloke, back in England, who Francine used to go on about.'

'Oh, him! That was two or three years ago, wasn't it?'

'Something like that.'

Junior paused, frowned and then added, 'What did you just say, George? That bloke's won ten million quid?'

George nodded, and said with a grin, 'We're going to tell him what to do with the money, Junior. He can't be left to look after it all by himself, can he?'

It was a question that didn't need answering.

Junior grinned. 'You're right there,' he said with a chuckle. 'That wouldn't be right at all. An amateur with all that money? No way!'

'And that's what I want you to do,' George continued. 'Show him what's good for him. First, though, I want you to put Davey away — permanently.'

'Permanently?'

'Yeah. It's sad in a way, but he knows too much about our business for this family to let him just walk away. It wouldn't make sense.

'I don't mind how it's done, Junior, but I always think car accidents are a gift from heaven when it comes to solving a problem like Ed Davey.'

'Understood.'

George brooded for a moment. Then he said, 'Something similar may be necessary with Francine's ex-husband, if he doesn't see sense. But we'll give him a chance first.'

Junior nodded and got his feet. 'I'll get right on it, George.'

CHAPTER TWELVE

A man emerged from the doorway of the building. Standing under the porch roof, shielding himself from the rain, he watched me park well away from the only other vehicle in the gravelled car park, a much newer Land Rover than mine. It looked like a Defender that had been tarted up a bit with strip lights, roof rack, et cetera. There must be money in nature reserves these days, I couldn't help thinking.

'Jason?' I called, as I set off in a hurry to splash across the waterlogged ground towards him.

'Yes. You Frank Doy?'

'That's me. Phew!' I added, shaking the rain off as I joined him in the porch. 'What a night.'

'Isn't it? Come on inside. I've got coffee on the go.'

We entered a big room that looked like the main exhibition space, judging by the array of maps, photos and piles of pamphlets adorning walls, tables and freestanding display panels. Jason led the way through and into one of several small rooms off a corridor. A glowing halogen heater was installed in one corner, throwing out a lot of welcome heat as it gently swung from side to side.

'My office,' he said. 'It's easier and cheaper to keep warm, and a bit more snug.'

'No leaks in the roof?'

'Not yet,' he said with a grin.

Truly, his home-from-home, I thought, glancing around. He probably spent more time here than he did in his house. I didn't suppose for one moment that I was the only one capable of arriving at that conclusion, though. Whatever he thought, he wasn't safe here. Not now. I had to tell him he needed to be out, and soon.

'So you and Uncle Jim are neighbours, eh?' he said, handing me one of the two mugs of coffee I had watched him pour.

'That's right. Pals, as well. We see a lot of each other.'

'At Risky Point?'

I nodded. 'We help each other out, whenever we can, which is why I'm here now. Your uncle asked me to come and see what I can do. I gather you've got serious problems?'

He grimaced. 'It's nice of you and my uncle, though,' he added with a wry smile, as if all effort to help was bound to be futile.

I wondered if he was always this calm. Was it a front, a posture, to help him carry what was obviously a pretty heavy load? Or was it just his nature? That was something I needed to find out, and fast, before I started dispensing advice.

'Your sister, Amy, has given me a quick summary, but I don't suppose she knows the full story. From what she told me, though, the first thing I need to tell you is that you've got to get out of here, and out of Rosedale, urgently. You're not safe here, Jason.'

'Now, hang on just a minute!' he protested, losing the smile. 'I've got a lot of responsibilities, including to this place and the people who work here. I can't just walk away from them.'

'Every minute counts, Jason. I mean it. This is a serious situation. You've got to get out fast.'

'What the hell do you know about it?' he asked, sounding annoyed now.

'Not a lot, but it's straightforward enough. You've been threatened in your own home by people who are actively looking for you. Let's not beat about the bush. They want the money you won. It's as simple as that.

'And they are an organized crime outfit, one organized more like a business than a street gang. People who run things like that don't make empty threats, Jason, and they don't waste time. They mean what they say.'

He glowered at me, seemingly stunned.

'What did they tell you?' I demanded. 'Exactly, I mean.'

'What makes you think they told me anything?' he said in a truculent tone.

'Come on, Jason! Stop playing games. Amy and your uncle expected to find you waiting for them at your cottage, because you had arranged to meet them there. When they arrived you were gone, with no explanation. That means something. It means a lot, actually.

'To me, it signifies an emergency. Your wife's family had probably got to you in the meantime. I'm not saying you panicked and fled, but something happened. And you felt you had to get out immediately.

'Your office, here, was the only place you could think of to go. But it's not safe, Jason. You must know that yourself. This is the first place the people hunting you will look when they find you're no longer at home.'

He looked devastated now, confused and anxious. Plain speaking, and simple truths, had broken through the protective cover he had fashioned around himself. The question was: could I get him moving before what I was predicting came true? My feeling was that we wouldn't have very long to find out.

'What the hell makes you think you know so much?' he demanded.

'Experience,' I told him. 'My work. That's security work, amongst other things. I've been doing what I do for a long time. I know about criminal gangs, and how they operate. I deal with them a lot.'

'Amy said something about that.'

I nodded and said, 'I take it you haven't contacted the police?'

He shook his head. 'They warned me not to, if I valued my family — and this place, the reserve where I spend so much of my life.'

'You were right not to ignore that advice. But what are you thinking of doing instead?'

He sighed, shook his head and said, 'Just thinking about it, in odd moments, is as far as I'd got until today.'

'With any conclusions?'

He shook his head again.

'So what happened today?'

'I got a phone call. They said that either I transferred the money by noon tomorrow or my widow would do it for me.'

That was plain enough, I thought. A bit dramatic, perhaps, but you couldn't fault them for lack of clarity.

'Then what?'

'I came here — to do some more thinking.'

And much good had it done him.

'I wasn't just going to roll over,' he said indignantly, mistakenly sensing what I was thinking.

'Fair enough, Jason. But the time for thinking is over now. We've got to get moving. We need to find a safe place for you.'

Suddenly, above the sound of wind and rain, I heard engine noise approaching. I pushed my chair back and jumped to my feet.

'What?' Jason demanded, his head jerking up, startled.

'They're here. Let's go!'

CHAPTER THIRTEEN

Junior planned the elimination of Ed Davey with care. He knew without being told that there had to be no comeback on the family. Especially at present. They couldn't afford it. They were in enough trouble already, one way or another. All because of that bloody hotel!

George's usually sure touch seemed to have let him down this time. Or, rather, Fate had. The hotel and casino complex had looked like a sure winner until Covid arrived on the scene and undermined the business plan. Now it would make a lot of sense to walk away from the hotel, just give it up, and try to save the rest of the family business. But George was obviously dead set against doing that.

Getting rid of Ed Davey didn't seem all that great an idea, either. They needed an accountant, especially at a time like this, and finding one they could trust who was prepared to work for them, and who could hit the ground running, was not going to be easy. Anyway, what would happen if the new guy gave George the same advice as Ed Davey had given him?

Junior shook his head and sighed. George was the boss, and he had his instructions. He'd better get on with it.

At least he knew what he wanted to do about Davey. It would be straightforward, and nothing he hadn't done before, but he would plan the job properly anyway. That was how he'd been brought up. He did a recce first, and identified the best spot for Ed Davey to have his accident. It wasn't hard to find.

The accountant kept pretty regular hours at his downtown office in Puerto de la Cruz. He liked to get home by seven in the evening, and there he usually stayed with his family until he went to work again the next day. Junior knew that whatever Davey was doing with all the money he made out of Reagan Enterprises, it was very unlikely that he would ever be a good customer at their new casino, if and when it ever opened. He wasn't that kind of guy.

Late in the afternoon, Junior parked at a safe distance from the building where Davey had his office and waited patiently for the accountant's Bentley to emerge from the underground car park. It duly did that at six-thirty. He set off to follow it home to the enormous cliff-top villa the Daveys had built, largely with the money earned from Regan Enterprises.

* * *

Joey Jackson, a cousin, and a mechanic, was the man Junior turned to first. They had worked together often enough on special jobs, although Jackson's day job was responsibility for maintaining the Reagan Enterprises fleet of vehicles. The special assignments were a welcome bonus for him. They gave him extra money and sometimes a lot of excitement as well. Maintaining vehicles all day long wasn't always a lot of fun. Sometimes a man needed an adrenaline rush.

'The Bentley?' Joey said slowly, wanting to be sure he'd heard right. 'Davey's car?'

Junior nodded. 'He's gotta go. It's been decided, high up.'

'Oh, boy!' Joey said, his eyes gleaming.

'It has to be total, and we don't want any fingers pointed at us afterwards. So nothing dramatic. More like wear and tear, natural ageing. Whatever.'

'No bomb?' Joey asked with a wry grin, a little disappointed now. 'No catastrophic failure?'

'Definitely not. And nothing else that might raise suspicions either. So what would you recommend? Myself, I was thinking brakes.'

'Brakes would be good. Easy to do. Nothing obvious. Just very unfortunate. One of them things.'

Junior nodded. They were on the same page.

Joey frowned for a moment. 'Not working. Due to a loss of brake fluid, maybe because of a loose or corroded connection causing a leak.'

'That would do it?'

'Absolutely!' Joey assured him with a grin.

* * *

'All set,' Joey said the next day, when he met Junior in a downtown bar.

'You got it done?'

'Yeah. Shouldn't take many minutes before the fluid drains out. Then — whoosh!'

'No one saw you?'

Jackson shook his head. 'Them underground garages are not places where anyone wants to hang around, and no one came in while I was there.'

'Good. Maybe by tomorrow, then?'

'I would say so. It will take a little time, not being a catastrophic failure, but definitely by tomorrow morning. The first big hill he goes down on his way to work should do it.'

Junior nodded. That sounded fine. Not as fine as a bomb, but it would do. Then he could get himself to the UK to look after the other task George had given him. He was looking forward to that. There was nothing like variety.

'Junior, there's something else I wanted to ask you about.'

'Mmm?'

'When are we going to get my dad out of Belmarsh? Any idea?'

Junior shook his head. 'Not really. It's up to George to decide when it's a good time, and how to do it. It'll be soon, though. You can be sure of that.'

'Do you think it might be brought forward, with this job being done right?'

'There's every chance, Joey. It ought to put George in a good mood. I'll have a word when we're done, and see what he thinks.'

'Thanks, Junior. He's been there long enough.' Joey added wistfully, 'It's time we got him out. He'll be thinking the family's letting him down.'

'Jesus Christ, Joey!' Junior said with exasperation. 'Don't you think George has enough on his plate at the moment, what with the pandemic and that fucking hotel? Give him a break!'

Joey nodded, knowing all that was true. Everybody in the family knew it. Even Uncle Oscar, despite what he had to say about things. These were hard times. It wouldn't be any different if someone else, Oscar or Junior say, took over from George. He knew that.

Realistically, Junior thought as Joey left, it wouldn't happen any time soon, if ever.

One, there were too many other problems, some of them more urgent. Two, getting Harry Jackson out of Belmarsh, the UK's top high-security prison, wouldn't be easy, even if actually possible. And, three, the guy wasn't really family anyway. He didn't share their blood. He'd just married Aunt Katy, his father's sister. It made a difference.

Whatever his dissatisfaction about his father's situation, Joey's work couldn't be faulted. Things worked out perfectly. Junior followed Davey the next morning at the start of the accountant's working day, and thrilled as the Bentley failed to slow on the long descent into the canyon, didn't make the bend at the bottom and plunged off the sea cliff onto the rocky beach below, where it burst into flames.

Now George needs to step up his efforts to find a new accountant, Junior thought with satisfaction and a faint smile. *This one's done.*

CHAPTER FOURTEEN

The talking was all done. We had to go — now!

Whoever it was out there, I feared they were here to make Jason's wife a widow, and put an end to negotiations about money. Francine — or the Family, probably — was intent on getting it all.

Looking panicky now, Jason whispered, 'They're going to kill me!'

I was almost relieved he'd come to the same conclusion as me. Not having to argue with him about that would save time.

'Not if we're quick. Is there a back way out of here?'

I heard car doors slam. And voices. Several of them.

'This way!' Jason said, snapping out of it and reaching to grab a backpack on a chair near his desk.

We left the room and dashed along the corridor, Jason in the lead. I pushed him on when he paused, his fingers automatically reaching for the switch to put out the lights.

'Leave it!' I snapped.

It was no time to be thinking of saving electricity, and incidentally letting our visitors know for sure there was someone in here.

He left it.

Outside, we dived into the shadows. I resisted looking over my shoulder until we were behind some dense bushes. Then I grabbed Jason by the shoulder to stop him, and spun round to see what was happening.

There were four of them, four figures. And two cars. One a Jag, the other an Audi, it looked like. In the driving rain and the darkness, apart from the feeble light coming from the lamp over the front porch, it was hard to see either men or cars in detail. One man stayed in the Jag. The boss, I assumed. The others went inside, and moments later one of them came back out to stand under the porch roof and have a shouted exchange with the man in the car. I couldn't hear what was being said.

'Know any of them?' I asked.

Jason shook his head. 'No.'

'Can you hear anything they're saying? I can't.'

He shook his head again and pulled the hood of his jacket up, which meant he would hear even less. I was resigned to rain creeping off my hair and down my neck. It was a filthy night, but one of us had to continue listening, and hearing, in the hope of learning something.

We did. We learned that the man who had stayed in the car was definitely the boss. He gave some final instructions and then drove away. I guessed he was returning to the village, possibly to Jason's cottage.

I wondered for a few moments what the others planned to do. Then it became obvious. Having not found us, two of them returned to their car, opened the boot lid and took out a big jerry can. I could only assume it contained petrol.

'What are they doing?' Jason demanded.

Best not to think or say too much about it. We couldn't stop them anyway. Jason wasn't a fighting man, and I didn't want him trying to act like a hero and getting himself killed in the process. Nor could I match up to the three of them myself, men who were probably carrying weapons, when I was not. It was time to get out — if we could.

'They're going to set fire to the offices, aren't they?' Jason gasped.

'Come on! Let's go,' I said brusquely.

'We can't just let them do it!'

'Offices can be rebuilt, Jason — but only if you're alive to do it. Now come on!'

I was thinking we might be able to reach my Land Rover if we moved quickly enough. Reaching Jason's was out of the question. The visitors' car was parked right alongside it. But mine was well this side of both those vehicles, and not far from where we were stood. Ten or fifteen yards. No more.

The engine would still be hot, and dry, I was thinking. So it should start easily. If it did, we could be inside and out of here before the gang realized what was happening. If it didn't, the likelihood was that it would be torched along with Jason's vehicle and the building. Us, too, probably. Getting to it would be a risk, but we had to take it. I didn't know if we could survive a night in weather like this out in the open, miles from anywhere.

'We can't just go!' Jason protested in an agonized whisper. 'I can't leave them to burn the place down.'

'Forget it,' I said roughly. 'We're going!'

If we were to try, it had to be now. Wait any longer, and the flames that were soon going to erupt from the building would leave us with no cover at all, and probably no Land Rover left to reach either.

I grabbed Jason by the upper arm and pushed him out in front of me. We broke cover and dashed for the vehicle, ignoring the shouts that meant somebody had seen us.

The doors of the Land Rover were unlocked. I bundled Jason through the passenger door. Then I ran round to the other side, got in and fired up the ignition. The engine turned and started first go, a rare event and welcome treat.

I swung the Landy round and we bucketed across the parking area and out between the timber posts just as the first flames roared skywards from the office building. Out on the road, I switched the headlights on. They didn't make a lot of difference, given the rain and general blackness of the night, but we needed every incremental advantage we could get.

I put my foot down hard and got the Land Rover moving as fast as it had done in a long time. That still wasn't very fast. If the guys with the Audi — the Tenerifes, as I was thinking of them now — chose to follow us, it wouldn't take them more than a couple of minutes to catch up. I wasn't too worried about that. However fast they caught up, they wouldn't be able to overtake us. Not on this road. It was single lane most of the way back to the village.

What did trouble me was the boss man in the Jag who had left first. I had to assume he would somehow be notified, and would make it his business to stop us. That meant I didn't believe we would be able to reach the village, and the main road out of it. All he would have to do was swing the Jag round to block the road, and then wait for his buddies to arrive and fence us in.

I had to assume, as well, that guns would probably appear at that point, the time for talking over. These were serious criminals, and there was a lot of money at stake. Jason wouldn't be meant to survive the encounter. Even more certainly, nor would I.

We didn't have much speed with my old Landy. What we did have in our favour, though, was all-terrain capability. My much-stressed brain did well and came up with a way we might be able to use that capability. But I needed Jason's detailed local knowledge.

'How can we get up to the old railway?' I shouted over the noise of the labouring engine.

'What railway? There isn't one.'

'The old mineral line I'm talking about.'

'Oh, that! I thought you . . .'

'Can we get up to it? Do you know how?'

'Well . . .' he began uncertainly.

'Jason, there's no time to think about it! Yes, or no? If we can reach it, we can get out of the valley.'

'But the village isn't far!' he yelled back. 'Get there, and we can take the main road out.'

I shook my head. 'They'll probably have the road blocked.'

'They can't do that! What makes you think . . . ?'

'Your millions, Jason! Your bloody money!'

That shut him up. I hoped it got him thinking, as well.

'If I'm wrong,' I said more gently, 'no harm is done. If I'm right, it would be suicidal to carry on into the village. But we won't know if I'm right or not until it's too late to do anything about it. We've got to choose now.'

That got through to him.

'I see what you mean,' he admitted. 'Good thinking. In a Land Rover, you can reach the old mineral track, the rail bed at least. There haven't been actual rails there for about a hundred years. And they won't be able to get there in their cars.'

'That's the point!' I snapped, switching into a lower gear to get us through a series of tight bends. 'How do we get there? Think, man!'

Fortunately, I got an answer this time.

'There's a little street village coming up in a minute. Hill Cottages. There's a track from there up to the old railway.'

Thank Christ for that! I thought with relief. Jason had his brain in gear. And we could do it — maybe!

Already I could see a light on the end of a terrace of cottages not far ahead. It wasn't much — possibly an old streetlight — but it was a beacon representing hope.

'Where's the track you were on about?'

'Just past the first house, on your left.'

Ignoring the fast-approaching headlights behind us, I leaned forward and peered harder through the mucky wind-screen. The lights from behind were dazzling me now. I reached up to the rearview mirror and knocked it aside.

'The track? What's it like?'

'Good enough.'

'Tarmac?'

'No. It's a farm track. Gravel all the way until you hit the rough ground just before the start of the railway.'

How rough would it be? I wondered. Very, I hoped. The rougher, the better. The Landy wouldn't mind.

We were close to the end of the terrace now. I stared ahead, looking for the turnoff. Saw it. But there was something to do before I turned on to it.

'Brace yourself!' I yelled. Then I knocked the stick out of gear and stood on the brake pedal, emergency style.

CHAPTER FIFTEEN

The Audi slammed into the back of us, right into the winch mounted on the rear end of the Land Rover. We jerked forward sharply and Jason cried out with shock as he hit his head on something. I just gritted my teeth and stayed focused, confident the bump wouldn't have done us much damage. Not at the speed we were travelling, and given the strong mounting for the winch. Hopefully, it would be a different story with the Audi. The winch was an effective weapon I had used once before against a chasing posh car that posed a threat.

As I pulled away again, the screech of tortured metal could be heard even above the noise the wind and rain were making. With a final scream, we lurched clear. I saw immediately that one of the Audi's headlights had gone out altogether and the other one was pointing at the sky. Hopefully, there would be more damage than that, a lot more. A busted radiator ought to be near the top of the list.

The Audi had stopped moving. Great! I just hoped it had become a major repair job. In my rearview mirrors, the Audi receded fast as we sped away. I couldn't have begged for more from the winch.

Meanwhile, Jason was trying to recover from the impact, which had taken him by surprise despite my warning. Now he griped, 'What the hell was that for?'

'To slow them down. Take a look in the mirror.'

He glanced at the mirror. Then he turned all the way round to peer through the rear window. 'They've stopped!' he shouted.

'Yeah,' I told him with satisfaction. 'Let's hope it's permanent.'

'Good move!' he said now, fingers tentatively exploring the damage he had sustained.

'Sorry about the head, Jason.'

'Don't worry about it,' he said graciously. 'The only thing that matters is that we stopped them.

'Well, at the very least, we've slowed them down and given ourselves a bit of time and space. I didn't want them getting in front of us as the road widens nearer the village. We'd have been in trouble then. Is this the turnoff, by the way?'

He turned back round to peer ahead. 'Yes. Just past the first house in the row.'

I slowed down and swung round on to a broad gravelled track, and we began to climb up the hillside. The Audi was out of sight, no longer in my mirrors. That really was a relief.

We made our way in second gear up the track, hemmed in by fences on each side of us as the track narrowed. We ran through an open gateway and across a farmyard, and then past a farmhouse that had no lights showing.

After that, for a while, it was just as well that we'd crippled the Audi and left it unable to follow us. The track was now running across gently sloping, open grassland and it would have been possible for us to have been overtaken. The rain might have made the grass greasy and slippery but a determined driver could have done it. I didn't like to think about what might have happened after that. Nothing good, that was for sure.

'We should stop to check for damage?' Jason suggested.

I shook my head. 'Not yet. No need, anyway. There won't be any damage, not to us. It's a different story with that expensive bit of German engineering behind us.'

'I wouldn't have thought this old Land Rover would take a hit like that?'

'I've got a winch mounted on the back, on a specially strengthened steel base. That's what did the damage. We're OK because I've also had the chassis strengthened, as well.'

That seemed to get him thinking. After a few moments he said plaintively, 'I just wish now that I'd put a fire blanket over my Land Rover.'

'Or installed a sprinkler system?'

'Yeah. That might have worked, too.'

'Might have,' I said, smiling.

Jason chuckled.

Things were looking up.

* * *

'They don't seem to be following us,' Jason said a few minutes later, after studying the wing mirror on his side for a while.

'No. I didn't expect them to be. Not up here, on a night like this — and with their front end stove in!'

He considered that for a moment and then said, 'So what's the plan now?'

'Working on it,' I said with a grin.

Actually, the plan had been to save our lives, and we'd done just that. For now, at least. Now we needed a new plan. But for the moment, I concentrated on the driving. That was challenge enough.

CHAPTER SIXTEEN

Junior took Joey Jackson and two others with him when he flew to the UK. Like Jackson, Mike Pearson and Seamus Reagan were cousins of Junior. They were all of a similar age, thirty-something, and were hard, experienced men who knew how to fight and do nasty stuff, as well as having other skills in their repertoire.

'Do you need all them?' George had asked him before they left.

'Dunno. But it's better than going under-resourced, and having to call up more support later on, isn't it?'

'You asking me or telling me?'

Junior shrugged and tried to hide his irritation.

'Just get on with it,' George said in a tone of dismissal. 'And do it right. Send a couple of them back if you find you don't need them. We're supposed to be cost-cutting, remember?'

Junior nodded and turned to go.

'I can understand it now,' George said suddenly, chortling.

'Understand what?'

'How you got the nickname.'

Junior stared at him.

'Putin. Isn't that what some of them call you behind your back?'

'I wouldn't know.'

'Using a sledgehammer to crack a nut!' George said with delight.

Junior departed, in a sullen mood. As he left the room, he could hear his father killing himself laughing. He scowled but kept going.

One day! he reminded himself. One day he would no longer have to put up with crap like that.

* * *

They landed at Heathrow, and then took another flight to Leeds-Bradford, where they rented a couple of the most expensive cars the hire company had on its books. To hell with cost-cutting! If they were going to be doing that, Junior thought, why were they still building that bloody hotel?

George's vanity project. That was all it was, really. His fucking legacy. Well, the way things were going . . . Anyway, when he took over from George he would have the bloody thing demolished. Show the old fart what his legacy was really worth. The business didn't need it, and the family didn't need it either.

* * *

They made their base in a cottage on a farm just outside the village of Rosedale Abbey. It was a holiday let, part of a holiday complex converted from redundant farm buildings. There were several cottages in the group, all of them empty now either because of the time of year or because winter holidaymakers were able at last to go abroad again in search of the sun.

The emptiness suited them very well. So far as Junior was concerned, the location was ideal, although his cousins were not all of the same mind. Distance from the village pub was one complaint — and distance from everywhere else that might provide fun and entertainment another!

'Whitby would have been better,' Mike Pearson suggested. 'Plenty of pubs there, I remember. Good for fish and chips, as well. Not that we're here on holiday, of course,' he added, seeing Junior frown. 'It's just that . . .'

'For crissake, shut the fuck up!' Seamus Reagan said. 'It's not a holiday. We're here for a reason. There's work to be done. The quicker we get it done, the sooner we get back where we can eat and drink in sunshine.'

'I'm glad you said that, Seamus,' Junior said. 'It saves me having to say it. If any of you feel we are here on holiday, you can leave right now. You can walk back to Tenerife, for all I care, and you can stand in front of George and tell him why you didn't do the job he sent you to do. Do I make myself clear? Have you got that?'

There were a few nods and silent assent, which satisfied Junior for the moment, but he knew now there was a weak link in the group who would have to be watched. Mike Pearson might not be fully committed.

'You all right with this, Joey?' he asked Jackson. 'This suit you?'

'It's fine. We won't be here long anyway, will we?'

Junior shook his head. 'A day or two maybe. That's all.'

'Tomorrow,' he said, turning the page, 'we start work. Who knows? We might even get done by the end of the day. Then we can piss off out of here and enjoy yourselves.'

'So what are we doing tomorrow?' Joey asked.

'Not sure yet,' Junior admitted. 'It all depends how cooperative Francine's husband is going to be.'

'Very!' Seamus chortled. 'If I have my way, we'll be done and out in no time at all.'

'That's the spirit!' Junior said with approval. 'You're going to make George a very happy man, talking like that.'

CHAPTER SEVENTEEN

We powered on up the track, passing through more open gates and past a huddle of sheep sheltering in a hollow. Soon after that we hit the start, or the end rather, of the old railway that had been built in the 1860s to serve newly opened iron ore mines in East Rosedale. It had linked them with blast furnaces that had been sprouting along the banks of the River Tees in the previous decade.

For seventy years, the Rosedale railway had done its job well. Then depletion of the ironstone and economic problems had in 1929 brought an end to its life. A scavenger company had bought the failed mining company and ripped up the rails for scrap. But the rail bed remained, and in time it had become a fine route for walkers and, more recently, mountain bikers. With a couple of pals, I had even walked along it myself as a youth. That was what I had in my mind when I was noting the lack of a road out of the northern end of the dale.

The Audi would have been really uncomfortable on the rugged track we were following. It would probably have bottomed out and got stuck in a muddy rut full of rainwater before now. My old Landy took it all in its stride, of course — the driver and passenger a little less well. It was tough going.

Eventually, I stopped for a few minutes to have a rest from the jolting and battering, and to think about what came next. To formulate a plan, though, I needed input from my companion, who I figured for an up-to-date local information source.

'When I was a youngster,' I told him, 'I walked along here with a couple of pals one time. That's how I knew the railway track existed. But walking is a bit different to driving. What I can't remember is where a vehicle can get off the track, if it's possible at all.

'I want to go where the railway used to go, over by the Lion Inn on Blakey Rigg to the Ingleby Incline, but I don't have any idea if we'll be able to drive up on to the Rigg. Do you know?'

'We'll be OK,' Jason said confidently. 'If we continue round the head of the dale, on the other side we'll cross a couple of farm tracks going up to the Rigg. We can use either of them.'

'That's what I wanted to hear!'

I engaged first gear and got us moving again.

* * *

We drove on past old calcining kilns, towering stone memorials to an industry long gone. They were once used to roast the raw ironstone in order to shed it of some of its impurities as well as to reduce the weight, and thereby the cost of transporting the material to the blast furnaces on Teesside. Only the track and the kilns remain from that era now, ruins that speak of what used to happen in this valley when there were five thousand miners plying their trade.

Just past a second group of kilns, high up on the hillside, there's a ruined terrace of miners' cottages called "the Black Houses". I couldn't see them that night, but the memory of them, even from that long ago summer's day when I did see them, made me shiver. They could never have been a good place to live. Little wonder people walked away from them when the mines were abandoned.

'The Black Houses are just up there somewhere, aren't they?' I asked.

'Yes. I can't see well enough to know how close we are to them, though.'

'Black Houses. Do you know where the name came from?'

'Not really. I just assumed it was because they didn't have chimneys to let the smoke out from the fires.'

'Like the Black Houses on Skye? That would explain it. The people living in them must have been kippered!'

'How they lived then,' Jason said with a wry chuckle.

'Terrible. Warm enough, perhaps, but not very good for your health.'

'Well, getting or keeping warm was probably all that mattered on a January night up here.'

I couldn't agree more.

* * *

We didn't get much further before I had to jam on the brakes in a hurry. I could no longer see the paleness of the stone on the gravelled track, however hard I peered. Switching the wipers on faster didn't help either. Nor did switching the lights between high and low beam. The way ahead remained dark and unclear.

'Where the hell's the track?' I wondered.

Jason leaned forward, peering hard through the windscreen. 'Looks like mud ahead — perhaps a landslip.'

'A landslip?' I groaned with frustration. 'Just what we need. I hope we can get through the bloody thing!'

I took a torch from a pocket under the dashboard and opened the door. Then I screwed my eyes tight and gritted my teeth as the wind shrieked and hurled sheets of rain, seemingly touched with sleet now, at my unprepared face. What a night!

Head down, I walked forward a few yards to the point where the grey gravel of the track became black with oozing mud from the peat-clad hillside. As far ahead as the torch could reach the picture was the same. Liquid mud all the way. Truly, a landslip.

With the toe-end of my boot, I stirred the mud immediately in front of me. It was only a few inches deep here at the edge. The Land Rover could handle that all right, but what was the depth like further on?

'It will be deeper in the middle!' Jason yelled at me.

I nodded. 'That's what I was thinking.'

Then I grimaced and turned back to the vehicle. Jason followed me.

Back inside, under cover, we went into deep thought mode. I wiped the rainwater from my face and ran my hands through my hair while I wondered what to do. It wasn't hard to reach a realistic conclusion.

'We're stuck,' I concluded. 'For now, at least. We'll just have to wait here till daylight. I don't want to risk trying to get through that lot in the dark. If the mud's still moving, it could take us over the edge.

'I'm not going to risk trying to turn round, either. The track's too narrow, and the ground at the edge is going to be soft with all this rain. We're on a steep hillside here, and I don't want to end up at the bottom of it.'

'I think you're right,' Jason said, nodding.

That was a relief. If he hadn't agreed, I would have told him to get out and walk. We simply had to stay put until we had light enough to see what the situation ahead was. There wasn't really any sensible option.

'This will happen from time to time, does it?' I asked.

'Landslip? Yes, it does. Only in this section, though. As you said, the hillside is really steep here. So this section of the track is a bit perilous.'

Perilous? I thought with a rueful smile. I liked that description. It seemed very apt.

I was getting to like Jason, as well. He was decent company, and we were doing well together.

'Let's just settle down for the next few hours,' I suggested. 'First, though, I'll reverse twenty or thirty yards, to make sure we're well away from the danger ground. Can you guide me?'

'Makes sense,' Jason said. 'Let's do it.'

I couldn't really see anything much at all behind me, and I was concerned about the danger of inadvertently reversing over the edge of the track and plummeting several hundred feet into whatever was down there. So, with Jason waving and calling guidance, I stuck my head out of the window and backed up far enough to be out of immediate danger from the moving mud. Then I pulled into the side of the track and stopped hard against a rock wall that offered some protection against a widening of the landslip.

All we had to worry about now was a possible avalanche of boulders and stones dislodged by the heavy run-off from seasonal rain. That, and the gang from Tenerife, of course. We couldn't afford to forget about the Reagans. One way or another, we still had more than enough to worry about.

'What time will it get light around here?' I asked, when Jason was back in the cab. I figured that, being a nature watcher by profession, he was more likely than me to know.

'Dawn will be about six, and sunrise about seven. Given the weather, though, I don't expect to see the sun much at all tomorrow.'

'But sometime between six and seven-ish there should be daylight enough for us to see what's what?'

Jason nodded.

The weather meant the light would probably be late coming, and visibility would remain poor all day. That suited me quite well. It meant the opposition would struggle to find where we were.

'I feel sorry for the guys from Tenerife,' I said cheerfully. 'They won't enjoy our weather.'

'I'm very sorry for them, as well. Maybe they'll just pack up and go home?'

Nothing like hoping. Still, it was a thought that gave us something to smile about at last.

* * *

So, we had a few hours to wait before daybreak. It seemed sensible to sort ourselves out a bit and try to find a little comfort. That wouldn't be an easy thing to do in the Land Rover, but it was worth trying.

'What have you got in that backpack you brought?' I asked. 'Anything to eat, or that's otherwise useful to people in our position?'

'Not much. There's a couple of energy bars. Otherwise, it's mostly personal junk, and stuff for banks and lawyers.'

'Only energy bars, huh? Well, you're in luck. I can bring a bit more than that to the table.'

Of late, I'd been carrying more than my usual emergency supplies, as I'd been doing a bit of travelling in remote country. Happily, I'd not yet got round to emptying the back of the Land Rover.

I fished out a couple of sleeping bags, for a start. 'Wrap yourself up in this,' I suggested, handing him one. 'Or get inside it, and stretch out best you can in the back of the vehicle. There's not a lot of room, and it'll be a bit of a squash with all the other stuff in there, but I know it can be done. I've done it myself.'

'I won't sleep.'

'Perhaps not. But if nothing else, you'll keep warm and you'll be resting.'

Next, I came up with a small camping stove, a kettle and a big bottle of water. 'Coffee or tea?' I enquired.

'You came well prepared, Frank!' Jason said with a chuckle.

'Oh, I'm a regular boy scout! Didn't you know? I've even got something to eat, somewhere in here.'

In the back of the vehicle, I got the water heating on the stove and started to rummage through a big cardboard box.

'Self-heating meals!' I announced triumphantly, holding up a couple of packets. 'I knew I still had some.'

Jason peered suspiciously at what I was holding up for inspection.

'Army field rations,' I told him. 'Chicken or meat balls. What's your preference?'

CHAPTER EIGHTEEN

We settled down to rest, if not to sleep. Given the pounding rain and the rocking of the Land Rover when the screaming wind hit it, sleep would have eluded all but survivors from World War One battlefield trenches. But cocooned in the sleeping bags, fed and watered, we were dry and warm, and at least able to rest. Thinking was possible, too, and I had plenty of that to do.

Hopefully, we would find a way through the morass of mud when daylight came, and get out of here. Assuming we could carry on round the head of the dale and up onto Blakey Rigg, we would have a multiple-choice question to face then: where to go next, out of the many possibilities. The answer would largely depend on how Jason saw the future — his future, that is.

Flight had been forced on us, but it wasn't sustainable. It was clear to me that sooner rather than later, the appropriate authorities, and the forces of law and order, needed to be brought in to take charge of the situation. That meant we ought to go as fast as we could to the nearest police station. For me, that would be job done then. I couldn't solve all Jason's problems. I would like to, but I was only one man. I couldn't save the world either.

All that was long-term thinking, though. Right now, we were a long way from a police station, and we couldn't call for help either.

I decided to leave the long term to look after itself. There was enough to worry about in the short term. Survival was the immediate priority. Big questions, like what to do after we got out of Rosedale, could wait until our wheels were on Blakey Rigg's tarmac. Just getting there, perhaps getting through the night even, was going to be enough of a challenge.

'I suppose you do this sort of thing all the time, do you?' Jason asked after a restful period of silence.

'What? Sit out a storm in my Land Rover?'

'You know what I mean,' he said with a chuckle. 'Security work. Bodyguarding, or whatever it is you do.'

'Working as a close protection officer, as we say in the trade?'

'Yes. I suppose so. Helping people like me, anyway.'

I decided he wasn't trying to take the piss. He was either filling in a silence that had become oppressive, or else he was genuinely seeking information. Perhaps he was just curious about the life I led, and how I could make a living out of it. Sometimes I wondered that myself.

'I've done my share of close protection work,' I admitted, 'but I'm not a specialist. I can't afford to be. I'm a one-man band, not a company that employs lots of people, all with different skill sets. I take on whatever comes in. Sometimes it's a private enquiry, like looking for a lost dog or husband. Or it can be setting up security for a vulnerable place or person. Occasionally, I just have to deal with trouble that arrives unexpectedly.'

'Like mine!' he said ruefully.

I chuckled, but he wasn't wrong. Emergencies happen. And if you're standing in their way, you have to do something.

'How do you get paid in your line of work? I've sometimes wondered about that. You see these movies featuring private eyes, but unless they find a gold bar that they're allowed to keep, you never really learn how they make their living.'

'Sometimes a cheque arrives in the post,' I told him. 'And sometimes I have to submit an invoice first, or go round afterwards banging on doors and making threats. Not all clients are eager to pay once their problem is solved. And some can't pay.'

'Just like any business, then?'

'Yes. I suppose it is.'

'Do you make a standard charge or does it depend on the job, and what you have to do?'

I had a wry smile about that. There were no fixed rules, much as sometimes I would like to have some.

'For most jobs I charge a daily rate, a working day being either twelve or twenty-four hours, depending on the situation. Other jobs, it depends entirely on results.'

I shrugged and added, 'Well, how do you get paid, Jason?'

'My salary is paid into my bank account every month.'

'Always the same amount?'

'Yes, unless we've had a pay rise or income tax has gone up.'

'Regardless of what you've actually done?'

'Yes.'

I smiled. 'Well, it's not like that for me. Actually, it used to be, once upon a time. But I got bored with it, and gave up on that way of making a living.'

'That's about where I am,' Jason said, surprising me.

'Oh?'

'I've got plans that will lead to a different way of life.'

I assumed he was talking about the estate, or farm, that he wanted to buy and rewild. Nice idea, rewild. You had to wonder, though, how it was going to compensate for the loss of a regular salary. Maybe it wouldn't, and he'd just have to dip further into the ten million quid he'd won. He ought to be able to manage for quite a while doing just that.

'Want to tell me about your plans?'

'I don't mind,' he said with a sigh. 'First, though, there's something else I want to ask you. Could I retain you to work for me? I'd pay your daily, or twenty-four hour retainer, of course.'

That took me aback a bit. Jason had come in at an angle and taken me by surprise.

'Retain me to do what, Jason? And for how long, or until what happens?'

'I would like you to do your best to keep me safe until the end of next week. For doing that, I'll pay you your usual rate.'

'That's a thousand quid a day, Jason.'

'Fine. Will you do it?'

'Let me think about it,' I said.

CHAPTER NINETEEN

Junior tired of waiting to hear what was going on and drove back down the valley to see for himself. What he found was Pearson and Reagan sitting in the Audi, out of the rain, and an exceptionally wet and bedraggled Joey Jackson working feverishly under the bonnet to try to get the damned thing started and working again.

'What the hell's happened?' Junior demanded, looking at the damaged front end of the Audi.

They told him they weren't sure.

'All I know,' Seamus said, 'is we were up close behind your man in his vehicle when there was this big crash, and everything went kaput after that.'

'Who was driving?'

'Me,' Pearson said.

Junior grimaced, pulled his coat collar up in response to a ferocious gust of wind-driven rain and leaned down to look Pearson in the eye through the open window. 'You mean you crashed into him?'

'I wouldn't say that, exactly.'

'What would you say?'

Pearson just shrugged, as if to say what had happened was beyond his comprehension.

Junior curbed his tongue and went back to Joey, who was still doing things under the bonnet. 'Any good?' he asked.

Joey straightened up and shook his head. 'It's a knacker job. I can't fix it. Not here. The hire firm or the dealer needs to collect it.'

'What's the problem?'

'The entire front end is smashed in, including the radiator. It was a hard hit, too hard. One thing we've learned,' Joey added, almost with admiration, 'is that the back end of a Land Rover isn't a soft touch.'

Junior straightened up, disgusted, and getting very wet himself now. 'And he just got away?' he said, meaning the Mack kid.

'Looks like it,' Joey admitted. 'Nothing we could do about it.'

'Where did he go? I passed no one on the way back here.'

'Off-road, I would guess. Maybe some farm track? I don't know.'

Junior bit his lip for a moment and took a decision. 'Come on,' he said. 'Leave it. I want you all in the Jag. We're getting out of here.'

'What we going to do, Junior?' Seamus called.

'We're going to abandon that heap of junk, get new vehicles and look harder for that kid. He's not going to be hard to find, wherever he went.' Junior paused and then added, 'There's other things we can do, as well.'

'Other things? What other things?'

'Stake out his house, and one or two other places. Get at his family. There's plenty we can do.'

'We haven't got the resources to do all that,' Pearson pointed out.

'We'll get more. Come on!'

* * *

'I need more men here, George.'

'More men? More? Why?'

67

Junior winced at the hint of sarcasm in George's voice. It looked like being as difficult a conversation as he had anticipated.

'It's night here and foul weather, and the target has run. He's going to be hard to find in the time we have. We need to stake out a few places. I also want to put more pressure on him.'

'Pressure? Like what?'

'He's got family, hasn't he? He can hide, but they can't.'

George was quiet for a few moments, thinking it over. Then he said, 'That's good, Junior. Good thinking. Get on with it. And, remember, if pressure on the family isn't working, don't hesitate to take the short cut. The Mack kid doesn't have to survive. Understand me?'

'I've got that in mind, George. What about some extra help?'

'I'll get on that right away. Any preferences about who you want?'

'Not really. I want them mainly for stakeouts. We don't need anyone special.'

'That's good. We're a bit stretched at the moment, as you know. The hotel is taking up a lot of our resources — and it's not even open yet.'

That fucking hotel! Junior thought with a scowl. *There it is again. It's getting to be all anyone thinks about. And George . . . Well, it's an obsession with him. It wouldn't be if I was in charge. We'd be walking away from the damned thing. Let the bloody Italians have it!*

'OK, George. That's good. Let me know who to expect, and when.'

CHAPTER TWENTY

I didn't know enough about Jason's situation to be able to answer his question immediately. I needed more information, a lot more.

'I want to know more about what's going on,' I told him. 'There wasn't time for Amy to say much, and your uncle told me nothing at all. So, although I thank you for your offer, I need to hear more about what I would be getting into before I can tell you yes or no.'

'What do you want to know?'

'Let's start at the beginning. Give me some context. How long have you been working at the nature reserve, for a start?'

'Ten years. Ever since I completed a degree course in environmental studies at Huddersfield University.'

'So you're well settled?'

'Very. At least, I was. I've been doing what I wanted to do, and this is a good area to do it in. So I've been happy to be here.'

'But things changed for you when you got married, I gather. How long ago was that?'

'Coming up to three years.' He gave a wry chuckle and added, 'They didn't really change then, you know. Not much anyway. The marriage only lasted three weeks. Then Francine announced that it wasn't for her and took off back to daddy's in Tenerife, which was where we'd got married.'

'Was that because of you or the place, do you think?'

'A bit of both, probably. Plus the poverty. I mean, by her standards. I earn a decent salary, but Francine has been brought up in the lap of luxury — with anything she wants, that money can buy, provided for her.

'When I met her she seemed to be going through a phase where she wanted a different kind of life, a simpler one. Living closer to nature with me appealed to her — briefly. That didn't last long.

'And I'd never met anyone like her. Vivacious and full of life. Spoiled and temperamental, as well, but I thought I could cope with that. I disregarded it. We were good together.

'So after a blissful few days Francine announced that she would like us to be married, and we just went off and did it. Got married — Vegas style! Well, it would have been, if Vegas had a beach.'

'You got married on the beach in Tenerife?'

'Yeah.'

It wasn't necessary to ask if he, too, had soon come down to earth once he was back home. Unnecessary, and unnecessarily painful too. He must have often wondered since whatever had possessed him.

Instead, I asked if he'd known about Francine's background.

He shook his head. 'Not really. Not at first. She just told me her father was a businessman, and had something to do with property. Nothing about the family's criminal activities, if that's what you mean.'

'Did she know herself?'

'I've thought about that a lot. She can't not have known. It would have been damn near impossible.

'But perhaps that was part of why she fancied a change of lifestyle, to get away from all that. Either that or it was just a temporary, emotional thing. Perhaps she'd had a row with her father, or he wouldn't buy her something she really, really wanted. I don't know. But I wouldn't be surprised. She could be very lovely and a lot of fun, but she was also very flighty and materialistic.'

I couldn't help thinking it must have been an earth-shattering change of scene for them both, that marriage. They weren't the first people to have made that kind of mistake, though, and they wouldn't be the last. It wasn't always the young who succumbed, either.

'So Francine just took off,' I said. 'What did you hear from her after that?'

'Nothing. Not a thing.'

'Until you won a pile of money on the Lottery?'

'Yes. Exactly. I couldn't say I'd forgotten about being married. You can't do that. But I'd known since she left that the marriage was over. I just hadn't done anything about it, about getting a divorce or whatever.'

'I wanted to avoid difficulties, put it all out of my mind, I suppose. I wanted to get back to normal life — my real life — as fast as possible.'

'I don't believe you're unusual in that respect, Jason. I understand perfectly. I'd probably have been the same myself.'

'Would you? Would you really?'

Who can say? I nodded anyway, and moved on.

'So you won a lot of money, and that was when Francine reappeared in your life?'

'Yes. Legally, she's entitled to lay claim to some of it, I suppose. Maybe even half, from what I've read. But I had plans for it already. Mind you, so did she!'

'Tell me about your plans, Jason.'

'I want to buy a farm, an estate actually, and rewild it.'

'You mentioned it before. That really would be something, wouldn't it?'

'I think so. You know what I do for a living. I'm a committed wildlife guy, and I've thought over the years how wonderful it would be to take part in the rewilding movement. Make a living from the land while still protecting the environment and keeping it fit for all the creatures that live there naturally. Now I have the opportunity to do that, thanks to the Lottery.'

'Nice. But, from what Amy told me, Francine disapproves?'

'I don't know if she thinks about it one way or the other. She just has plans of her own for the money, and they conflict with mine.'

'What does she want to do with it?'

'Her focus is on residential property. She wants a villa in southern California, where all the celebs live, and another one in France. Maybe an apartment in London or Paris, as well. She's dreaming. The money wouldn't go anywhere near paying for all that.'

Dreaming. Like Jason, I couldn't help thinking, but didn't say. Jason's dream seemed infinitely more worthwhile than Francine's did.

'Her wish list does sound a bit expensive. Even if you gave her everything you won, it wouldn't be enough, would it?'

He shook his head. 'Nowhere near. When I offered her half a million quid, because I have to accept she probably has some sort of legal entitlement, she just laughed at me and said she would see what her father had to say about that.'

'And now we know.'

He nodded.

I mulled over what Jason had just told me, and wondered if I could usefully play a continuing part in his travails.

'Why would you want my services only until the end of next week?'

'There's a deadline. I found an estate that's up for sale and that I really like. It would be perfect for what I want to do. Bids were invited. So I bid, and had my bid accepted. A week on Friday I'm due to sign the legal documents and pay the money.'

'And that's the deadline?'

He nodded. 'After that, a substantial part of the money will be gone. So it won't matter then what Francine's family threaten and do.'

Hmm. I wasn't too sure about that. It seemed to me that there was a fair chance that the family might want to finish him off anyway, for business reasons, or even if it was just out of rage or in a spirit of pure vengeance. Then they — Widow Francine, technically — would be able to claim all of Jason's assets, and possibly put the estate back on the market and gather the proceeds from its sale.

Francine's dad was a successful businessman, after all. Whatever else was a clear-eyed, forward-looking, tough, experienced businessman — criminal or not — going to do but look ahead and chart the most rewarding course to take?

'So will you help me survive to the end of next week?' Jason asked.

I nodded. 'I wouldn't be able to look your Uncle Jimmy in the eye ever again if I turned you down.'

'That's a yes, is it?'

'It is.'

'Deal!' Jason said with a chuckle.

'Deal. Right, now we've got that settled, let's try to get some sleep before the sun comes up.'

CHAPTER TWENTY-ONE

I didn't expect to see sunshine when I woke up, and I didn't. What I did see, through a windscreen thick with condensation, was grey light and swirling tendrils of mist. The Landy was still shaking a bit with the wind, but nothing like it had been at the height of the storm. And the rain seemed to have stopped, or perhaps just paused.

I lay still for a minute or two, eyes open, listening to the world outside, acclimatizing myself. Then I sat up, opened the driver's door and clambered outside to stretch and ease the stiffness I could feel in every joint. I have to admit, you don't get a comfortable night's rest in a Land Rover, not one like mine anyway.

The air was chill and damp. But not fresh, which it is when it comes off the sea at Risky Point. This air smelled of mud and decaying vegetation. It was the universal scent of land that mariners know so well.

I gazed around. Visibility wasn't good, but I could see all I wanted to see. Nothing was moving on the track, either behind or in front of us. There was plenty of swirling cloud in the dale below our position, but from time to time I glimpsed a farm down there. What was the betting it was called "Dale Head Farm", I wondered?

I turned round and studied the mudflow that had stopped our progress. It was still moving. Smelly and dark brown, and very liquid, it was still oozing down the hillside and across the old rail bed, then to disappear over the edge and plop into the depths.

A signpost bearing a notice warning of the danger of landslips had been dislodged and pushed aside. I picked it up and used the pole to test the depth of the mud in front of me, without wading out into it. Even near my feet it was several inches deep, and getting deeper as I reached out a bit further. I grimaced. The mudflow was a good thirty or forty yards across, and it would be much deeper in the middle.

A car door slammed shut behind me and I turned to look at Jason.

'Welcome to the new day,' I told him. 'What kept you?'

'Yeah,' he said with a scowl. Then he nodded at the mud and added, 'What do you think?'

'We'll have to find another way of getting out, Jason. It's too deep, too risky. I'm not going to try to go through it.'

'Pretty bad, eh?'

'I wouldn't even risk your Landy in this, never mind mine. If you still had one, that is.'

'Don't remind me,' he said with a grimace.

'Come on! Cheer up. It's insured, isn't it? Let's have a couple of all-day breakfast packs while we think about what we're going to do.'

'Breakfast, as well? You're very well equipped, Frank.'

'I have to be. You get to some funny places, at strange times, doing what I do for a living.'

We cut open the bags, added a drop of water to the heat pouches and warmed up a couple of breakfast packs for the ten minutes that was all it took to get them steaming hot. Then we gorged ourselves on the contents, mostly baked beans and little sausages, while we waited for the kettle to heat the water for coffee. Not gourmet dining, but hot nutrition. And very welcome, given the situation in which we found ourselves.

We got back in the Land Rover with our mugs of coffee and I pored over the OS 1;25,000 map for the area. I was looking for a way out of our predicament that didn't require us to return to Hill Cottages, where the Tenerifes might still be waiting for us. I had no success until Jason piped up.

'A little way back,' he said, 'they've been doing some forestry work in an ancient wood in a small side valley.'

'Yeah?'

'They had to put in a little track from the bottom of the hillside to reach the wood.'

'That right?'

'And from that track you can get to Dale Head Farm. Well, one of them. There's two with that name. I'm talking about the one on the east side of the dale.'

I had to smile. Dale Head Farm, eh? I wasn't wrong. But two of them!

'The one on our side?'

'Yes. And from the farm, there's a good track through a couple of other farms, and then another one up to the road on Blakey Rigg.'

Ah! This might be it. I closed the map and turned to look at him. 'Does this new forestry track come up here to the old railway?'

He shook his head. 'No, unfortunately. But I'm wondering if we might be able to reach it anyway, somehow.'

'That would certainly solve our problem.' I pushed map and torch behind the seat and gulped the rest of my coffee. 'Let's find out.'

CHAPTER TWENTY-TWO

With Jason's guidance, to make sure I didn't fall off the edge, I got turned round and we set off back along the track.

'It's not far,' Jason said. 'Maybe half a mile. A bit more, perhaps.'

We didn't actually get that far. Far sooner than I would have liked, we spotted two vehicles in the distance coming towards us. They looked like all-wheel drive SUVs, or the equivalent. Not Land Rovers anyway.

'It's them!' Jason gasped, sitting up straight and staring hard ahead.

My thoughts, exactly. Unfortunately.

'How much further till we can get off the track, Jason?' I demanded abruptly.

'Not far.'

I put my foot down.

Something started happening up ahead of us. The approaching vehicles stopped. Figures emerged. Fingers were pointed towards us. Urgent consultations took place. Then the figures got back into the vehicles, which started moving again.

Through all they had lost a couple of minutes, which we had gained and used.

'How far now?' I yelled, my foot jammed down hard on the accelerator.

'The edge of the woodland coming up!'

Couple of hundred yards only. But could we make it? It would be touch and go. The approaching vehicles were starting to fill the windscreen.

I gritted my teeth, screwed up my eyes and listened to the inner voice screaming at me to *Keep Going!*

Another few seconds. That's all we needed.

Come on, come on, come on! I urged the Landy. *You can do it! You can, you can, you can . . .*

Then I knew we weren't going to make it. The Tenerifes would reach the edge of the woodland before we did, and block off any possible exit.

'We'll have to jump!' I yelled. 'Grab your pack!'

Jason reached behind the seat. While he was doing that, things ahead of us changed. The lead vehicle approaching us swerved sideways to block the track. The second vehicle stopped behind it.

I kept going. Only fifty yards to the first vehicle now. Forty yards, thirty . . . I still couldn't see an escape route. The valley side fell away below us far too steeply for me to see anything at all down there.

Only one thing left to do now. No option. We'd run out of space and time.

'Hang on!' I shouted.

Then I swung the steering wheel round, clamped my teeth hard together and steered straight for the edge of the track and the open sky beyond.

CHAPTER TWENTY-THREE

Jason screeched with alarm. I slipped my foot off the throttle, braced myself and clung tightly to the steering wheel as we went over the edge. For a brief moment there was quiet, and I saw clear sky all around us. Then the front end of the vehicle dipped and all was blurred images and confusion as we dropped precipitously and hit the steep slope with an almighty bone-shaking crash.

There was no logical way we could have avoided toppling end over end down the hillside, but somehow we did. My head slammed into the roof. My body was thrown one way and then the other, ignoring the constraint of the seat belt, in a sickening, stomach-turning sequence of jerks and wrenches. And the noise was terrifying.

The Landy hit the ground hard, but somehow stayed upright as it bounced forward several times before swinging sideways to lurch and crash down the hillside, constantly on the brink of turning over. Saplings lashed at us. We hit trees, trunks and branches that may have slowed our descent a little, but I don't really know. Everything happened so fast, and there was nothing I could do about any of it. I hung on to the steering wheel desperately, but without being able to influence how or where we moved in the slightest.

Somehow we missed the big head-on collision with a massive tree trunk that would have brought our descent to a summary halt. Without any help or guidance from me, the Landy crashed downwards until we hit the forestry track Jason had told me about. Then, shaking violently and sounding like a bag of tin cans, the Landy settled at last on its own four wheels.

I eased out of it too, gradually returning to the familiar world. Heart hammering, pulse racing, I blinked a few times and swallowed experimentally as my body tried to do normal things. Then I turned my head cautiously and looked for Jason. It seemed bad. He appeared to be unconscious, or worse.

But after a few still moments, an eye opened. I sagged back with relief and closed my own eyes again while I gave thanks.

'Jesus Christ,' Jason mumbled through bloody lips. 'You mad bugger!'

I wiped my own lips with the back of my hand, blinked hard and managed to reply.

'I agree totally,' I told him.

That was all I could manage for the moment.

But it wasn't a time for talking, anyway. Overcoming my desire for inertia, rest and silence, and ignoring the symphony of metallic creaks and groans from the Landy, I reached for the ignition, wondering if the stalled engine would ever start again.

The starter motor whirred long and hard. At least, that was still working, but nothing more happened.

I stopped, waited a minute and gave it another go. Same thing. Jason opened his door, looking as if he was ready to abandon ship.

'Wait!' I urged, grabbing him by the arm. I gave the starter motor another go. And this time the engine roared into life.

I forced my door open with difficulty, as it or the frame had been distorted by our descent. Then I eased myself out and checked to see if we still had four wheels before I tried to get the vehicle to do anything else, like moving. We did. Four wheels. I glanced up at the hillside, and wondered how on earth we'd kept them, when I saw where we'd just come from.

Then I jumped back inside, engaged first gear in a hurry, and got us moving. I had seen faces peering over the edge of the track, and moments later heard the crack of what sounded like gunfire. Something hit the roof of the Landy and ricocheted off with a screech. The Tenerifes weren't mad enough to follow us, but they were obviously angry enough to do everything they could to stop us leaving.

A bullet hit and knocked out the wing mirror on Jason's side of the car. Then we were deeper amongst the trees, and if more shots were fired, we knew nothing about them.

We slipped and bounced down the hillside, moving as fast as we could reasonably go, which wasn't very fast at all. There was no question of piloting a route either. I just focused on what was immediately in front of us, and did my best to avoid a calamity.

In the poor, early morning light, in misty conditions and amongst the trees, it didn't seem as if we were on a track cleared by foresters. Soon it was obvious that we weren't. I kept going anyway. We just needed to get as far away as we could, as fast as possible.

'Does this feel like the right way to you?' I shouted, trying to make myself heard above the roar of the engine and the bumping and banging as we lurched downhill between the trees.

'More or less!' Jason shouted back.

I left it there. From what I could remember from the map, we would come out somewhere near Dale Head Farm. Then we would be able to make our way over to Bush Farm, and after that pick up the track leading on to Blakey Rigg. Maybe.

Provided we didn't hit a tree or fall into a ravine in the meantime. This wasn't a difficult drive. Not really a drive of any description. It was more like falling. We slid and slithered, and crashed our way through the undergrowth, all the way down to the bottom of the hillside. And there we stopped for a couple of minutes to have a rest.

'Were they really, actually shooting at us?' Jason asked wonderingly.

'That's what they were doing,' I admitted. 'With a rifle, as well. Not just handguns.'

'I can't believe it,' he said.

Myself, I didn't have any doubts at all about what had happened. I wasn't even surprised. It was more or less what I had been expecting all along, ever since first talking to Amy. They were a tough lot, the Reagans.

By now, they had probably given up thoughts of persuading Jason to put his money into their investment project. It would seem simpler just to make Francine a widow. A couple of times already they had come perilously close to doing just that. I knew I was going to have my work cut out trying to keep Jason alive until the end of next week.

But I would do my best, and after that, somebody else could have the job!

CHAPTER TWENTY-FOUR

Somehow or other, mostly by sheer luck, we had reached the foot of the hillside and now had emerged from the woodland to find ourselves facing a five-bar gate that barred entrance to a field. I kept the engine running, in case I couldn't get it started again, but switched off the lights. We didn't need them now we were out of the wood, and there was no point advertising our whereabouts. Then I sat for a few moments, massaging my aching hands.

'Tough drive,' Jason said with a grin.

I smiled and agreed. Fundamentally, though, I was just surprised that we'd made it. All the way down, I'd been anticipating the Land Rover slipping into a gully or jamming itself inextricably between rocks and trees. It seemed like a miracle that that hadn't happened.

'They must be tough machines, these old Land Rovers,' Jason added. 'Stronger than the modern versions anyway. I don't believe mine would have emerged in one piece from a journey like that — if I still had it.'

'I appreciate that remark, Jason. And so does my Landy. Thank you very much indeed. You certainly know what you're talking about. Now, get out and open that bloody gate, please! And while you're at it, see if you can work out where we are.'

'I know that already,' he said, opening the door. 'If we go straight across two fields, we'll get to the track to the east side's Dale Head Farm.'

'Thank God for that!'

* * *

We ran as quickly as we could across the fields and along the farm tracks that took us to the other side of the dale, passing very close to two farms without stopping at either of them. It was still pretty early for me, if not for farm folk with cows to milk, and I preferred to pass by as little noticed as possible.

I would have liked to stop somewhere and make another mug of coffee to help me recover from having been so badly used that morning. Not just yet, though. I wanted to be up the other side of the valley and out of Rosedale before we did that. If the Tenerifes had bothered looking at a map, they would know what I knew: that if we didn't go back to the village where our journey had begun, the farm track up to Blakey Rigg was the only exit from Rosedale by vehicle. I didn't want to find them up there, waiting for us.

'Assuming we can get up on to Blakey Rigg,' I said, 'what do you want to do next, Jason?'

'I'm paying you to look after me till next Friday, remember? You're in charge. So you think of something. What do you bloody well suggest?'

'Heading for the nearest police station,' I responded with a grin. 'That's what the smart money would say.'

'Stuff that! Can't do that.'

'Why not?'

'Two reasons. My sister, Amy, and my Uncle Jimmy.'

'They've been threatened?'

'Through me, they have. Neither of them is likely to survive a failure to reach agreement with the family, I was told.'

I grimaced, but I wasn't surprised. It was what I'd expected. Organized crime outfits work with a broad brush, and the nearest and dearest invariably come into the picture when they encounter an intractable obstacle. Jason was lucky he hadn't been presented with an ear or a finger from one of his relatives already. There was still time, of course.

'Let me think about it,' I told him.

We hit the track leading up to the ridge. The engine growled in protest but accepted the challenge. Gravel and mud spurted out in our wake. Sheep in adjacent fields lifted their heads at the noise made by something that wasn't the usual tractor. The noise we were making wasn't what I usually heard either. Something was wrong with my poor old Landy. But this was no time to stop and try to find out what it was.

'I'm just hoping we don't have a reception committee waiting on top,' I confided.

'Yeah. Me, too.'

'Assuming there isn't, I want to get up there and then disappear. Normally, I would have suggested my place at Risky Point, but we can't go there.'

'Because of Uncle Jimmy?'

'Amy, as well. I told her to take him there.'

Thankfully, the road seemed to be clear when we breasted the ridge and emerged, astonishingly, into clear blue sky and sunshine. The mist, or cloud, was all down in the valley. It was a different world up here.

I stopped at the edge of the tarmac and looked questioningly at Jason, who seemed to be struggling with something he wanted to say. 'Left or right?' I asked him.

'I know where we could go, Frank — where I'd like to go, at least,' he said hesitantly.

'It wouldn't be a farm in Northumberland, by any chance, would it?'

He smiled and nodded.

'OK. We can do that. First, though, there's something else we need to do.'

CHAPTER TWENTY-FIVE

'What do you think?' Joey Jackson asked.

They were stood on the edge of the track, peering down into the cloud swirling over the woodland, wondering what had happened to the Land Rover.

Junior shook his head. 'Madness,' he said.

It was beyond him. But somehow the Mack kid, and whoever was helping him, had survived yet again. He heard the engine roar as the Land Rover came back to life.

'Put the rifle away, Mike,' he said. 'It's no good now.'

'Maybe I got him?' Pearson said hopefully.

'Yeah. Maybe you did. So who's driving the fucking vehicle, you moron!'

Junior turned to Joey Jackson, who was still looking at him, awaiting an answer to his question.

'They're away, Joey. And we're not following them down there. We'll just go back to the village. Maybe we'll intercept them there. If not, there's other things we can do.'

'Like what?'

'Like I told George, Mack has family. That's his weak spot.'

Joey nodded and headed back to the SUV he was driving. *Trust Junior*, he thought. *He's like his dad. Always got something up his sleeve.*

'Come on!' Junior said to the others. 'We can't stand around here all day.'

CHAPTER TWENTY-SIX

Northumberland, eh? Well, OK. But I didn't think we could make it that far, not in this vehicle, given the shape it was in. The noise from under the bonnet was becoming very worrying. It was far too loud. And the roar from the engine was accompanied by a lot of clanking and anguished squealing from unhappy moving parts elsewhere in the machine. The suspension system had obviously taken a beating, as well. All that without even thinking about the cracked and starred windscreen and windows.

All in all, my poor old Landy had taken a rare thrashing in the last hour or so and was understandably feeling its age. I didn't believe tea and sympathy would help much either. What was needed, and badly, was time out for rest and recuperation. Preferably in a well-tooled garage with people who knew what they were doing and had access to ample spare parts. That added up to one thing for me. I knew where to go.

I turned left on to the road that runs along the top of Blakey Rigg. After a couple of hundred yards, I turned right on to another gravel track, a continuation of the old mineral railway from Rosedale to Teesside.

'Frank?' Jason said, puzzled. 'What are you thinking?'

'Bear with me. We've got problems with the vehicle.'

'I was wondering about that. How bad is it?'

'Hard to say. But bad enough.'

We trundled down the track gingerly for a few hundred yards until we rounded a small hillock. I stopped there, where we couldn't be seen from the road, and got out to check under the bonnet. I didn't see any obvious problem there that I could fix on the spot. No loose pipes or connections. Nothing like that. But I knew a lot was wrong, and I had serious concern about how far the Landy could take us now. Not very, probably. And certainly not as far as Northumberland.

'What do you think?' Jason asked again, coming over to join me.

'We need to change vehicles.'

'I thought as much,' he said with a grimace. 'Just our luck! We're going to really need a four-by-four, as well, if we're going up to Northumberland.'

'We'll get one. Don't worry about that. I was thinking of changing vehicles anyway, just in case they're able to track us in this one.'

'How could they do that?'

'Oh, there's ways and means, especially if you have plenty of money to throw around.'

'Well, Francine's family certainly have that.'

'Number plate recognition technology is one possibility, perhaps by hacking or bribing their way into the police or DVLA systems. Or the Department of Transport's. I'm not saying they will have done that. I'm just saying it can be done, and I want to avoid the risk.'

'So what do you think we should do?'

'I'm going to make a phone call, if we have server coverage now we're out of Rosedale.'

* * *

I called Roy Thwaites in the imaginatively named Liverton Mines, an old ironstone mining village in my part of

Cleveland. Roy is . . . well, more of a collaborator than a pal, I suppose. But a very handy guy to know anyway. I do a fair bit of business with him and his garage.

Thankfully, we did have server coverage, and my call was answered.

'I've got a bit of a problem, Roy. The Landy has taken a battering, and it's in need of a major overhaul. I need another vehicle urgently.'

'What's wrong with the Volvo you got from me? You haven't totalled it, have you?'

'No, no! But it's at home. I'm not there at present. Besides, I need four-wheel drive capability. I was wondering if you have any Land Rovers in stock?'

'Maybe,' he said after a pause. 'You thinking of hiring or buying?'

'Whatever. I just need a vehicle.'

'So it's urgent?'

'Very. I would need it brought to me, as well, and my Landy taken back to your place for repair.'

There was a lengthy pause then as he considered the situation. He was probably wondering if he would get any vehicle he loaned me back in one piece, and if he had one he could afford to lose, if it came to that. He knows what I can do to a car.

I cupped my hand over the phone and said to Jason, 'We may have to buy a replacement.'

Jason nodded. 'That's OK. Go ahead. I don't mind buying.'

'I don't know what the price tag will be if we have to buy. I'll try to hire first.'

'Just agree to pay — whatever the price. I'm going to need another Land Rover anyway, when this is all over.'

'You sure?'

He nodded.

Roy came back on the phone. 'There is one I can bring. You'll have to look after it, mind!'

'I'll do my best.'

'Yeah. Right. So where are you?'

'Blakey Rigg. But I want to meet you near Ingleby Greenhow, at Bank Foot. Know it?'

'The farm at the bottom of the incline?'

'Yes.' I glanced at my watch and added, 'We'll be there in about an hour's time, if things go well.'

'Across country, I take it?'

'That's right.'

Roy knew, or could work out, what I was intending to do. No need to spell it out.

'Bring your recovery truck,' I added, 'just to make sure you can get back home again.'

'Point taken. I'll be there.'

Roy ended the call.

'We're in business,' I said to Jason, pocketing the phone.

CHAPTER TWENTY-SEVEN

The track we were on was still the old Rosedale railway line. We were following it northwards, on the route the trucks laden with iron ore would have taken when they headed for the blast furnaces of Teesside. What the ironmasters and the railway engineers did to build the line all those years ago must have seemed fantastical to the handful of folks who lived then along the banks of the Tees and in the farms and villages of the Tees Valley. A railway climbing up the escarpment of the Cleveland Hills and striking out across the moors for a distant, lonely valley to the south . . . The very idea!

But it was done. The hard part for the railway builders would have been working out how to get up and over the north face of the hills and onto the moors beyond. They had done that by building the Ingleby Incline, a long, diagonal, slanting route up the face of the escarpment that took the railway a thousand feet up from the sea-level farmland in the valley of the River Tees.

It was far too steep a route for a locomotive to climb. Instead, a combination of gravity — the laden trucks going down pulling the empties back up — and power supplied by a stationary engine at the top of the incline did the job. It had all worked fine for seventy years, until mining in Rosedale ceased.

Now we were heading for the Ingleby Incline ourselves, coming from the south. It wasn't far from Blakey Rigg, only a dozen miles or so, and I was hopeful that the Land Rover would get us there. My thinking was that if we could manage to potter on for the next few miles, we could then freewheel down the incline and a good way along the track, if not quite all the way, to Bank Foot. Despite our present sorry state, I was prepared to carry on and hope for the best.

We took it easy, trundling gently along in a low gear. The rugged condition of the track hereabouts wouldn't have permitted us to go much faster even in a better vehicle. The surface of the hardcore bed wasn't too bad, considering it had been about ninety years since the rails were lifted, but there were plenty of flooded holes and significant depressions to navigate carefully through and around. It was slow going, and would have been even if the Landy had been in better shape.

The going was also a bit tedious, which may have been why it wasn't long before Jason said, 'I'm hungry again, Frank. Got any more of them food packs left?'

'A few. But I was thinking we could go straight to the meeting with Roy, and have a brew up and a bite to eat then.'

'Why not stop now?'

It was a fair question, and I couldn't think of an over-whelmingly good reason why not. We were well out of sight here, and making good time. Besides, Jason wasn't the only one who was hungry. So I pulled up.

'All-day breakfast suit you again?' I asked, pulling a couple of packs out of the box in the back. 'We seem to have plenty of them left.'

'Fine. What's in it, by the way? Have you ever worked that out?'

'What are you more of, Jason — inquisitive or suspicious, or just plain hungry? There's beans in it, and little sausages. I don't know about anything else. But whatever else there is, it all adds up to 400 grams of nutrition — it says so on the packet — and it comes hot! That's good enough for me.'

'Me, too,' Jason admitted, with a big grin.

While the packs heated up, I got out the stove and put the kettle on.

'Tea for me, please,' Jason said.

'Oh? The coffee not to your taste? Fussy, aren't we, this morning? OK. Tea, then. Incidentally, may I ask again what you brought to the party?'

He grinned, delved into his backpack and came up with a miniature bottle of whisky, which he held out for me to see.

'Wow!' I said admiringly. 'Now we're motoring. Keep it for tonight, though. Whisky for breakfast might put me over the limit and send me back to sleep.'

'And me,' Jason admitted. 'I just carry it for emergencies.'

'Good to know. Anything else in there you want to tell me about?'

He shook his head. 'I'm afraid not. I came ill-prepared.'

It wasn't much, not side-achingly funny anyway, but the banter served us well. We were getting on together pretty good, a lot better than initially I had thought we would. I had come to feel Jason was a decent guy, and I wanted to do my best by him. It was no longer just a matter of loyalty to his Uncle Jimmy, or even the pay packet he'd offered me, for that matter.

'This bloke we're going to meet,' Jason said. 'Who, and what, is he?'

'Roy Thwaites. A good man. I've known him a few years now. We've done a fair bit of business together, usually involving me wrecking cars and him patching them up again.'

'He has a lot of cars, does he?'

'Quite a few. He has a garage business in Liverton Mines. He buys and sells vehicles, does them up, repairs and services them. All that. He has a good business.'

'Thanks to you?'

'Only in part,' I said with a chuckle. 'He's a hard-working feller, and he has a good name in the area.'

'It's really great that he's prepared to do what you asked him.'

'It is. This way we can slip away unnoticed by your in-laws. They'll have no idea where we are, or what we're driving. That reminds me . . .'

I had finished my meal and drunk most of my coffee. I got up and went to get a screwdriver out of the back of the car. Then I used it to take off the licence plates from front and back of the Land Rover.

'So no one will know whose it is, in the unlikely event they even see it,' I explained.

'Will you get it back eventually? I mean, is it repairable?'

'Oh, yes. And I expect it to be in mint condition by then, courtesy of Roy.'

'That'll take some doing. He must be a helluva mechanic.'

I nodded. 'He's that, all right. He was in the Army, with a battlefield tank recovery unit. Mechanics don't come tougher, or more skilled and resourceful, than those guys. They are the ones who are asked to get disabled tanks moving again while being bombed, shelled and generally shot at.'

Jason shook his head. 'Impressive CV.'

'You're right, there. Come on! Let's get moving.'

CHAPTER TWENTY-EIGHT

But we didn't move off immediately. I checked my phone, confirmed that we still had server coverage and decided to try Henry again. It was still a little early for him, but I thought Maggie might have got him up by now. She didn't strike me as the sort of woman who would let people lie in bed half the day. Tough lady, Maggie.

Henry Bolckow, by the way, is my go-to guy, when I need some research doing and lack the time or ability to do it myself. He's based in Middlesbrough, and he's good. Especially with IT. But he has problems. Some stem from smoking too much and drinking too much beer, but the main ones come from his tendency to upset dangerous, powerful people. As a result, his rackety life is lived on the edge. Somehow, though, he stays afloat.

The good news is that Henry has a forensic nose for wrongdoing, and the people he upsets are mostly corrupt or criminal. And sometimes both. He's a good man, in short. I wouldn't say we're blood brothers, but we do share a certain mutual affinity and respect. We help each other out from time to time. Henry comes up with the goods, and in return, I pay him good money that's always much needed.

The phone rang for a long time, but eventually Henry answered it. He'd probably recognized the number and hoped I would give up waiting.

'That took you long enough!' I grumbled.

'Been busy. What do you want?' he growled in a voice suffering even more than usual from excessive cigarette smoke.

'Henry! Is that any way to greet an old friend?'

'Old friend, huh?'

'Possibly the best one you have, apart from Maggie.'

'I tend to run into trouble doing things for you.'

'I always pay you well for the inconvenience, though, don't I?'

Stony silence. He wasn't going to admit to anything, let alone that I was right.

'Where are you right now, Henry?'

'Maggie's.'

I'd thought as much. That was a run-down pub in run-down Port Clarence, where Henry often sought refuge from danger, or the solace of friendly human company. I'd even stayed there myself once, not long ago, when I needed a place of safety and obscurity, and mistakenly thought that might be it.

'She still mad at me?' I asked, meaning Maggie.

'For running out in the middle of the night when the bad guys came? Nah! You'd paid upfront, hadn't you?'

True. I had. But it had been an unseemly departure, spurred on by a spot of violence outside that had not been initiated by me.

'That's good, Henry. I'm relieved. I wouldn't want to be in her bad books.'

'So what do you want now?'

'I've got a job for you, if you're able to take it on. It's urgent.'

'Tell me about it.'

I smiled. The tone of the conversation had changed. Henry was interested now. I could tell. He knew how I made my living, and the jobs I sent his way were often ones that he liked doing. They intrigued him. Also, I paid for them, usually upfront.

'I want to know what you can find out about the Reagans, a criminal family formerly of Essex, and now based in Tenerife.'

'An organized crime gang, then?'

'Yes.'

'Successful?'

'It looks like it. They're said to be very wealthy.'

'What do they do?'

'No idea, really. I would be guessing.'

'And you're interested because?'

'I'm trying to help a young guy called Jason Mack — Jimmy Mack's nephew, actually — who made the mistake of marrying a girl from the family. Francine, she's called. The marriage didn't last five minutes. Then she went home to Daddy, probably because she couldn't stand the poverty.'

'I know that feeling myself. It's not nice, poverty.'

'Well . . .'

Briefly, it crossed my mind to wonder what Henry's daddy was like, or had been like. Somehow, I couldn't picture him ever having had one.

'Anyway, the lad didn't hear from Francine again until he came into a bit of money. Then she reappeared, demanding a share, and set Daddy on him when he wouldn't cough up what she wanted. Since then, he's literally been running for his life.'

'With you, I take it?'

'Yes. He's with me now. The family are going to a lot of trouble and expense over pursuing him, and I'm wondering why.'

'How much money did the lad come into?'

'Ten million quid. He won the Lottery.'

'Then that's the explanation right there! Ninety-nine point nine-nine per cent of crime is for a lot less than that.'

'It's certainly a lot to the likes of you and me, Henry, but I wouldn't have thought it would be to them. I'm wondering if for some reason they really need the money, or if it's all about revenge — family honour, or whatever — because of the failed marriage and imagined betrayal of the daughter.'

He thought about that for a few moments, and then said, 'OK. I'll see what I can find.'

'Call me on this phone, Henry, not the landline. For security reasons, I'm not at home at present.'

'That's funny,' Henry said with a wry chuckle. 'Neither am I — for the same reason!'

CHAPTER TWENTY-NINE

Jason had wandered away while I was on the phone. When he saw I was done, he came back.

'Who was that?' he asked.

'Henry.'

'Henry?'

'My go-to guy for IT stuff, and all sorts of research. I've asked him to find out what he can about the Reagans.'

'You know enough already, surely?'

I shook my head. 'Nowhere near enough. There's a lot more I need to know.'

'Like what?'

'How big the family is, how their business is structured, how they make their money, how much they're worth, where they live . . . Do I need to go on?'

Jason shook his head. 'I guess not.'

'I just need to know what we're up against,' I added. 'Their strengths and weaknesses. So far we've just been running away from them, and we've been lucky. That won't last. We need to do better than rely on luck.'

Looking thoughtful, Jason nodded. He was having to get used to the idea that he was in over his head, and all this was actually happening to him.

* * *

We moved on. Towards the northern edge of the moors we passed over the Bloworth Crossing on Rudland Rigg, an ancient track running from Kildale to Kirkbymoorside. While the railway was operational, a level-crossing gate had been needed at this point. A house on the spot had been home to its attendant and family. Now there was almost nothing to mark what once had been. No gate. No house, or ruins of one. Not even an information panel with the history of the place. All had been cleared away, all except the name on a signboard, and the track bed where the railway had once run.

We pressed on, and in a few minutes came to the top of the Ingleby Incline, where there were a few relics of the glory days in the form of scattered bits of weathered timber and rusting ironwork, remnants of stone walls and mountings, and an information panel together with a cast-iron model of the buildings that used to be there. We paused for a couple of minutes to give the Landy a rest and for us to savour the view down over the Tees valley.

'I've never been here,' Jason said. 'Terrific view, isn't it?'

I nodded. 'Where industry and town meet countryside,' I said, not altogether fancifully. 'But we have no time to stand and stare. Come on — let's go!'

Staying in the lowest gear and keeping my foot on the brake, we began a slow, steady descent of the incline, which is about three-quarters of a mile long. A gate with attached locks might have given us problems on another day, but it was neither locked nor even closed now.

'We were lucky there,' I remarked. 'The gods must be on our side.'

In just a few minutes, we reached the foot of the incline without incident. From there, the old railway track ran north for a couple of miles to Bank Foot, where I hoped Roy would be waiting for us. We were still in good time, and nearly there now.

We were also well out of the sight of the Tenerifes. The only people we were likely to see around the meeting venue were dog walkers and possibly a couple of farm workers. They wouldn't matter. We were incognito now, our licence plates removed, and we were legal so long as we kept off the tarmac road into the nearby village of Ingleby Greenhow. My only concern was that Roy might not have been able to come up with a replacement vehicle.

We ran gently along the smooth, level track, passing the half dozen terraced cottages that had been built back in the day for railway men and their families, but now seemed to be owned and occupied by Urbs living in Rure. Coming round a bend, and emerging from overhanging trees, we could suddenly see our destination half a mile ahead. Roy was already there. At least, his truck was.

'That's him!' I said with relief.

'He must have got here early,' Jason pointed out. 'He's got that vehicle he brought off the truck already.'

I nodded. I'd seen that for myself.

'He doesn't hang about,' I said.

Things were looking good.

* * *

'You made it, then?' Roy called, as I drew up behind his truck.

'With a little bit to spare. I don't think she'll go much further, though. How are you doing, Roy?'

'Good. You?'

'Not bad. This is Jason, by the way.'

'Now then, son,' he said with a nod.

The two of them shook hands. Roy didn't ask any questions about what we'd been doing. He knew better than that. All he knew, and all he wanted to know, was that he'd been called out to a breakdown. That suited him, as well as me.

'What have you done to it this time?' he asked me, glancing at the Landy.

'Came over some rough ground.'

'You must have done.'

Walking around the vehicle, running his professional eye over it, he said thoughtfully, 'Rough ground shouldn't have been this much of a problem.'

'Steep downhill slope at speed, then, between trees, and we flew a bit before landing heavily.'

'Ah!' He nodded. 'You didn't roll it, though?'

I shook my head.

'The glass is messed up, which is understandable. But what's this?' he asked with a frown, running a finger along a groove on the passenger-side door. 'It wasn't a bush or a tree that did that.'

'Probably not, no. There's one or two other marks just like it on the roof.'

'Ran into a shooting party, did we?'

'Something like that,' I admitted. 'Anyway, I'd like the vehicle properly fixed up, Roy. Expense no problem. And keep it as long as you need. Take your time, and fit it in with whatever else you're doing. But I want it kept out of sight for now. That's why I've taken the plates off.'

'The police looking for it?'

'No. They're not the problem.'

Roy glanced over his shoulder at Jason, who had moved up close to the replacement vehicle Roy had brought. 'The lad?'

'Jimmy Mack's nephew. He's run into a bit of trouble — not of his own making, by the way. Just some bad people looking for him.'

'And . . . what? You're looking after him?'

'Trying to,' I admitted with a rueful smile.

''Nuff said. Give Jimmy my regards, by the way. Now, let's see if what I've brought will suit you. It's all I have at the minute, but it might be OK.'

* * *

OK? I could see at a glance that it was phenomenal.

Jason had seen that, too. He turned as we approached and said, 'This isn't a normal Land Rover Defender. I've got one myself — or I had — but I've never seen one like this before.'

Neither had I.

I stared with amazement. From a distance, it looked like an ordinary Land Rover Defender. A lot younger than mine, of course, but from the same family. There, the resemblance stopped.

'It's very clean,' I said hesitantly.

Roy chuckled. 'It won't stay like that for long in your hands, though, will it? I could throw a bucket of muck over it myself to get you started, if you like?'

'No, that won't be necessary, thanks, Roy. We can mucky it ourselves. It's just that . . .'

I began to circle the vehicle, astonished by what I was seeing.

'It's called "the Beast",' Roy advised quietly.

I nodded and said, 'It's well named.'

CHAPTER THIRTY

It was a shiny, sleek, black beetle of a vehicle, recognizable as a Land Rover only by virtue of its boxy shape — and, perhaps, by its tough, rugged appearance: immense wheels and heavy-treaded tyres, the square front, upright windscreen, foldaway running board, roof rack, strip lights and spotlights, and . . . I won't go on. It just looked impressively magnificent. Fit to cross the Sahara or the wastes of Siberia.

'What the hell is it, Roy?'

'The best Defender ever built — or so they claim.'

'A Defender?' I gave a little chuckle and shook my head. 'I don't think so. I've never seen anything like it. It's . . .'

'Twisted?'

It took a moment, but then it clicked.

'Ah!' I said, understanding. 'Not one rebuilt by that guy in Thirsk?'

Roy nodded.

I shook my head now and spun round on my heel, chuckling. 'We can't take this, Roy. We can't afford it! Whatever were you thinking?'

'It's all I have.'

'Roy!'

'We'll take it,' Jason interrupted. 'I like the look of it.'

'Keep out of it, Jason! You have no idea what . . .'

'A 6.2 litre, supercharged, petrol V8 engine,' Roy intoned, 'delivering 430 brake horse power, but with the traditional ladder-frame chassis and independent suspension.'

I'll admit it. I was severely impressed. Like Jason, I did a double take when we heard the specs recited by Roy. We were both stunned.

Then my companion, aka the Money Man, repeated in a calm voice, 'We'll take it.'

'Jason,' I said despairingly, 'you have no idea what it will cost! These Twisteds are out of this world.'

'What are you asking for it?' Jason asked Roy.

'A hundred and twenty grand. Not me, though, son. It's the guys in Thirsk. I just told them I would showcase it for them. I do that from time to time, and they push a bit of work my way.'

'That's still OK. We'll take it,' Jason said doggedly. 'We need it,' he added, with a sideways glance at me.

'How would you pay for it, if you write it off?' Roy asked, not unreasonably.

'That's not going to happen. But I've got the money, if it does. Anyway, I want to buy it. I can write you a cheque or do a bank transfer right now, if you like?'

It was Roy's turn to look sideways at me. I could see what he was wondering.

I nodded. 'It's right enough, Roy. He has the money, and it's up to him what he does with it.'

'That what the bad guys are after? The money?'

I nodded again. 'He won it fair and square on the Lottery.'

'OK, son,' Roy said to Jason. 'Let's do a bank transfer. Then she's all yours.'

The wonders of online banking — and the internet! It only took a couple of minutes to get it done. Then Roy handed Jason the keys, saying, 'I'll sort out the paperwork and let DVLA know about the change of ownership. In the meantime, temporary insurance comes with the vehicle. It's good for a couple of weeks, giving you time to sort something out for yourself.'

Turning to me, Roy said, 'Let's get your vehicle loaded, Frank. Then we can all be on our way.'

I wasn't happy, neither with Roy for bringing such an expensive vehicle nor with Jason for buying it. Yet it was all he had, and we were in an impossible situation. We needed transport, and we needed to get out of here. It could well be a matter of life or death still. And, in the end, Jason did have the money. So it was a time to be pragmatic.

Roy knew that, too. 'It's the only four-wheel drive I have at the moment,' he said quietly, as we manoeuvred my old jalopy onto his truck.

I just shook my head.

'Cheer up, Frank. It's not your money! And if the worst does come to the worst, it will be an insurance job. The vehicle will probably have been stolen and crashed. There, does that make you feel better?'

'Not really. But thanks, anyway. And Jason's right. We really do need it.'

'There you are, then. You know your trouble? You worry too much about what might never happen.'

'Get out of here! You're nothing but a con man.'

He laughed and got in his cab, and he was away and gone before we could even bring ourselves to sit inside the Beast.

CHAPTER THIRTY-ONE

'You need to keep your eye on Mike,' Joey Jackson said.

Junior nodded. 'I know.'

'He's not happy. I'm getting sick of him, moaning and criticizing all the time.'

It wasn't news. Junior had ears and he had eyes. He understood body language, too. In a way, it was good that he'd brought Pearson with him. He hadn't known beforehand that Pearson was a dissenter. He knew now. Pearson was Oscar's man, not his, or even George's. That was as plain as the rain and mud in this fucking country.

Well, the time was coming when members of the family were going to have to decide where they stood and take sides. George couldn't go on forever, with or without his bloody hotel. And he, Junior, wasn't going to stand aside for Oscar. He had prepared and waited too long already to claim his inheritance, and everyone knew that George regarded him as next in line. But he knew that some, apparently including Pearson, wanted Oscar to be the next head of Reagan Enterprises. Well, it wasn't going to happen.

'Don't let him bother you, Joey. Just ignore what he says and hints. For the moment, we need him. We're undermanned. But I'll get rid of him when the time comes.'

'Send him back?'

'Not necessarily.' Junior grimaced and added, 'A more permanent solution might be better. I don't want enemies in the camp, and George doesn't either.'

'That's wise thinking, Junior. We need everyone to pull together. There's no place in the family for them that can't do that.'

Junior patted him on the back. Then they left it there, with Junior not quite ready to spell his thinking out any further. But the time would come, in the not-too-distant future. The way things were going, it was inevitable.

CHAPTER THIRTY-TWO

Jason had paid for it. So I let him drive it. That seemed only fair. Besides, I wasn't sure I could handle a vehicle like the Beast, with all that horsepower and capability, never mind the technology behind the scenes. Jason might be a better fit. He was used to a more modern Land Rover. Also, I felt he needed something to take his mind off the problems besetting him, while I had some thinking to do.

I have to admit I was a lot happier now we'd broken the chain linking us to Rosedale. Changing vehicle had been exactly what we needed to do. Now the Tenerifes would have no idea where we were.

My old Defender was going to be out of sight, tucked away in the darkest recesses of Roy's extensive premises until he found time to start restoring it. He could take all the time he needed, so far as I was concerned. In the meantime, we had the Beast, and I would have the Volvo back at Risky Point to use when I got back home.

'Will he be able to fix it, do you think?' Jason asked, breaking into my thoughts.

'Oh, I think so. Apart from Roy being a master craftsman and top-grade mechanic, those old Land Rovers are pretty near indestructible. That's the beauty of them.'

'We gave it a hell of a hammering.'

'No worse than it's had before.'

'Really? If you say so.'

I smiled. 'You're not a believer, are you?'

'No, not really.'

'Well, let me tell you something. Those old Landys. You can take 'em apart completely and rebuild them, throwing away and replacing the bits that are too far gone.'

'Can you get spare parts for them, though?'

'From scrap yards and specialist dealers, you usually can. If you can't, Roy can make them himself.'

Jason laughed. 'Like any battlefield vehicle recovery mechanic would!'

'Exactly. He's done it before, to my certain knowledge.'

That pretty well put the subject, and the doubts, to bed. I knew what Roy could do, given the time and money needed to do it.

'Jason, there's a couple of things I want to run past you. If we head straight up to Northumberland, we're going to have to spend a lot of time up there in that boggy wasteland doing nothing but wait.'

'That's fine by me.'

'Because of the birds and wild flowers, and things?'

'There's not so much to see at this time of year. Mostly sheep, actually. And maybe a few wild goats.'

'As I was thinking. So we'll stand out like a sore thumb. And Northumberland is where the Tenerife guys are probably going to go next, now they've lost us down here. They probably even know the actual estate you're interested in.'

'Yes, I'm sure they do. Francine will have told them.'

'So their next move will probably be to try to stop you paying out the money for the estate, which I don't suppose is to happen down here, is it?'

'No. That's set up for a solicitor's office in Morpeth, in Northumberland.'

'Why don't we break the journey, and spend a few days where the Tenerifes won't be looking for us?'

Jason frowned. 'Like where?'

'How about Hartlepool?'

'Hartlepool?'

I could tell from the tone of voice how much that appealed to him. So I moved quickly to counter any negative thoughts before they found expression.

'I wouldn't mind seeing the seals again.'

'What seals?'

'On Seal Sands, of course, and in Greatham Creek. Both places are just past the Saltholm RSPB reserve, which I'm told is one of the most important bird places in the country. But it's the seals I like.'

Jason reflected for a moment. I could hear his brain humming.

'Seals, huh?'

Definitely more interested now.

'We could go past them on the way to Hartlepool.'

'That right?'

I rubbed it in.

'If we go into Middlesbrough, we can cross the river to Port Clarence, using the Transporter Bridge. Then just follow the road through the marshes to the coast at Seaton Carew, and on into Hartlepool.'

'I've never been that way,' Jason said, very thoughtfully now. 'And I'd forgotten about the RSPB reserve at Saltholm.'

'And Seal Sands?'

'Yes. There, as well. OK, then. Let's go that way. Maybe we could find somewhere to stay in Hartlepool?'

'Now you're talking! I'm sure we could,' I said shamelessly, hiding my smile of relief.

There was no way I wanted to sit in the Northumberland hills for the better part of the next two weeks.

'What do you think of your new vehicle, by the way?' I added, just to distract him further.

CHAPTER THIRTY-THREE

In other circumstances, I might have felt a bit frustrated about crossing the River Tees via the Transporter Bridge. It's slow going. The Transporter is not a bridge that carries a road, or even a footpath, and in that sense, it's not a bridge at all. It's a structure that spans the river, all right, but vehicles and people crossing the river ride on a little moving platform, known as the gondola, which is suspended on cables from the arch high overhead.

Better than the ferry that preceded it, certainly, but using it to cross the hundred-yards wide river is a slow, cumbersome process. It usually starts by hanging about for at least ten minutes until the gondola returns from the other side of the river, where it invariably is when you arrive.

So although the Transporter is a breathtaking iconic structure for Middlesbrough, and for Teesside, there's little wonder that only another three like it were ever built anywhere in the world.

My other reservation about the Transporter is from the security point of view. Once you're on the gondola, you're locked in there until you reach the other side of the river. The only escape, if trouble were to arrive, would be to jump into the Tees, and I've never heard of anyone surviving such a desperate measure.

Jason and I were fine now, though. No worries. Almost a holiday mood upon us, now we had left our recent troubles behind. No one who meant us harm knew where we were. Judgement Day, in the form of running the gauntlet to sign legal papers and write a cheque, was still ahead of us, and hopefully, there wouldn't be another outbreak of trouble until then. Nothing to do now but take in the sights and relish a sense of well-being.

'I've never been on this thing before,' Jason confided as we stood at the rail watching Middlesbrough fall behind. 'It's fascinating, isn't it?'

I nodded and grinned. 'Possibly not as interesting as when both sides of the river were lined with iron and steel works, but I know what you mean.'

'And there's still the river,' he pointed out, 'just as there was before all the works were built.'

'Thinking of rewilding it?'

He laughed.

'You'd only have to turn the clock back two hundred years,' I pointed out. 'What's that in the lifetime of a great river? Next to nothing.'

'I'll stick to the farm in Northumberland. That will be enough for me.'

* * *

When we reached the Port Clarence side of the river, Jason was gracious enough to offer me the opportunity to put the Beast through its paces. I have to admit that it performed most impressively. I'd never driven anything like it for power. Even so, the frugal part of me wondered what the 430 bhp engine — petrol, not diesel, as well — would deliver in terms of fuel economy. Not much, probably. Possibly single figures, when it came to miles-per-gallon.

We were all right for now, though. We had a full tank, courtesy of Roy. No doubt the cost of that had been added to the bill and already paid for by Jason.

'We'll take some catching in this!' I chortled as we belted along the A178 towards Hartlepool.

'Do you think they could catch us?'

'Nah! Not where we're going. In this thing, we'd run rings around Jags and Audis, and anything else they're likely to bring out.'

'Maybe even a normal Land Rover,' Jason said. 'The one I had at the reserve was pretty new, and a lovely vehicle, but it didn't have the power this one has.'

With a bit of luck, I was thinking, we wouldn't need all that power, but you never knew. You just couldn't tell.

* * *

We called in at Saltholm to let Jason give the birds the once-over, but neither of us was really in the mood for bird watching. So we didn't spend long there. It's a great place, though, as Jason readily agreed.

Then we spent a little time watching seals from the observation hides overlooking Greatham Creek, just off the main road from Port Clarence to Hartlepool. It was pretty much low tide and there were plenty of seals hauled out on the muddy banks of the creek and its tributaries. They weren't doing much, though. Just sleeping, or at least resting. Low tide is their time for doing that. Once the tide turned, they would be back in the water and off out to sea again for the fishing.

'It's amazing to see them here,' Jason said, 'amongst all this industry.'

I could only agree. It was. On the north shore of the Tees, there was historically an enormous area of wild marshland, but over the past two hundred years, ninety per cent of it has been reclaimed — to use the developers' term for wild land destruction — and used for industry. Only a small patch remains now for the seals, and they disappeared altogether when industry was at its height. In the '70s and '80s, though, as industry dwindled and water pollution declined, they began to return. They have kept on coming ever since, both grey seals and common seals.

Once, the marshes and tidal creeks would have been home to legions of wild things. Now, as far as the eye can see, they're home to chemical plants, oil refineries, a nuclear power station, a giant incinerator, and a place where a specialist company dismantles clapped-out ships that are laden with toxic waste. Yet the sea still returns every six hours to what is left, and as long as it does that, the birds and seals will make their home at Seal Sands and the tidal creeks and pools that still run through this land.

'Shall we move on?' Jason asked, when we'd seen our fill.

I nodded. We needed to find somewhere to stay. The afternoon was drawing on, and the light fading.

CHAPTER THIRTY-FOUR

I scanned my phone and opted for a guesthouse on the seafront in Seaton Carew, a Victorian seaside resort just a mile or two south of Hartlepool. Without Jason and his current predicament, I would have chosen to stay on the Headland, or "Old Hartlepool" as it used to be called, a far more interesting place. It's the location of the original town, which was in existence for more than a thousand years before the Victorian town of West Hartlepool was built. It's the latter, though, that's by far the greater part of the modern borough of Hartlepool.

The trouble with Old Hartlepool is that it's on a headland jutting out into the sea, from which there are few escape routes, if one should be needed. I wasn't expecting trouble, but escape options have to come into the picture when you're operating as a close protection officer.

Jason was happy enough with Seaton Carew anyway. We had an early evening meal of fish and chips at a chippy that was part of an amusement complex on the seafront, at the centre of the town. Then we wandered back to the guesthouse. Jason wanted to look around some more, but I didn't think that was a great idea. We might have got out of the line of fire, but it was too soon to relax our guard.

'Let's just have an early night, Jason. Get out heads down and make an early start in the morning. Sleep with your clothes on, by the way, and don't lock the door.'

He stared at me. 'You're joking?'

I shook my head. 'No joke.'

'What on earth are you expecting to happen?'

'Nothing. These are just-in-case, standard precautions in this line of work. There's no sense taking risks we don't need to take, or in not being ready if something happens. We've been through enough trouble already. We don't need any more.'

'I don't believe this!' Jason said, sounding and looking annoyed.

'So fire me. Look, Jason, do it my way or I'm no use to you, and we might as well part now. I can get back home by train easily enough, if it comes to that.'

He stared a moment longer, considering his options. Then he turned on his heel and headed for his room, with a curt, 'Good night.'

'Good night. Sleep well.'

I didn't suppose he would, any more than I would myself. The danger Jason was in had not come to an end. It was merely in abeyance, and would be for a while yet.

* * *

The guesthouse was a pleasant, quiet little place with everything we needed, and our hosts were friendly, helpful people. After running his eyes over the Beast, the husband, Geoff, recommended parking at the rear of the house, in a part of the garden designated for the purpose.

'Leave it in full view out the front,' he said, 'and such a beautiful machine might be irresistible to any of the local bad boys driving past.'

It was sensible advice, and we had taken it. Bad boys might have trouble controlling the Beast, if they ever managed to get through its defences and break into it, but there was no point denying its attractions. It wouldn't only be career criminals who found it attractive, either. Boy racers and joy riders are still out there, always on the lookout for thrills. That's the trouble with high-end vehicles in general. They're collectors' items. In contrast, nobody would look twice at my old Landy, which was another good reason to keep it going.

* * *

Sleep proved as elusive as predicted, but I was content to lie there anyway, just resting. I could hear light traffic passing by, and the distant sound of music and happy voices from the amusement arcade not far away. None of that troubled me any more than the soft murmur of waves breaking on the beach closer by.

I wondered what I was going to do with Jason for the next few days. He was a nice lad and I liked him, but he really was in desperate trouble. I was going to have my work cut out trying to protect him.

That was a thought that started me wondering about bringing someone in to help. It would make a lot of sense. There's a limit to how long one man, or woman, can stay vigilant when the need is for twenty-four hours a day.

One name came immediately to mind, but I had no idea of availability. High-quality personal protection officers are rare people, and in great demand. I would have to think it over, and consider putting out feelers when I had the time.

For now, the best thing to do might be to stock up with provisions and hide away in the hills until a week on Friday, when Jason was supposed to pay the money and take ownership of the farm. After that, he wouldn't necessarily be out of trouble, but the situation would be very different. Apart from anything else, he would no longer have a pile of money sitting in his bank account doing nothing.

The question then would be how far a grasping, estranged wife and covetous family would be prepared to go. Surely a few thousand acres of boggy moorland wouldn't be much of an attraction? Once the sale had gone through, they might as well pack up and go back to Tenerife. But would they?

After all, this was the Family we were talking about, not an ordinary family. They would still have the option and capability of making the daughter a widow, and accessing assets and property through the laws governing inheritance. I grimaced. That scenario didn't seem quite so fanciful, now I'd seen something of how far the Reagans were prepared to go.

Then I wondered again why they were so determined and relentless in their pursuit of the money, which reminded me how little I knew about them.

That was when, right on cue, Henry phoned.

'I thought I'd better get back to you straightaway, Frank.'

'Hi, Henry! What have you got for me?'

'Not a lot yet, but enough to make me want to be sure you know what you're getting into. The Reagans are a bad, bad bunch. And I'm not exaggerating when I say that. It looks to me like you're in a lot of trouble if you're messing with them.'

'I do know that, Henry. What have you found out?'

'They're an extensive family, involved in all sorts of legitimate business, as well as a variety of criminal activities. A bunch of them are located in Tenerife, as you know, but not all of them. Some are still in London and Essex. And a couple are in prison, serving life sentences for murder.'

I grimaced, but it wasn't news to me. I'd already been told that.

'George Reagan is the boss of the family, and of the family business, Reagan Enterprises. Junior, his son, is his deputy.

'I don't know if George literally runs everything himself. Probably not. It's a pretty extensive empire. Some things in the UK, for example, will have to be run locally, I would imagine. But he's top dog in Tenerife, and probably he takes the big, strategic decisions elsewhere as well.

'The long-standing family accountant, Ed Davey, recently came to a bad end, seemingly after displeasing old George.'

'Oh?'

'The brakes failed on his posh car. Locals believe it wasn't an accident.'

'So what had he done?'

'Failed to borrow the money George wanted for some construction project.'

'Disciplinary action for professional incompetence, then?'

'Looks like it. Don't you get any ideas, though!'

'Henry, Henry! Would I ever?'

'It's a good thing I don't have a car to drive. That's all I can say.'

'You ungrateful wretch!'

'That woman you mentioned, by the way? Francine. She's his daughter.'

'Yes. I thought I'd told you that. Henry, I have to remind you of something else. The young guy I'm helping is Francine's estranged husband. She estranged *him*, by the way. Walked out on him after three weeks of marriage.'

'And that's the fella with the money?'

'That's him.'

'Oh, boy!' Henry said.

'Like I said, they seem to want his money badly, but I don't know if they really need it, or if they're just trying to get some sort of revenge on Francine's behalf. Perhaps they imagine she's been insulted in some way. Any ideas there?'

'Well, not really. I know they're a wealthy organization. There's no doubt about that. But they could still have a cash flow problem, and be in need of ten million quid. They could be like the late Queen Elizabeth.'

'I really don't think they're much like her at all, Henry! What on earth do you mean?'

'Well, she has an enormous property portfolio, doesn't she? But if she's out walking and fancies a cup of coffee, she doesn't have a penny in her pocket to buy one. Someone has to do her a favour. A courtier, or whatever they're called. She doesn't carry money.'

'Ah! You mean the Reagans could be capital rich but cash poor?'

'Exactly. I'm not saying they are. I'm just saying they might be. And if they are, that could explain why they want your guy's money so badly. But I don't know. I'll have to look into it further.'

'If you would, Henry. That would be great. Thanks.'

He ended the call, having given me a warning about the Reagans I didn't really need, and also having given me more to think about.

CHAPTER THIRTY-FIVE

Something woke me. I didn't know what it was. Just . . . something. I lay still, senses on full alert, feeling rather than listening, trusting my instincts and trying to work out what had agitated them. Now I was conscious I wasn't picking up anything out of the ordinary.

I pushed the covers aside, swung my feet to the floor and got up. Then I stood still for a few moments. Still nothing.

All I could hear was the low hum of the sea massaging the beach. No traffic now. Not surprisingly. It was two-fifteen, according to my watch. The house creaked a bit, but nothing unnatural about that. It was cooling down for the night. No wind moaning around the house either. Not even a stiff breeze.

I stepped over to the window, fingered a curtain slightly aside and glanced out. A car had drawn up outside. Doors were open. No lights on inside, but I could see enough. Figures were emerging.

I spun round. Without switching a light on, I grabbed my jacket and the small bag I had brought into the house with me. Seconds later, I was out of my room and opening the door to Jason's. I dashed across the room and pulled the quilt from him.

'Get up, Jason!' I said in his ear, pulling him gently by the shoulder. 'We've got company. We have to go — now!'

He was very groggy, but he rose to the situation quickly enough. 'They're here?' he whispered.

'Yes. Come on!'

I helped him to his feet, pleased he had taken my advice to keep his clothes on. Once he'd grabbed his jacket and backpack, I urged him towards the door.

Using a small pocket torch of mine to light the way, we made our way out of the guesthouse, via the emergency staircase and then a door opening into the back garden. It was a route I'd sussed out before going to bed.

'Just in case?' Jason had asked at the time with a smile, scarcely able to contain his amusement.

I hadn't bothered saying anything in response. I didn't say anything now, either. I just hustled him outside and into the Beast.

The engine started first go, as we had every right to expect, given what Jason had paid for it. In seconds, we were moving quietly down the back lane. I hoped we would have two or three minutes' start. Our visitors wouldn't take longer than that to determine that we'd gone.

As we neared the end of the back lane, a black car pulled across the entrance, effectively sealing it off. I grimaced and swore. Obviously they'd guessed right about what we might do.

'Hold on!' I snapped.

I dropped down a gear and put my foot down on the throttle. The engine roared and our wheels gripped and threw out a shower of gravel and dust.

'Frank!' Jason yelled with alarm.

I ignored him. No way was I stopping or holding back.

Stop, or even slow down, and we'd be sitting ducks. It was time to see what the Beast could do when asked to rise to the occasion.

Two figures jumped away from the black car at pretty well the last possible moment. Then we hit it, hit it hard.

I had angled the hit, which meant we crunched into the side of the car, towards the back, spun it round and effortlessly sent it flying. As it went, it rolled and then fell upside-down in what I took to be a drainage ditch. Perfect! We'd caught it just right.

Then we were clear and racing away from the scene, The mighty Beast surging with power and a throaty roar, seemingly of delight.

'OK, Jason?' I called, after we'd turned a corner and got onto a tarmac street, and I'd eased my foot on the accelerator.

I glanced sideways and saw him nod and sit back, another terrifying moment survived.

'Now I am,' he spluttered. 'But you can't keep doing stuff like that, Frank. I'm a nervous wreck!'

'It doesn't show, Jason. You're doing fine.'

'We couldn't have . . . well, just stopped back there, could we?'

I shook my head. 'It would have been a bad mistake, possibly the last one we ever made. As I keep telling you, these people play for keeps. Anyway, I wanted to see what the Beast was made of. She came through fine, didn't she?'

'Yeah. But now we'll have a bashed-up front end, I suppose, and God knows what other damage. A brand-new car, as well!'

'Quit worrying. It'll be OK. You'll see.'

I stopped briefly a few minutes later, to allow him to confirm my confident prediction. He seemed amazed. I never had been worried.

When Roy had been giving us the guided tour, I'd taken note that the vehicle was well armoured, all round and underneath. The front end was protected, and reinforced, by a massive, military-style bumper and by steel bars over the radiator grille. The Beast was a true go anywhere, anytime kind of machine.

'Well,' Jason said, sounding relieved, 'Not a mark on it. Better than your old Landy!'

'Not a mark on us, either, which is more to the point.' I grinned. 'You worry too much. Come on! Let's get moving before the Tenerifes find a replacement vehicle.'

* * *

Rather than take the A179, the main road connecting Hartlepool to the north-south A19 and the rest of the country, I headed north on the slow road along the coast. I might have been wrong, but I was hoping the Tenerifes would assume we had opted for the fast way out of the danger zone.

Jason had nothing more to say, and for a few minutes, I ignored him and concentrated on the driving. My right foot itched to press down hard on the accelerator pedal, but I held back.

'Surely it will go faster than this?' Jason said eventually in a surly tone.

'I'm sure it will. But I don't want to attract attention by making a lot of noise and exceeding the speed limit. How ready are you for a high-speed chase by the Tenerifes or a police patrol car, and possibly the police helicopter as well?'

'Hmm,' he grunted.

'You're awake now, I gather?'

'Yeah.'

'Sorry our departure had to be that way.'

'Me, too. I assume it really was them, by the way? You are sure about that?'

'Not entirely. But how likely is it that what I saw was just a carload of new guests arriving at . . . what?' I glanced at my watch. 'At two-thirty in the morning?'

'Not very, I suppose,' Jason said grudgingly.

Then, perhaps thinking better of it, he added, 'It was lucky you heard them. But I suppose you expected them all along, didn't you?'

I shrugged. 'Not really. It was just a possibility. That's all. But I'm on guard when I'm working, and I always have an exit plan in mind.'

'Well, you did OK. A lot better than me, anyway. I was out like a light.'

'I'm used to this sort of situation. You're not. You've got no reason at all to feel bad about going to sleep.'

All that was true. Experience counts for a lot, nearly everything. Once you've been there, you don't sleep deeply if you're on call or under threat. Folks like me have to live their lives in almost a feral way at times. When the raptors are out there looking for us prey creatures, we know we can't just go to sleep without a care in the world.

'How could they have known where we were?' Jason asked.

I'd been wondering that myself, without getting a grip on it yet. I'd been too busy escaping.

'Beats me,' I admitted. 'The phones are an obvious possibility. Not mine. Yours. But you haven't phoned anyone, have you?'

He shook his head, and then said hesitantly, 'Only my sister.'

'What!' For a moment, I couldn't believe it. 'You phoned your sister?'

'Last night. To tell her what was happening. She has a right to know.'

'That's it, then,' I said, suppressing my anger that he'd done it, and that I hadn't thought to tell him not to. 'No need to wonder any longer.'

'What do you mean?'

'They'll be tracking your phone, having got your number through calls you and your wife exchanged.'

'Oh, shit! I never thought of that. Is it easy to do?'

Privately, I cursed myself for not telling him not to use his phone. The lack of server coverage in Rosedale must have encouraged complacency, not that that was an excuse.

'It's not hard for the tech savvy, or for organizations — including criminal gangs — that have IT capability in their ranks.'

'So what will they have done — listened to our phone calls? Recorded them?'

'I doubt it. All they needed was your number. Then they could follow the electronic marker — the locator — on your phone.'

'Is there anything we can we do about it?'

'Either throw the phone away or disable it. Take out the Sim card and the batteries.'

'Then it will be no good!'

'That's the idea. We'll still have my phone. They don't know about that. So we can continue using it. And we can buy you a cheap burner — a pay-as-you-go, throw-away phone.'

'I've heard of them. You read about them in crime thrillers.'

I nodded.

'Now do me — do us — a favour, Jason, and sort out your bloody phone! We don't want them following us any further.'

I left him to fiddle with it for a couple of minutes while I concentrated on driving and using the satnav. We were getting into territory I didn't really know in detail.

'Done!' he said with satisfaction. 'I've disabled it.'

'Good.'

Something else was bothering me now. We'd swapped vehicles, breaking the link between us and my old Land Rover. The trouble was that the Tenerifes might have learned at the guesthouse about our new Land Rover. They might even have the licence plate number, if our landlord had recorded it. But had he? Not to my knowledge, but I didn't know.

Neither did I know what we could do about it, even if he had. Make the plates illegible? Smear them with mud? Maybe. We could try it. Either that or pinch the plates off another Land Rover. I couldn't think of anything else we could do, and decided to stop worrying about it. We would just have to continue travelling hopefully.

CHAPTER THIRTY-SIX

'We've lost 'em,' Mike Pearson said, looking up from his laptop.

'Lost 'em?' Junior snapped.

'They've disabled the phone, or got rid of it.'

'And that's it?'

'There's nothing we can do about it. There's no signal now.'

'So we can't follow them anymore?'

Pearson shook his head. 'We might as well just go home, and forget all about this caper. George will have to accept that we can't do anything about it. Personally, that won't bother me. This place . . . Hartlepool, is it? Well, it does nothing for me. We're just wasting our time.'

'Not going to happen, Mike. We have our orders, and we'll follow them. Come on! Take a little walk with me, while we work out what we're going to do next.'

Pearson closed his laptop with a sigh and got up to follow Junior, who was already moving away from the car.

'I don't know what he thinks I can do,' he said to the others, who were still inside the car. 'I can't magic a signal out of thin air.'

Nobody said anything. Pearson shrugged and set off.

They were parked on the Headland, in a museum car park close to the promenade that skirted the little peninsula. When Pearson caught up with Junior, he was standing leaning against the low sea wall, staring out at the lights on the far side of Tees Bay.

'That town over there,' Junior said. 'Do you know what it is?'

'Redcar, I think. According to the Google map. Why? We going there?'

Junior shook his head. 'No, I don't think so. Nothing there for us. It's just that the lights are pretty, and the town looks so peaceful.'

'Yeah?' Pearson peered across the water, but couldn't see anything of interest.

'It's good at a time like this to rest your eyes on something like that, something pretty and peaceful,' Junior confided. 'Good for the soul.'

'If you say so,' Pearson said, bored out of his mind nearly, and shivering in the cool wind off the sea.

'Those ships out there, as well,' Junior added, swivelling and pointing to lights far out on the dark horizon. 'Beautiful.'

Pearson kept quiet. Maybe if he didn't argue, Junior would see sense and call this whole thing off. Then they could get out of this miserable country and see some sunshine again.

'I gather you're not too keen on what we're trying to do here, Mike?'

'Well . . . I just think it's impossible, especially now. There's nothing we can do now, even if it ever did make sense.'

'You think George got it wrong?'

'I do. He should have listened to Oscar. Then this would never have happened. Oscar usually calls it right.'

'And George doesn't?'

'Not any more. Not often, anyway.'

'Maybe Oscar should be head of the family? That what you think?'

Pearson hesitated for a moment, and then said, 'George has had his time, hasn't he? Someone else should have a go now.'

Junior nodded. Then, seemingly distracted, he swung round to stare back out to sea. 'That ship,' he said. 'It seems to be signalling.'

Pearson leaned forward to stare where Junior was pointing, but couldn't see flashing lights or anything.

Junior took out his Beretta and shot him in the back of the head. Then he gave him a helping hand to topple over the low wall and fall into the sea.

* * *

Back at the car, Seamus said, 'Where's Mike?'

'He's staying here, he's decided,' Junior said. 'Now we've lost the signal, there's nothing more he can do. We no longer really need him anyway.'

'Staying here?' Seamus said doubtfully.

'Only until he can catch a train down to London. He's not planning on putting down roots in Hartlepool.'

'Oh.'

Joey Jackson caught Junior's eye and nodded understandingly. 'What about us now? What are we going to do?'

'We're going to Newcastle Airport to meet our guys arriving this morning. Some of them, I want to head up to this farm the Mack kid wants to buy in Northumberland. The others, we'll take with us back to the base in Yorkshire.'

Joey nodded.

'So let's get rolling!' Junior concluded.

CHAPTER THIRTY-SEVEN

Traffic was light and there was no sign of pursuit. I began to feel easier. Perhaps we had got away with it again. We ran through quiet former pit villages with empty streets that would once have been teeming with men going on or coming off shift. Not now, though. Not at this time of day anyway, and not since King Coal came to the end of the road. Now these places are more like retirement villages, which is more or less what they are, I suppose, although there isn't much wealth in them.

Just before Easington Colliery, a bigger place but one still with empty streets, we switched across country to join the A19. Then I pulled into a big twenty-four-hour service area and stopped.

'Frank?'

'No point hammering on, Jason. It's still only three in the morning, the roads are empty and we have time to kill. We need to get some rest and have something to eat, and then we need to talk about where we're going and what to do next.'

'We're going to Northumberland!'

I shook my head. 'Eventually. But it's still only Tuesday, and we have to stay out of trouble for another ten days or so.

Let's just take our time and go carefully. I want to get a bit of shuteye first. Then some breakfast.'

'I don't think I could eat another of your all-day breakfasts,' Jason confided.

'No?'

'No.'

'Well, let's get some rest. Then we can head over to the restaurant over there and see what their all-day breakfasts are like.'

'Or get something else, perhaps?'

'Like what?'

'Oh, I don't know. Muesli? Toast and marmalade? Bran flakes?'

'I can ask if they have caviar, if you like?'

'Muesli would be better.'

'OK. Now shut up — please! I want to get some kip.'

* * *

It was just after six when I resurfaced. I felt much better, and the world was different by then too. The once almost-empty parking area was bustling now. Giant trucks were pulling in, brakes squealing. Others were leaving with a roar of their engines, diesel fumes trailing behind. I could see cars at the petrol pumps, and the figures of their drivers waiting inside the shop to pay.

'The world has woken up,' I murmured.

Jason, watching it all, said, 'Some time ago, actually.'

'You didn't sleep?'

He shook his head.

'Feel like some breakfast?'

'That would be good.'

'Let's go.'

* * *

It was pretty warm in the cab. Two bodies throw off a bit of heat over time. But when I opened the door, and fresh

133

air rushed in, it was a different story. I shivered and braced myself in the icy wind. Jason pulled his hood up as we set off for the restaurant. Despite being a bird watcher, he really wasn't any hardier than me, I decided.

We joined the queue and collected what we wanted as we passed along in front of the serving places. Jason got his muesli and some other stuff. I opted for scrambled egg and coffee, feeling the need for something hot. We paid. Then we settled at a table I chose that was shielded from anyone looking through the window by a clump of giant plastic ferns and trees.

'Nice,' I said, nodding at the plastic vegetation as we sat down.

'Mmm. I suppose they don't need any watering — and will last for ever, unfortunately.'

'But the accountants will approve.'

'True.' He grinned. 'Even though I work for a nature reserve, I can't ignore the accountant's opinions.'

'Mine's the same,' I assured him.

Brothers in arms, breakfasting together. Not a care in the world, so far as the casual observer was concerned. We needed moments like that. It had been a rough thirty-six hours, or whatever it was now.

* * *

Afterwards, we visited the washrooms and then headed back to the vehicle.

'Something I need to tell you, Jason,' I advised. 'But, first, let me ask you something. Did you have your phone hooked up to your Land Rover? So you could use it without holding it, I mean, and make calls from the screen and so on?'

'Sure.'

'I can't do that with mine. There's no screen in my car, for a start. So I've never learned. Do you know how to do it?'

He nodded. 'It's pretty easy, actually.'

'Good. So can you hook my phone up to the Beast?'

'Probably.'

'Well, let's sort that out before we get going.'

It wasn't all that easy to do. It took him a good minute. Then he sat back and said, 'Who are you going to call?'

'I already did. Now I'm waiting for him to call me back, like he said he would. You'll be able to hear what he says. It might be interesting.'

'Who are you talking about?'

'Henry.'

'Henry? The guy in Middlesbrough?'

'That's the one.'

As we got moving again, I told him what I'd asked Henry to do.

Jason said nothing for a few moments. Then he just said, 'You're running things, Frank. It's your show.'

I didn't know what he thought of how well I was doing. Not much, probably, his response suggested.

CHAPTER THIRTY-EIGHT

'Tell me the programme for next Friday,' I suggested.

'If we survive that long, you mean?'

'Don't worry about that. We'll survive, all right. What's supposed to happen then?'

Jason struggled for a few moments, seemingly finding it hard to start thinking about the future.

'It's straightforward, supposedly,' he said with a yawn.

'Not tired already, are we?'

'Fuck you!' he responded.

That was a shock. I hadn't expected such language from him. But the belligerence wasn't unwelcome. On the contrary, I wanted to see more fight from him. I just hadn't thought him capable of it.

'Jason, Jason! This is a brand-new day,' I said with a grin. 'And we've only just got started.'

'Yeah, well. Anyway, next Friday. I have an appointment with the solicitor in Morpeth. I go to see her in her office.'

'Is it in the centre of the town?'

'Yes.'

'What happens then?'

'The groundwork's already been done by the solicitors on both sides. So I sign a few documents. Conveyances, or whatever. Then I pay the money. That's it, basically.'

Provided you don't get shot first, I was thinking but didn't say. No need for gallows humour. Jason probably wouldn't appreciate it this morning.

'How do you pay?' I asked. 'Gold coin, cheque — or what?'

'Bank transfer, like with your mate Roy.'

'Who to?'

'The solicitor's firm.'

'Then they pay it to the vendor's solicitor?'

'Presumably.'

'Straightforward, then.'

'Yeah. If we get there.'

I smiled but I didn't know if Jason was joking. I did know he was right, though. It ought to be straightforward, but only if we could get there — if the Tenerifes didn't stop us, that is.

Afterwards might be difficult, as well, though. I didn't rule out anything, before or after. Hitting us, destroying the solicitors' IT systems, shooting the solicitors — anything!

Still, all that was for another day. What I had to focus on was keeping Jason alive until then. That was more than enough to think about.

Looking at it from the Tenerifes' point of view, the game had changed now Jason had escaped them in Rosedale. The idea of forcing him to change his mind and hand over the money was no longer such a simple option. They didn't even know where he was right now. But their focus now might well be on killing him before he could transfer the money. Straightforward enough. Just more brutal.

'Have you met the solicitor?'

'Yes. A couple of times.'

'What's she like?'

'As a solicitor, or as a woman?'

I laughed. 'Let's just stick with the professional person!'

'Efficient and highly competent, I would say. Although I haven't had much to do with solicitors,' he added with a shrug.

'Have you told her there might be difficulties?'

'What would be the point? She might have to rerun the auction if I did.'

'Fair enough.'

'Mind you, that probably wouldn't take long. I don't think there were many bidders. I might even have been the only one.'

I chuckled until I realized he wasn't joking.

'Are you serious?'

He shrugged. 'She more or less told me that, when she said my bid had been accepted.'

'That's a little hard to believe.'

'Wait till you've seen the farm!'

'Oh. Bad as that, is it? What grows there?'

'Grass, mostly. Just rough grass, reeds, moss and heather. And patches of gorse.'

'Sounds lovely. Livestock?'

'A small number of sheep — and some feral goats.'

'Timber?'

'There's a few copses of scots pine down in the valley.'

'And that's it — all there is?'

'Yeah. It's in the Cheviots.'

All in all, I wouldn't have been surprised if Jason really had been the only bidder. It was a wonder the vendor hadn't paid him to take it off his hands.

'Hill sheep farming,' I said thoughtfully. 'It doesn't pay much, does it?'

'Next to nothing. The future for farming in the hills is going to be more about land and environment management than food production. For some farmers, that's how it is already.'

'And for you, too, I gather?'

'Rewilding,' he said, with all the confidence of the young, and the still to be disappointed. 'That's the future for me. There's a living to be made out of it, and I want to give it a go.

'I want to make it a demonstration project, too, somewhere that will attract naturalists and other scientists and specialists from far and wide. From abroad even. I have a lot of contacts with people in Europe who do what I do. It would be good to have some of them visit, observe and even take part with experimental projects.'

'Where would they stay, though?' I asked, being practical.

But Jason had thought of that as well.

'I'm going to build accommodation for them underground. Eco-friendly accommodation that will be a closed system, and won't impact anything on the surface.'

'An eco-hotel, then?'

He chuckled. 'Something like that. I know it must sound crazy to someone like you.'

'Not at all! I'm all for it. It's just that it's likely to be expensive.'

'It is,' Jason confirmed. 'But I've got detailed designs for what I want to do, and they've been costed. It can be done.'

'Now you have the Lottery money, presumably?'

'Exactly. It wouldn't be possible otherwise. That's where most of the ten million is going to go.'

'That's fine, Jason. Just be sure to keep enough back to pay me!'

CHAPTER THIRTY-NINE

So we kept on heading north, bound now for the Tyne Tunnel, and beyond that Northumberland. It was time to talk about where we were going in a bit more detail.

'We've got quite a few days to go, Jason. Any thoughts about where and how we might spend them?'

'Not really. What do you think?'

'I'm not sure,' I admitted. 'But the Tenerifes will certainly be looking for us. We can count on that, I think.

'Hotels are difficult. There won't be that many of them where we're going, and they can easily be checked out. Guesthouses are safer, holiday lets even better. Perhaps we can find an out-of-the-way place not too far from Morpeth.'

Jason didn't say anything. No doubt he still had the farm in mind.

'We'll do that, then. We'll just hunker down somewhere, be careful and stay on guard.'

That didn't seem much of a plan. It might get us through to the end of next week and allow Jason to pay the money that would give him ownership of the estate, but what then? That probably wouldn't end it. He would still be at risk. Perhaps even more so, given there would be only way left for them to get money from him.

Hmm. I didn't like where my thinking had taken me. I needed to start again, and try to come up with a better plan.

We drove on steadily. The Tyne Tunnel wasn't far ahead now. We had crossed the River Wear a few minutes earlier and were approaching the outskirts of Jarrow. Once across the Tyne, we could stop, look at the map and decide exactly where we were going.

Then Jason pre-empted me, but it wasn't a surprise.

'I'd like to go to the farm,' he said. 'That would be my preference, given that we're just going to be filling in time.'

'The farm? Or the estate?'

'It's both. There used to be a couple more farms on the property, but there's only the one there now, Highup Farm. The others were abandoned long ago. All you can see of them now is the ruined houses.'

'Highup Farm, eh? Sounds lovely,' I said, hoping he knew what he was getting into up there in the North Country.

'Yes, it is.'

I smiled and said, 'Anyway, we can't do that, occupy the farm. You haven't paid for it yet, remember?'

'Doesn't matter. It'll be all right. There's no one there now.'

'You know that for sure? The farmhouse is empty?'

'Very much so. It has been for quite a while.'

'Us trespassing might complicate things legally, though?'

'I really don't think so. It's not as if we would have to break in, or anything. I know where there's a key.'

That shut me up. I needed to think about this, and there was a lot to consider. How did Jason know about a key, for instance? And might there not might be legal consequences, whatever he thought?

Even more important, Jason had already told me the Family knew which farm he was intending to purchase, and if we could get there in advance, so could they.

We arrived at the Tyne Tunnel, and I had to concentrate then on working out how to pay the fee for using it.

It wasn't easy. Most of the entry points were cordoned off by lines of traffic cones, and the signage was almost non-existent. We were in a convoy now, a single line of moving traffic. None of the vehicles in front of us stopped to pay, or for any other reason. So we didn't either. We just kept going, all the way into the dark hole under the Tyne and out the other side.

Then it was the same thing all over again on the north side of the river, except there was a row of pay booths there. But they were cordoned off and the line of traffic kept moving past them as if they didn't exist.

'The attendants must be on strike,' I ventured. 'Either that or it's a free day.'

'No.' Jason shook his head. 'I recall reading something about how this was to happen sometime. You have to pay online now, I think. The Tunnel authority said they were going to do away with the pay booths.'

'And now they've done it?'

'Looks like it.'

'Well, that was interesting,' I remarked as we gathered speed again once we were clear. 'Free, as well!'

Jason shook his head. 'I think you'll get a bill, or a fine, in the post.'

'It will be you that gets that, Jason,' I said with a chuckle. 'Remember? You're the owner of this vehicle, not me.'

'Huh. That's something to look forward to then, if your friend Roy has done the paperwork.'

'Oh, he will have. Don't worry about that. Roy gets on with things. Now, where are we going? Morpeth initially, perhaps? I need to suss the place out, and see where your solicitor's offices are.'

Jason nodded agreement. So we headed for Morpeth.

CHAPTER FORTY

I really did need to check out where things were in Morpeth. Jason might have been there before, but I hadn't. I needed to make a risk assessment of what would be involved in getting him to and from where he needed to be a week on Friday. We had already experienced some of what the Tenerifes were capable of, and I wasn't going to rule anything out. They had to stop Jason, preferably before his meeting with the solicitor. It was as simple as that.

The town was pleasingly busy, and the centre a vibrant, old-fashioned high street with plenty of little shops and an absence of boarded-up windows and doors where shops had once been. I would have liked the solicitor's office to be right in the middle of Bridge Street, the main shopping street, but it wasn't. Instead, it was set a block away, between the shops and the River Wansbeck. That was a little too quiet for me. A more public place would have been better.

There was nothing to be done about that, though. We would just have to go there, and take the risk of being gunned down. Maybe there were things we could to reduce the risk, but it would still exist.

'Mind if I borrow your phone?' Jason said.

I looked askance at him. Jason phoning anybody didn't seem a good idea. He had such little appreciation of basic security measures.

'What do you want it for?'

'To see what time it is,' he said with a grin.

'OK, Jason,' I said, smiling reluctantly. 'I get the message. But you do know why I asked, don't you?'

'Security.'

'Damn right! Let's not shoot ourselves in the foot again.'

'I just want to call Lydia. Let her know what's happening.'

'Lydia?'

'My . . . Well, my girlfriend, actually.'

I was astonished.

'Your girlfriend, Jason?'

He nodded. 'Didn't I mention her?'

I shook my head. 'No, Jason, you didn't. Amy didn't either.'

'There hasn't been time, I guess.'

I didn't buy that. We'd had plenty of time together.

'Maybe not. But listen! If you call her, we don't want her telling anyone else where you are. OK?'

'Oh, she wouldn't! She's totally discreet.'

I wasn't his jailer. All I could do was take his word for it. So I took out my phone and handed it over. Then I left him to it, and hoped for the best, while I went to have a look at the river.

I was irritated, annoyed even, that Jason had a girlfriend neither he nor anybody else had told me about. It amounted to an extra dimension to the security situation. And nobody had thought it worth mentioning?

I sighed and shook my head. But when I thought about it, why was I surprised that a newly wealthy, handsome young man whose wife had left him several years ago had a new girlfriend? No surprise at all, really.

When Jason rejoined me, he said, 'I was thinking of heading for Alwinton, in the Cheviots, near where the farm is. There's a problem, though, but I think we should still go there anyway.'

'Because?'

He shrugged, awkwardly I thought. Then it dawned on me.

'Lydia lives there, perhaps?'

'Yes.'

Trying to keep a straight face, I asked, 'So what's the problem?'

'She says some people have just moved in, and she thinks they might be part of Francine's family.'

'Strewth, Jason! And you still want to go there?'

'We have to,' he said doggedly. 'You have to go through Alwinton to get to the farm.'

All my instincts said to turn around and go in the opposite direction, but Jason countered that argument before I could say anything more.

'Also, I think Lydia is in danger.'

Ah!

He said it with such a beseeching look in his eyes that all I could do was sigh and say, 'Well, I guess we'd better go to Alwinton, then.'

CHAPTER FORTY-ONE

'Tell me about Lydia,' I said as we set off again.

'She's wonderful,' he replied, flashing me a big grin.

'Of course she is. I'm sure she is. But how wonderful was she before she learned you'd won a lot of money?'

'It's not what you're thinking, Frank,' he said, sounding hurt now.

'Maybe it's not. You'll have to forgive me, Jason. Cynicism comes naturally to me now. Sadly, that's what experience does for you. But did you meet Lydia, I wonder, before or after you won the Lottery?'

'Before, long before.'

'That's good, Jason. I'm very relieved.'

I wasn't all that relieved, if I'm being honest, but at least the situation sounded better than I'd feared.

'We first met at uni,' Jason continued. 'We were on the same course.'

That sounded better.

'So she's a naturalist, as well?'

'Very much so. She works for WWF in Northumberland. Her main interest is entomology. Mine is ornithology.'

Insects and birds, then, I thought, still in cynical mode. What a fine couple they would make!

'And she lives in Alwinton?'

'She does. She's from the area, as well.'

'Oh?'

'Actually, Frank, there's something else I should perhaps tell you.'

Here it comes! I thought with a wry smile.

'What's that, Jason?'

He didn't disappoint me with his extra bit of information.

'This farm I'm hoping to buy, the estate?'

'Yeah. What about it?'

'Lydia's one of the owners.'

That shut me up.

'One of them,' he repeated, to make it crystal clear. 'She's a part-owner.'

It was almost too much for me. I just stared, flummoxed. It was hard to know what to say.

Then Henry phoned, and I forgot all about it for the moment.

'There's something going on,' Henry said. 'I haven't been able to put my finger on it yet, but I think you might be right.'

'About what?'

'The Reagans. It's not just about the girl, the lad's wife. There's something financial, as well. My sources tell me the Reagans — the whole lot of them! — have been doing strange things lately. It's as if someone has chucked a grenade into a football crowd, except it's financial.'

I winced at the metaphor, thinking I might have preferred a fox being put into a hen house. But that's Henry for you.

'That's all you've got?'

'For now. I'm still working on it. I just wanted you to know that I believe you're thinking along the right lines. The Reagans are a crazy lot, and they're running around more crazily than usual.'

'One other thing, Henry. Does the old man still do business in the UK?'

'George? I don't know. Maybe. Why? What are you thinking?'

147

'Nothing really. I'm just trying to get a picture of the guy — how he lives, and so on.'

'Well, like I said before, he'll have business interests in the UK still, but he's not necessarily running them himself. The Reagan family is a big clan. They're widespread, and a lot of them are still in London and Essex doing their own thing. As head of the family, though, George will probably still have overall control, won't he?'

'I don't know.'

'Neither do I. But I can tell you this much,' Henry added thoughtfully. 'From what I've seen, he travels to the UK quite often.'

'Oh?'

'I don't know why, or what he does when he's there, though.'

'How often?'

'I don't know. I'll have to check.'

'If you would, Henry. That might be interesting.'

The call ended. Henry hadn't given me much that was new but it was good to know his instincts matched my own. Moreover, I trusted them, his and mine. Something was up. Something was going on.

'So that was Henry?' Jason said.

I nodded. 'You heard him. What do you think?'

'I think he's dead right about the Reagans. They are crazy. Doesn't pull any punches, though, does he?'

'Not Henry, no. And he's usually right.'

* * *

Coming out of Morpeth, we were briefly on the A1 before switching to the A697, the main road to Coldstream on the Scottish side of the River Tweed. We were not on that for more than ten miles before turning on to a B-road going to somewhere called Rothbury.

'Rothbury?' I said, thinking I'd heard of it, but not quite sure how or why.

'Capital of Coquetdale,' Jason said with satisfaction, pleased no doubt to display his local knowledge. 'It's where Lord Armstrong, the Victorian industrialist, developed his Cragside estate.'

'Ah! That's it. Cragside. I knew I'd heard of Rothbury, not that I've ever been there.'

'It used to be a little village. Now it's a little town. Like everywhere else, it's been growing fast in the last decade or two.'

'That's what happens when your population keeps growing,' I said with a smile. 'You need more houses to put all the extra bodies in.'

'Yeah, well. It's not going to happen on my farm. That's going to stay a wilderness.'

'Said with feeling, old son!'

'We need wilderness areas. All of us. For our mental health, as well as everything else. We may not all realize it, but we do.'

'Just so you know,' I told him, 'I couldn't agree more.'

More comfortable, now I'd assured him we didn't disagree, Jason resumed.

'Anyway, after Rothbury we'll be on a steadily deteriorating little road that runs up to a village called Alwinton.'

'That's the end of the line, is it?'

'Not quite,' Jason said with satisfaction. 'The road continues after that, but only as a single track, all the way to Meckenden.'

'Which is?'

'The last farm in the valley. Just past Meckenden you reach a gateway that's the entry to the Otterburn Ranges, where the Army trains and practises with its big guns.'

'Good to know,' I said. 'We might need the Army before we're finished with the Tenerifes.'

Jason grinned. 'Actually, we turn off on to a gravel track at Alwinton, well before Meckenden. Or we would do in normal circumstances.'

'Gravel track, huh?'

'Yeah. But that's not for the Beast at the moment.'

149

'Why not?'

'Lydia says she thinks the Family have got people at the farm, as well as in the village, watching out for us. So we can't go to either her place or the farm.'

I grimaced. It felt like we were losing control again, just as I'd been starting to believe we were on top of things.

'I'm feeling out of my depth here, Jason. But I'm guessing you and Lydia have a plan, or you and I wouldn't be out here. You'd better run it past me before we get much further.'

'OK. What I've agreed with Lydia is that we'll walk over to the hut, which is on the estate, and stay there till it's time to go back into Morpeth. She'll join us there.'

'The hut? Sounds kind of . . . rustic?'

'Oh, it is! But we'll be safe there. It's an old shed, out in the wilds, for hunters.'

Hmm. I had to wonder about that. Was it really what we wanted?

Jason added, 'We'll leave the Beast in Alwinton, and walk in to the hut. It's about eight miles over some rough country. No track or path to get there either. The Family won't know about it. Even if they hear of it, they'll never find it.'

'Will we, though? It sounds delightful, but I hope you know the way, Jason.'

'I do,' he assured me with a grin. 'Lydia and I have stayed there a couple of times.'

I wasn't sure I liked the plan, and found myself thinking how much I hoped the hut could do more for us than offer Jason happy memories. Still, we did need somewhere safe and out of the way while we worked out what to do next. The hut might do, I supposed.

But so far, all we'd done was react and run. We couldn't keep on doing that. Somehow, we had to bring this mad vendetta to an end. Time to think, while we were somewhere safe, might help us do that.

CHAPTER FORTY-TWO

The light was going fast when we pulled into Alwinton an hour later. It didn't look much of a place. Just a pub and a handful of cottages, mostly on one short street. We had stopped not long before to sort out what we would take with us on our hike. We didn't have much we could have taken, but we had to make sure we were only taking essentials, given that everything had to go into my rucksack and Jason's little backpack.

Most of what we packed was food — my self-heating, ready meals. Otherwise, we took the sleeping bags and the rug from the back of the Land Rover, together with a couple of empty flasks and the stove and kettle. No clothes to pack, because we were wearing all the clothes we'd brought with us.

'Is there water at the hut?' I asked.

'Not a kitchen tap, but there's a stream nearby.'

'Dead sheep in it?'

'I hope not.' Jason grinned. 'But you never know, do you?'

'Indeed you don't.'

I'd been a little worried about Jason's capabilities if we had quite a big trek in front of us. But now I decided there was no real reason to worry. He seemed to be a fit enough guy, and out here he ought to be in his element. The out-doors was where he belonged, and this particular bit of it seemed to be where he wanted to spend his life from now on.

So why on earth had he ever got himself involved with a woman from Tenerife, one who lived in such a very different world? You had to wonder — until you remembered about human nature.

When we were done packing, we got back aboard the Beast and motored on into Alwinton. We left our vehicle there, on a patch of grass between a couple of other vehicles, and set off walking. I was a bit worried about leaving the Beast, but accepted Jason's assurance that it would be all right in Alwinton. They were used to vehicles like Land Rovers, SUVs and pickups there, he said. It was a jumping-off spot for lots of walkers, cyclists and overnight expeditions.

He also said we were leaving the car well away from Lydia's cottage, just in case she was right about Tenerifes watching it. I supposed that made sense, although I couldn't see how they might know who Lydia was. Were they that far into Jason's personal affairs?

Whatever. It sounded to me as if Lydia was a sensible young woman, and I looked forward to meeting her. Jason said he wasn't too sure when that would be, when I asked him. All he could tell me was that she would eventually join us, probably at the end of the night. Apparently, she was currently monitoring some nocturnal insects and reptiles.

Hmm, I thought. Sensible woman? Perhaps I should have reserved judgement until I actually met her.

* * *

We set off walking in a rising wind, just as it started to rain. The darkening sky hadn't been only because of the time of day.

'November now,' Jason said with a wry chuckle. 'Not my favourite month.'

'Nor mine,' I assured him. 'Risky Point is bad enough at this time of year, but I imagine it will be a lot worse up here.'

'Yep. Cloudier and wetter. And darker. Up here, you just have to make sure you use what daylight there is.'

'So setting off like this is a mad thing to do, really?'

'Absolutely! What fun we'll have.'

So things were OK. I'd been a bit worried about Jason's spirits, but he seemed fine. He knew this territory, and he was looking forward to seeing his girlfriend again. For the moment, at least, the Tenerifes had been shunted aside.

That was good, because I soon realized we were probably going to have a rough time that night. Already the rain was becoming steadily heavier, and it was being driven into our faces by a strong nor'westerly. We were both wearing decent boots and outdoor jackets, but our lower halves were not clad in waterproofs. So legs and, probably, feet as well were going to get wet, very wet. No doubt, the ground conditions would be a challenge, too. It was that kind of night, and that kind of country.

'I assume you'll be able to find your way, all right?' I asked again.

That was very much on my mind. Travelling in dry conditions in sunny daylight is one thing. Making the same journey on a dark, stormy, wet night is something else entirely.

'I'm a Ranger,' he said cheerfully. 'Trust me!'

I had to. I didn't have any choice. Had I detected any hint of a doubt in his voice, I would have aborted the hike and turned back.

Anyway, I reminded myself again, he was an outdoors guy. And he knew this country well, apparently, and liked it so much he was planning to buy a big chunk of it. I had to trust him to get things right.

To begin with, we walked side by side on a broad track in a wide valley as we left Alwinton behind. The wind shrieked at us and hurled the rain in our faces, effectively putting an end to conversation. After fifteen minutes, Jason touched my arm and led the way over to the foot of the steep hillside. Then we began to climb. I couldn't see a path. Even if there had been one, I probably wouldn't have been able to see it in those conditions, but Jason seemed to know exactly where we were. So I just followed him.

It was hard going. The route was very steep, and the rough grass and heather underfoot pretty slippery now it was so wet. The only good thing to report was that we were shielded in part from the ferocious wind by the curve of the hillside, but I guessed that wouldn't last long.

I was right. We reached the top of the hill, and wind like an express train hit us full on. With gritted teeth, we headed out across a broad grassy plateau in the teeth of what was fast becoming a gale. At times, forward progress was difficult, and at times it was a struggle just to stay upright.

We kept going. After half an hour of it, I sensed that Jason was struggling and I steered him into a small hollow to get us out of the wind for a few moments. We hunkered down and put our heads close together. I gripped the front of his jacket with both hands and gently shook him.

'How are you doing?' I yelled, alert for signs of exhaustion.

'OK,' he insisted, pushing his head into my chest. 'I'm just a bit breathless.'

'Me, too. How far do you reckon we have to go?'

'Just a couple of miles.'

Just? A couple more miles in these conditions wasn't going to be easy. I was also worried that Jason might lose his sense of direction if fatigue and cold took their toll. If that happened, we really would be lost. I wouldn't know where the hell we were. We had to get going again before we reached that point.

I grimaced as we climbed back out of the hollow and the shrieking wind hit us again with fury. 'Which way?' I demanded, ducking my head and turning towards Jason.

He consulted a little compass, pressing a button that made it light up. I saw then that it was pinned to the back of his glove, and felt reassured. He still knew what he was doing.

He took a reading and pointed ahead, roughly in the direction in which we had been heading. A particularly violent gust of wind sent him staggering, and he tripped and fell.

I reached down, grabbed his pack and pulled him back up. Then we got going again. Somehow.

I wouldn't say I was in great shape myself, but I knew by then that I was stronger than Jason, and had more left in the tank. I also knew that I had to take the lead now. As long as Jason could do the navigating, I could keep us going. If necessary, I promised myself grimly, I would even carry the skinny little bugger!

It hadn't quite come to that yet, but it wasn't far off. With one of my arms clamped around him, we pressed on, staggering rather than walking, on into a wall of blackness. I could see nothing of the rough, broken ground at our feet, and just had to hope there were no yawning chasms or even potholes to trip us up. It was a stumbling, awkward way to proceed, but we had to keep on doing it if we were ever to reach refuge in a hut that was beginning to seem as mythical as any desert mirage.

I knew, too, that we were well past the point where we could have given up and turned back. That was no longer an option. We would never have made it. Keeping going forward was all we could do now.

To Jason's enormous credit, he played his part well. He focused on his little compass and navigated us all the way there, all the way until I realized there was something big and solid right in front of us that had taken away the power of the wind.

I came to a stop, raised my head and peered forward. But I couldn't see anything. It was more a matter of feeling than seeing. I just knew there was something in front of us. I reached out and felt rough timber beneath my fingers.

Is this it? Are we here? I wondered, scarcely daring to hope.

CHAPTER FORTY-THREE

I gently leaned Jason against what I took to be a timber wall. Then I pulled the tiny emergency torch that I always carry out of a sodden pocket in my jacket. Switching it on, I used the little beam to hunt for a door. It was good enough for that, even though it wouldn't have been any use to us coming across the moor. Needless to say, I had to go round three barren sides of the hut before I found a door. Nothing was easy that night.

Then I sought and found a door handle. I turned it. The door stayed closed. I searched further and found two bolts, one high up and the other low down. With some difficulty, I managed to ease them aside with fingers that had very little feeling left in them. After that — at last! — I could open the door.

I went back for Jason, dragged him round the fourth side of the hut in the teeth of the wind and pushed him inside. We tumbled over the threshold. Jason tripped and sprawled across the floor, and I tripped over him. But I got back up fast, the wind screaming in my face, found the door and put all my weight behind it to slam it shut.

Then I slumped against a wall I couldn't see, having pocketed my torch for safekeeping. I slid down until I was sitting on the floor. For a few moments I just sat and listened to the wind trying to get inside the hut after us, hearing it shriek in frustration as it realized it couldn't. Rain like nails clattered on what seemed to be a metal roof.

'Christ!' Jason muttered in the darkness.

I said nothing. I was still catching my breath, and just so relieved and thankful to be out of the wind and the rain. Nothing else mattered just then.

'You OK, Frank?' Jason asked, after a little while.

It irked a bit that he seemed to be recovering faster than me. 'Almost,' I said grudgingly. 'You?'

'Fine. Never better.'

'That's good,' I said with a reluctant smile, remembering how he couldn't stand up by himself not that long ago.

Then I stirred and dug the little torch back out of my jacket pocket. Switching it on, I swept the slender beam around the hut, seeing in the dim light a big table and a couple of wooden bench seats nearby. Most of all, and best of all, I saw a big, empty space that looked completely dry. Lastly, the beam caught Jason, who was sitting up and shielding his eyes from the feeble light.

'There's a lamp on the table,' he said. 'A big one. Either there or hanging on the wall.'

'I take it you're not planning on getting up to look for it?'

'Not just now, Frank, if it's all the same to you. I'm all right here for the moment. I'm knackered!'

'Good to know. Me, an' all,' I assured him.

I stirred myself and struggled back up on to my feet. One of us had to do it. The torch beam showed me that there was indeed a big lamp on the table, a battery lamp. I reached it, found the switch and turned it on, bathing the hut in a lovely warm glow.

'That's better!'

Jason agreed. 'It's maybe worth me getting up now.'

I reached out a hand for him to clasp and hauled him to his feet. Recovery was underway for us both.

Stumbling across the room to a long timber bench set against a wall, I pulled off my dripping-wet jacket and slung both that and my sodden rucksack onto the big wooden table. Then I slumped on to one of the benches, leaned forward, elbows on knees, and listened to the pounding rain and shrieking wind.

Only just in time, I thought. We had probably got here just in time. Neither of us could have gone much further.

Jason staggered across to join me. I grinned ruefully at him. 'It's worse than Rosedale, this. I can't imagine why you ever thought it would be a good idea to move up here.'

'Neither can I, just now,' he admitted, with a weary smile. 'But Lydia says it's better here for insects and small reptiles.'

'Why am I not surprised? Are we talking midges and baby crocodiles?'

'Something like that.'

I got up after a few moments of rest and hung my jacket on a nail in the wall. Then I did a bit more stock taking. One thing that struck me immediately was Jason's resilience. He seemed to be recovering fast from our ordeal, mentally, at least, if not physically. That was good. The big lamp was good, too. I was glad we had that for company. What else was good?

Looking around, I spotted a wood-burning stove. Fine, but we hadn't brought any firewood with us. A large, transparent, plastic water container looked half-full. That was a particularly welcome sight. We needed a drink, preferably hot.

I began pulling things out of my rucksack and setting up the camping stove. I hadn't brought the kettle, but I did have a small billy can with a lid we could use to heat water. For food, we had the meal packs. So if we could warm and dry ourselves a bit, we would be all right here for a while.

Then I grimaced as I remembered Jason's girlfriend, poor girl, and how she was supposed to be joining us sometime during the night.

'What about Lydia? She's going to be in trouble, if she's out on a night like this.'

Jason shook his head. 'She'll manage,' he said, seemingly with great confidence. 'Lydia knows what to do when it's like this. She's lived here all her life.'

I wasn't so sanguine. I had my doubts. But there was nothing in a practical sense that we could do to help her right now. We had no idea where she was even. She could be snug in her own bed for all we knew. I hoped she was.

* * *

Later, when we were slightly drier and a fraction warmer, and after we'd drunk coffee and eaten chicken casserole straight out of the self-heating bags it had come in, I asked Jason to tell me more about Lydia. She was obviously a player in this game, and I still knew next to nothing about her.

'Lydia?' he said, as if surprised by my question.

'Yes. Who is she? What is she? Apart from her being your girlfriend, a part-owner of the farm and interested in bugs, I know next to nothing about her. You're expecting her to meet us here, but when? And where is she coming from? And what did you actually mean when you said she was a part-owner of the farm?'

'She's the granddaughter of the head of the family that's selling the estate. As such, she gets a settled portion of the money that the sale raises. An eighth, I believe.'

'So the farm is owned by a family trust?'

'Yes. That sort of thing, anyway. Her grandfather set it up that way.'

'I take it the family don't live here?'

'Not any more. Lydia is the only one of them left living in the area. She grew up on the farm, with her parents, but no one in the family has lived here permanently since her parents gave up farming and moved to London. They wanted to be near the rest of the family — not to mention shops, theatres, concert halls, museums, et cetera.'

'Of course not. I'm sure such things didn't come into the decision at all. Her parents probably just got sick of living in the back of beyond, and working themselves to a standstill for next to nothing as reward.'

Jason nodded, as if he accepted my cynical take as gospel truth.

'But Lydia came back,' he resumed. 'After she got her degree, she took a job with the Wildlife Trust and came to live in Alwinton. It was perfect for her.'

''Cos of the insects and lizards, and things?'

'Exactly!' Jason chuckled and gave a wry smile. 'You have to be a naturalist yourself to understand the allure of the place.'

'Probably.'

But I believed I could understand it, actually. Lydia isn't the only person ever to have been attracted by the Cheviots, and upland regions like it. I live in one not too dissimilar myself. Plus, her roots were here, and her childhood memories. This was where she belonged. It was home. I know that feeling.

'Presumably she knows all about your marriage and the Tenerifes?'

'Everything. She even met my ex-wife, down in Rosedale one time.'

'How did that go?'

'Not terribly well,' he admitted with a grin.

'I can imagine.'

We shut up then to listen to a particularly violent squall hitting the hut. I found myself thinking Jason and Lydia would have to get used to that sound, if they continued along the road together and stayed living out here. But perhaps they were used to it already.

'The hut seems well made,' I said, looking around and seeing no sign of it being troubled by anything the elements were throwing at it. 'No leaks anywhere. No sign of walls shifting or subsiding.'

'Lydia's grandfather had it built for his shooting parties. They needed somewhere dry and sturdy, I suppose, for when they were worn out shooting things in the rain and needed to sit down for a rest.'

'Do I detect a hint of censure there?'

'No, not really. Well, perhaps there is. When we get the farm, there'll be no more shooting. This land will be a place of sanctuary, a refuge for wildlife, not a killing zone.

'But I do acknowledge,' he added fair-mindedly, 'that people felt differently in the past, and I'm not going to condemn how things used to be. People have always killed animals, but for food, not for so-called sport. They still do, of course. But they mostly do it in abattoirs these days.'

That was quite a statement. I have to admit that I was becoming more and more impressed by Jason. I didn't agree with him about everything, but he was a very decent guy, and eminently sensible too. What he had just said struck a chord with me, as well. Unlike contemporary statue topplers and portrait removers, he had a civilized, rational view of the past, even though he was living firmly in the present.

'Well, let's just keep our fingers crossed that Lydia makes it here safely,' I said.

Or she doesn't even try, I was thinking, but didn't say. Staying wherever she was now would be by far the safer option, however much she was at home in these hills.

I got up to start sorting out somewhere to sleep, or at least to rest. It was hard to believe there would be any sleep for either of us until the storm abated.

'She'll get here,' Jason said confidently. 'Lydia knows how to look after herself.'

I just hoped he was right.

CHAPTER FORTY-FOUR

It was a wild night. A cold one for us, too. Jason accepted the sleeping bag when I insisted that I was warm enough without it, but he stretched it out on the concrete floor, and I don't believe he could have been much warmer than me. I laid on the big table, preferring to have wood rather than concrete under me, and did the best I could to kid myself it wasn't so bad. Not really cold. Quite warm, actually. Certainly compared with being outside in the wind, and in what at times sounded like hail.

Time drifted by, accompanied by the unrelenting barrage of the wind and sheets of particles of something hitting the hut on all sides, as well as the roof. Somehow, hearing all that commotion outside helped me feel warmer, but only relatively. Safer, as well, of course. No Tenerifes to worry about for the moment. That helped. I even managed to snatch a succession of cat naps that, although they didn't add up to sound sleep, at least gave limbs weary from the forced march to get here a bit of a rest.

In between my naps there was time to reflect on the route taken to get us here. It hadn't been a lot of fun. I can't pretend otherwise. Actually, I couldn't help feeling I would rather have been in Prague, even though I knew being with Leon Podolsky wouldn't have been much fun either. If anything, it would probably have been worse, knowing how close to the edge he lives. Always there are Russian assassins searching for Leon, so far unsuccessfully. But only so far.

It was tempting to wonder if I ought to give up this way of life, and associating with people like Jason and Leon, and become a local government officer or an accountant. Or a civil servant. A bank manager, even! Something, anyway. Something that held out a reasonable prospect of living long enough to retire.

Anyway, a few more days and my commitment here would be over. I would be free as a bird, free to go and see what Leon had in store for me. At least it would be something different, something that didn't involve me trying to get some sleep in a hut on a hilltop in the back of beyond while a storm was raging. But I would still have to keep the bad guys in mind, and wonder where they were now.

The future having come to mind, I began to think about what was going to happen here. With luck, we would get through the night, and Lydia would arrive with a few more things we needed, enabling us to hold out for a bit longer. Then, at the end of next week, we would go to Morpeth and run the gauntlet that was bound to have been set up by the Tenerifes around the solicitor's office. Jason would pay the money, and it would all be over. We would be done!

Or not, I thought with a grimace, as reality overcame fantasy. Wishful thinking wasn't going to do it.

Just coming up to four in the morning, a particularly violent squall hit the hut, putting all thoughts of further sleep entirely out of the question.

'You awake, Jason?' I asked quietly.

'Yeah.'

'For long?'

'All night. Never slept a wink.'

'Fancy a coffee?'

'Very much. Better than lying here shivering for a few more hours.'

My feeling, too. I sat up, dangled my legs off the edge of the table and reached for where I knew the lamp to be. My fingers, though stiff with cold, twiddled the knob until the hut was filled again with a warm, glowing light.

'That's better!' I announced.

Then I looked over at Jason. He was shivering wildly, and I realized it was a good thing we were getting up. Hypothermia probably wasn't far away, if he laid there much longer.

While we waited for the water to heat up on the stove I moved around the hut, exercising to get warm. Urged to do so by me, Jason did the same. Old-style PT. Arms swinging and knees bending. Movement. Anything helped.

I caught sight of a big wooden locker in one corner and wondered what it was for. I'd been too tired when we arrived to even notice it. Now I walked over to it and lifted the lid.

'It's empty,' Jason called, from the other side of the room.

But it wasn't. There was a kettle, for one thing. There were also half a dozen big candles, church candles as I thought of them. Plus quite a few other things, domestic items, some of them things we could use.

'Lydia must have brought it all,' Jason said, peeking over my shoulder to see what I'd found.

I took out the pack of candles.

'We'll get a bit of heat from these,' I said. 'And we need all we can get.'

I lit a couple of the candles and stuck one at each end of the table.

'That's better!' I stood back to admire my innovation. 'Heat, and more light.'

'Won't make much difference,' Jason said, still shivering.

Yet it did. Whether it was purely psychological or real, the hut seemed immeasurably brighter and warmer.

'Let's have some breakfast, as well,' I suggested, to lift Jason's spirits.

'Breakfast? At this time?'

I glanced at my watch. It was a bit early, but what the hell!

'Why not? You're not thinking of going back to bed, are you?'

He shook his head. I pulled a couple of all-day breakfasts out of my rucksack and tossed him one.

'Here you are, Jason. You know what to do with it. Get started!'

Having something purposeful to do, and the imminent prospect of hot food, woke us up some more. We watched eagerly as the packets swelled and issued little puffs of steam as our breakfasts heated up for the required ten minutes. We even laughed and joked as we held our hands over the packs in the hope of warming them.

'I hope there's a bit of bacon in mine this time,' Jason grumbled.

'A slice of fried bread is what I'd like to see most,' I told him. 'Two slices, by preference.'

Neither of us got what we wished for, but we did get a reasonable meal of baked beans, fried egg, sausages, and some bits of stuff that were unidentifiable. I thought they might be bacon. Jason just shook his head. It was hard to say what they were definitively. What we could say was that we each got 400 calories worth of something hot again, whatever some of it was. The information on the packet assured us of that.

Afterwards, we were sipping second mugs of coffee when Jason said, 'The wind's dying down.'

I listened for a moment and agreed with him. The storm seemed to be moving on at last.

Then, just coming up to half-five, something else happened.

CHAPTER FORTY-FIVE

'I'm here!'

I swung round with alarm when I heard the call, just in time to see the door burst open and a bundled-up figure cross the threshold.

'Lydia!' Jason cried, rushing to greet her.

I relaxed.

They hugged and showered each other with kisses and excited, affectionate words of greeting. I had to smile. Young love!

'You must be Frank?' Lydia said, breaking away from her beloved. 'How are you?'

'Astonished,' I said with a grin. 'We didn't expect to see you this early, if at all today. But otherwise fine, thanks.'

'That's good. I was awake, and thought I might as well get myself here.'

She was a very self-confident, cheerful young woman with a lovely, friendly smile. I was instantly ready to like her. I wondered how she had spent the night, but Jason asked first.

'Were you in the tent?'

'Only to start with. Then the wind got up so much I was afraid I was going to lose it. So I pulled it down and retreated into the cave.'

'Oh, yes. I'd forgotten about the cave. Was it all right?'

'It was OK. A bit draughty and damp — but so was everywhere else!' she finished with a chuckle.

'You can say that again!' Jason assured her. 'It was all right once we were here, but getting here was a struggle. Frank had to half-carry me.'

'Oh, I wouldn't say that,' I objected. 'But it was certainly a struggle.'

'But you made it,' Lydia said with satisfaction. 'Well done, both of you.'

Then, looking at me, she said, 'Thank you so much for helping us, Frank. It's really very good of you.'

'I've had to. Jason has employed me as his close protection officer.'

She looked at Jason, surprised. 'I thought . . .'

'I couldn't have survived and got out of Rosedale without Frank. I'm just covering his expenses for a few days.'

'Good,' Lydia said briskly.

Then she spun round and ran a critical eye over arrangements in the hut.

'Coffee?' I asked. 'Would you like a coffee?'

'Very much. Thank you.'

I got busy with kettle and stove, and kept my head down when Lydia began rebuking Jason.

'It's very spartan in here, Jason. Didn't you think of pulling out a few things to make your stay more comfortable?'

'I don't know where anything is,' he protested.

'Oh, Jason! Of course you do.'

'Well, I couldn't remember. I was too tired and too cold.'

'I can vouch for that,' I interjected. 'We both were.'

'Men!' Lydia pronounced with disdain.

I watched then as she marched to the timber wall at one end of the hut and opened a small door in it that I hadn't even noticed. She delved into the space behind and started hauling out various useful items, including sleeping bags and air mattresses, as well as boxes of tins and packets that looked as if they might well contain food.

167

Jason shrugged apologetically when I gave him a questioning look. That made me realize how utterly exhausted he must have been when we arrived here. His brain had almost stopped working. We'd been lucky. Our situation would have been far worse if we'd been out in the storm much longer.

I made three mugs of coffee. Then I took mine outside to do some thinking, and to give the lovebirds some space.

CHAPTER FORTY-SIX

I emerged from the hut into shimmering sunshine. With surprise, I realized that the storm had passed on and the world was a different and better place. Especially this bit of it. We were up high, on a little plateau, and I gazed around with wonder at a glorious vista of hills and valleys stretching away into infinity. Not a hint of a human presence in any direction. The sheer emptiness of the land and the profound loneliness was immediately awe-inspiring. No road, no buildings, no walls or fences. Only the hut, and ourselves, to show that Man had ever been here.

Perfect for insects and small reptiles, and probably for birds too, I couldn't help thinking with a smile. Ideal for them two — Jason and Lydia! I could understand why they wanted to be here, and could believe they had a wonderful time ahead of them as they tackled their life and their big project together.

Something else I believed was that I had to try even harder to help make sure it all happened for them. It wasn't going to be easy.

Wednesday now. Nine days to go. But even if we got through to a week on Friday, and Jason paid over the money for the farm, it wouldn't be over. I knew that for sure. The Reagans would still want Jason dead.

Something permanent had to be done to stop them threatening Jason, and not just for now. Running from them was no longer enough. It was time to do some fresh thinking.

That didn't take long. My thinking done, I knew what I had to do. Sitting here, on top of a beautiful hill for the next few days wasn't going to save Jason's hide. I needed to talk to Henry and develop an action plan. From up here I couldn't do that.

'OK, folks,' I said when I went back inside the hut. 'There's no point in me sitting around up here, waiting for the problem to solve itself. The Reagans won't stop or go away. I want to find a permanent solution.'

'I'm all ears,' Jason said, sounding amused. 'What have you got in mind, Frank?'

'Nothing yet. First, I want to see Henry. I need to talk to him. So I'm going to visit him.'

'What?' He looked alarmed now. 'Go back to Teesside?'

'Yes. Just me, though. Not you. It's not dangerous for me down there. I know my way around. After all, it is my home, remember? Besides, the Reagans know nothing about me.'

'Who's Henry?' Lydia asked.

'A guy I know. He's been doing some research on the Reagans for us.'

'Research? What do you mean?'

'I asked him to find out more about them. Right now, we know very little.'

'On the contrary,' she said, 'we know more than enough about them! They're a nasty, evil bunch of criminal . . .'

I held up my hand to staunch the flow of invective.

'They're all of that, but that's not what I mean, Lydia. So far, all we've done is run from them. That has to end. We have to do something positive.

'There'll be no peace for you and Jason, as well as Jason's family, if their pressure isn't brought to an end. Jason paying the money to buy the farm won't change the situation either. They'll just have even more reason to kill him then.'

'Kill Jason? What are you talking about? They're not going to . . .'

'You tell her, Jason,' I suggested.

'Frank's right, Lydia. They want to stop me paying for the farm, and blackmail and force me to hand over the money. If they can't do that, they'll kill me and hope to get the money through selling the farm that Francine will inherit. That's it, basically.'

There was a stunned silence then while a shocked Lydia digested what she'd been told.

'So far,' I said, resuming, 'all we've been doing is running and trying to stay alive. I want to stop and take the fight to them. To do that, though, I need to find a way of hurting the Reagans so badly that they'll give up chasing Jason.'

'But once Jason has bought the farm, surely that will be it?' Lydia said in a faltering voice.

I shook my head. 'I really don't think so, Lydia. It won't be over. An organized crime gang like the Reagans is not going to just give up and walk away.'

'You really think they'll . . . try to murder him?'

I said nothing more.

Jason came to my rescue again. 'Me or my family,' he said. 'Amy and Uncle Jimmy are in the frame, as well. That's why we can't go to the police, remember?'

'Oh, my God!' she said despairingly, when it had sunk in. 'What can we do — anything?'

'I don't know yet, Lydia. That's why I've brought Henry in. Now I need to find out what progress he's made.'

She seemed ready to debate it further, but thankfully Jason quietened her and put a stop to that.

'We've been through a lot in the last couple of days, Lydia. And Frank has taught me plenty about how organized crime gangs work. I believe him, and I trust him. He's had a lot of experience. So if this is what he thinks is the best thing to do, we have to let him go ahead.'

'You should both stay here while I'm gone,' I said, moving on briskly. 'I want you out of the reach of the Reagans. You're safe here. They have no idea where you are. And you've got each other for company, together with everything you need to survive for a few days.'

There was a silence for a minute or two. Then Lydia said, 'When do you want to go?'

'Right now. I'll return to Alwinton and find a way of getting back to Teesside from there.'

'Take the Beast,' Jason said.

'Oh, I couldn't do that!'

'Take it!' Jason insisted, holding out the keys.

'The Beast?' Lydia said. 'What on earth are you talking about now?'

'My new Land Rover,' Jason told her.

'What? You've bought a new Land Rover — when you already have one?'

'Had, Lydia. Had. The Reagans burned that one out in Rosedale.'

'Oh? You'd better tell me more!'

'I will.'

She glared at him and then said, 'The Beast? Why did you call it that?'

'I'll tell you that later, as well,' Jason said crisply.

'I shall look forward to hearing what you have to say!'

I smiled as I started pulling my stuff together. It looked as though Jason had got himself a true, hands-on, working partner this time.

'Call us and let us know what you discover and what you're going to do,' Lydia said, handing me a business card. 'Here's my number.'

'This won't be any good, Lydia. There isn't server coverage,' I said, puzzled. 'Not to here, there isn't.'

'I think you'll find there is, now the storm has moved on.'

I checked my phone and found it was true. I just looked at her.

'Don't ask me,' she said. 'I'm just an entomologist.'

'You never told me about this,' I accused Jason.

'I didn't know,' he protested.

'How did you know?' I asked Lydia.

She smiled sweetly and said, 'I've lived here all my life, Frank. I've learned that sometimes things work, and sometimes they don't. And that's it — all I can tell you!'

I left them to it. It seemed we all had some learning to do.

CHAPTER FORTY-SEVEN

In daylight, with no wind or rain, and with a watery sun instead of Jason to keep me company, it only took me two hours to reach Alwinton. It was downhill all the way, of course. That helped. It helped a lot.

The Beast was where we'd left it, untouched amid the three other vehicles parked there. I made my way straight to it without bothering to look for possible watchers from Tenerife. If Lydia believed there were some, I was inclined to believe her. This was her village. She would know the types of visitors it attracted, as well as its residents. Oddballs would stand out. But there was nothing I could do about it anyway.

Besides, I would be moving too fast for them to do anything about me even if they knew who I was, which still seemed unlikely. Without Jason alongside me, there was no reason for them to link me to him. Not even the Land Rover. They hadn't seen the Beast before, and the Landy they had seen was resting out of sight in Roy Thwaites's cavernous premises.

Anyway, nothing happened, and no one followed me. I had the road to myself as I set off out of Coquetdale.

I started thinking about the young couple I'd left behind. I liked Jason, as I've said previously, and now I'd taken an instant liking to his girlfriend as well. They made a fine couple. Jason was lucky. This time, at least, Jason was lucky! They both were. I smiled and shook my head.

Then I began wondering whatever had possessed Francine the other year. It hadn't only been Jason that had got married. She ought to have known he was not the one for her, given her background and family circumstances. Perhaps Jason was right, and she had grown tired of life with her family and wanted to try something else. If so, it hadn't taken long for her to decide she was wrong.

How long? Three weeks, wasn't it? Something like that. I smiled again, ruefully this time. Three days to get into the situation, and three weeks to get out of it. Sort of. Not bad, really, when you thought about it. Some folks spend the rest of their lives recovering from an unfortunate marriage.

My smile turned to a puzzled frown as I thought about the three-day lead-up to the marriage. Three days? That wasn't very long at all. How had they managed it? The arrangements for a wedding take time, especially if the bride's family have a part to play, and surely a family like Francine's would have insisted on involvement? Yet they couldn't possibly have got to know Jason well enough in just three days to have given the marriage their blessing. Had they even met him?

I thought back to what Jason had told me about the actual wedding ceremony. It had taken place on a beach, apparently, before a small gathering of people that Francine had invited. Family members and friends, presumably, but Jason hadn't said who they were. His equivalents had all been unknowing, back in England. Even so, according to him, it had been a lovely day and all had gone well.

Still . . . You had to wonder. I made a mental note to do just that.

CHAPTER FORTY-EIGHT

The Beast ran like a dream and got me down to Teesside in a couple of hours. I turned off the A19 just south of the junction with the main road into Hartlepool and ran down the B-road that goes around Billingham and skirts Saltholm before hitting Port Clarence. En route, I had already established that Henry would be at Maggie's place, the Station Hotel, again. Or, perhaps, still. He seemed to be there almost full-time these days. No doubt he liked having her look after him.

More likely, his office in the centre of Middlesbrough had become too dangerous a place for him to visit very often. Either that, or he couldn't afford to keep it warm and the electricity flowing. Who knows? There was a lot about Henry that I didn't know, but what I did know had long persuaded me that I really didn't want to know much more. He was dangerous company for me to keep — just as I was for him, to be fair.

'Oh, it's you again,' Maggie said when I walked into what Maggie liked to call "The Lounge".

'Hello to you, too, Maggie!'

She sniffed and said, 'I hoped I'd seen the last of you.'

'Is that any way to greet an old friend, and an even older friend of Henry's? Besides, I did send an apology for my rapid departure last time I was here.'

'In the middle of the night, like a pair of thieves.'

I winced. But I made no attempt to correct her. No way was I going to say that the lady in question, who I'd been protecting, was not a thief. She was, or had been, a contract killer who had fallen on hard times. It was complicated -- but that's what she was. Even so, I had quite liked Lady Day, as I had learned, to my astonishment, she was called. But Maggie would have barred me instantly and permanently if I had disclosed any of that.

'Henry in?'

'In his room. I gather he's waiting for you.'

'Thanks, Maggie!'

I headed for the stairs, and Henry's territory. Room Number Six, his home-from-home these days.

* * *

'Oh, it's you,' Henry said, sounding disappointed, when I knocked and opened the door.

'Has Maggie been coaching you? That's exactly what she said when I walked in.'

He grinned and waved me to an upright chair beside the bed. Henry was sitting on another one just like it, next to a little table supporting his laptop.

'What you got for me, Henry? Anything?'

'Not much, but it seems to be like I thought. The Reagans are over-extended. They have a big loan repayment coming up, and they're struggling to make it.'

'Who are they in hock to?'

'Everybody — everybody they've been able to think of. They're running around trying to borrow even more, but so far they haven't found another lender.'

'And they're due to make a big payment?'

'Next Monday. Ten million quid.'

'Sterling?'

'Yeah.'

'Which they haven't got, and are struggling to find?' I said thoughtfully. 'That explains a lot.'

177

Henry nodded.

I sighed. It all made sense now. Not that that helped. They needed Jason's money badly, unfortunately.

'What's happened to put them in such difficulty?'

'It seems to be down to a hotel and casino complex they're building in Puerto de la Cruz. That's what I hear.'

'Puerto . . . Where's that?'

'The north coast of Tenerife.'

'Is that where they live?'

'It is. The salubrious side of the island.'

'They must have ambitions to gentrify their business empire.'

'Could be. But the word is that the project, and the trouble they're in, is all down to George, the head of the family. Others, especially his brother Oscar, don't like it. But George sees it as his legacy plan and can't be dissuaded.'

'Legacy plan?'

'For when he's retired. It will tell the world who built it, and who and what he was. Like Raffles in Singapore, and Reid's Palace in Madeira.'

I just shook my head, as much at Henry's knowledge of the global hospitality industry as anything else.

'He thinks,' Henry added.

'But?'

'His legacy plan is a financial disaster, the way things are going. Anyway, I'll keep on it. See what else I can find.'

'If you don't mind, Henry.'

The discussion lapsed for a few moments while I digested what I'd heard, and what to make of it. Then the mental note I'd made earlier came back to mind.

'There's something else I'd like you to check for me, Henry.'

'You're going to get a helluva big bill!'

I waved the comment aside. 'That's not a problem. Let me worry about that.'

Henry grinned and said, 'Actually, you're just reminded me of something else I wanted to tell you. You know, you were asking how often the big man goes to the UK?'

'Have you found anything?'

'He goes twice a month, regular as clockwork.'

'That's a lot.' I thought about it for a moment and said, 'Sounds like he goes for a regular update, a financial report, maybe?'

'Could be. I'm not sure where he goes. But probably the old home town. That's where he flies to, anyway.'

'I'm surprised he passes muster with the authorities. Surely someone has something against him? Customs and Revenue, Immigration, the Met, the National Crime Agency — someone!'

'Seemingly not. He's just waved through like everyone else.'

'I'm tempted to offer the word "bribery" as explanation, but there's too many agencies he'd have to fund for it to be relevant. Perhaps he's just clean, legally?'

'Yeah, well. I'm not sure about that. Maybe he's just got good lawyers and accountants.'

'I'm sure he has. Anyway, Henry, if you pick up anything else, let me know.'

Then I told him something else I wanted. Henry chortled with amusement.

'It's not for me,' I assured him with a scowl. 'I'm not getting married, if that's what you think.'

'That's a pity. It couldn't happen to a nicer bloke!'

'I'm going to have to go to there, aren't I?' I said, with a grimace after a few thoughtful moments of silence.

'Where?'

'Tenerife.'

Henry became agitated. 'Do you think that's wise?'

'Wise? Maybe not, but I can't see any other way round it. So far, all I've been doing is helping Jason run away from the people hunting him. We can't go on doing that forever. It's not going to solve the problem.

'The boss man needs a poke in the eye, to stop all this. And he's in Tenerife. So I need to go there and sort him out. Otherwise, there'll be no end to it. '

'Sort George Reagan out? These are seriously bad peo-ple, Frank. And I don't want to lose one of my most valuable clients.'

I chuckled. 'That's very touching, Henry.'

'But you're going anyway, aren't you? You've made up your mind?'

I nodded. 'I'll have to.'

'What about the lad, Jason? Will you take him with you?'

'Oh, no! I've got him and his girlfriend stashed some-where safe. They can stay there till I get back.'

'You might need help? No! Don't tell me any more,' Henry said with a shudder, recovering quickly. I don't want to know. I'm just a desk warrior.'

'And a very valuable one,' I assured him with a smile.

It was true. Henry really was invaluable to me, even though he wasn't what I would need in Tenerife. And he was right. I would need help when I got there, and not just with carrying my suitcase, either.

CHAPTER FORTY-NINE

My phone vibrated. I glanced at the screen, failed to recognize the number, but answered anyway.

'Frank? Is that you, Frank? It's Amy.'

It was all said in a whispered rush that had me on instant alert.

'What is it, Amy?'

'We couldn't get away. Uncle Jim and me. They trapped us.'

Ah! Not what I wanted to hear. I grimaced and asked her what the situation was.

'We're in Rosedale still. Not the village, but somewhere nearby, I think. A cottage on a farm, maybe. I've heard cows not far away. We're locked up in a room that has shutters over the window.'

My plans were going to have to change. This was desperate. No way could I depart for Tenerife now.

'Are you hurt?' I asked, keeping it cool. 'Have either of you been threatened or mistreated?'

'Uncle Jim's not very good. He tried to resist, and got punched a few times. He's bruised and dazed. Maybe something worse. I don't know. I'm trying to help him.'

'What about you?'

'I'm a bit scratched and knocked about, as well — but so is one of them, now!'

'Have they said what they want?'

'Not directly, not to us. I've just picked up bits and pieces from what I've overheard. Basically, they want Jason, of course. I think they want to trade us for him.'

'Probably.'

I thought quickly, trying to guess how that might work, but there were too many unknowns.

'You're able to make phone calls?'

'This one, I am. I hid my phone when they caught us, and they're all out at the moment.'

'You can't be in Rosedale, then.'

'Because of server coverage? I think we are, or only just outside. Perhaps we're high up, and in range.'

It was possible. High up, there might well be server coverage in places. Knowing that might help me locate them.

'Any idea what they intend doing now?'

'Not really. But from what I've overheard, they're waiting for Jason to surface. They don't know where he is, but they do know where he'll have to be next Friday.'

Morpeth, I thought with another grimace. But they were not going to be able to make any progress before then, they would be thinking, until they got Jason on the phone and were able to threaten him about Amy and Jimmy.

'In the meantime, what's happening?' I asked.

'I think they have someone watching Risky Point, believing Jason, or whoever is with him, will try to make contact there with Uncle Jim. I suppose they might even move us there.'

It was a possibility, but unlikely. Best to keep the hostages somewhere nobody knew about, or was likely to stumble on.

'Is Jason all right, by the way?' Amy asked. 'Where are you?'

'He's fine. We've been in a few scrapes along the way, but we managed to get out of them. It's best if you don't know where we are.'

'Because I might tell them — or they might beat it out of me?'

She was clear-thinking, was Amy. But I didn't confirm or deny it. There wasn't much point. I said something else instead.

'We'll get you both out of there, Amy. That's a promise. And soon. Just hang on, and look after your uncle. Keep me informed about what's happening, if you can. Use texts, if you can't use voice. And I'll let you know what we're going to do.'

'Who? You and Jason?'

'Me and someone else. I'll keep Jason out of it.'

'Good.'

'One last thing, Amy. Do you think they know about the farm?'

'Oh, yes. I think they've even got someone there now, in case Jason turns up.'

* * *

After the call ended, the first thought I had was that they seemed to have a lot of manpower at their disposal, the Reagans.

The other thought I had was that it was time for me to make another phone call, this one a call for help. Help wouldn't come unless I asked for it, and I really needed it now. So did the Macks, all of them.

CHAPTER FIFTY

'It's Frank,' I said, when she answered the phone.

There followed a long pause before she said, 'Frank? How are you, Frank?'

'Pretty much the same. You?'

'Good, thanks.'

Just as brief and staccato as I remembered her being.

'So you've still got my number?' she said.

'I have. You didn't expect me to delete it, did you?'

She ignored that, and said, 'I'm assuming this isn't a social call?'

'You're right. It isn't,' I said, with a chuckle at last. 'I wanted to see if you were busy.'

'Ah!'

'And to find out where you are currently.'

'So it's business.'

'Yes, it is. I could do with some help, and naturally you came to mind.'

'Of course!' she said, chuckling herself now. 'For old times' sake. And before you say or think anything else, no, I'm not disappointed. It's good to hear from you, Frank.'

I smiled at last. It was going to be all right. We had experienced some tough times together, and grown very, very close in a short space of time. Then, for no very obvious reason, we had grown apart again and gone our separate ways. Neither of us was the staying kind, I guess. But some kind of bond was still there.

* * *

'So what's going on, Frank? And where's the action taking place?'

'Tenerife, eventually. Have you been there?'

'Know it well.'

'Fancy going back for a few days?'

'I just might,' she said after a brief pause. 'I'm getting a bit bored here at the cottage.'

So that's where she was. Her hideaway in Wasdale, in the Lake District, that seemingly nobody but me knew about. On her hols, perhaps, or between engagements? Possibly even retired, but I didn't think so. She liked the buzz of action too much. In some ways, she was like me.

'Tell me more,' she added.

Emma was a remarkable person, with capabilities I didn't have. She'd had a tough military background before she started freelancing and hiring herself out as a close protection officer. So I had no hesitation in outlining the situation to her. Then I just held my breath and waited.

'Yes,' she said, after a few moments thought. 'I like the sound of that. It's interesting. Count me in.'

'There won't be a lot of money in it,' I warned, 'but, like me, you'll get your normal daily retainer.'

'I would do it for free, Frank,' she said briskly. 'Jimmy Mack is a fine man. I remember him well.'

CHAPTER FIFTY-ONE

So there we were. Started. It hadn't taken much to get her on board either.

I began to talk details. I told her what had been happening. Then I told her about the farmhouse, and that I'd decided we needed to clear it of the Tenerifes as the first step. Clear the ground in Northumberland before we tackled anything else. If we did that, Jason and Lydia would be able to move out of the hut and set up base in the house.

Then we could travel south to do something about Amy and Jimmy. They seemed to be reasonably safe for the moment, and I was sure Junior wasn't about to do anything to them that might undermine his negotiating strategy with Jason and lead him to go to the police.

After that, if we were still on our feet, we could take off for Tenerife and sort out the big man there. George Reagan, himself. That was going to be a challenge, but we'd have to find a way.

None of this would be easy. I knew that. But it's in my nature, a fault if you like, to travel hopefully. So we would go for it, all of it. I have to admit that with Emma on board, I felt a lot better about our prospects. Together, we had tackled and bested bigger hoodlums than this pathetic bunch of low-life expat criminals. Besides, I was sick and tired of doing nothing but run and hide. It was time to give the other side something to worry about.

* * *

'How urgent is all this?' Emma asked.

'It is urgent. I can't tell you much more than that. But at least we have a few days to sort everything out. That said, the sooner you can get here, the better.'

'Where do you want to meet?'

'A little place called Rothbury would be good. It's . . .'

'I know it. I've been there. Coquetdale, isn't it?'

'That's right. I'm surprised . . .'

'I can be there by three this afternoon. That soon enough?'

'Perfect. Which way would you come?'

'Over to the M6 from here. Then north as far as Carlisle, and then turn on to the A69 to Newcastle. I'll leave that at Greenhead and take the Military Road alongside the Roman Wall as far as Chollerford. Then thirty miles on little roads to Rothbury.'

'You've been before,' I concluded, mightily impressed by her route knowledge.

'I have. I'll get started shortly. Weapons?'

'We'll need something, I think.'

'There's a car park called Beggars Rigg overlooking the river at the western edge of the village. I'll meet you there.'

I smiled with relief as I closed the phone down. Working with someone as well organized and capable as Emma was good. I wouldn't say it made the job simpler, but it certainly made it a lot more doable. We were in business!

CHAPTER FIFTY-TWO

The phone again, the damned phone!

'Yes, Henry?'

'Frank.'

I screwed my face up in irritation and hoped my impatience wasn't revealed by my voice. I was driving and in a hurry to get back to Northumberland, with a lot on my mind.

'You got something for me, Henry?'

'Dunno. I might have.'

I forced myself to relax. It was best to let Henry get to it at his own speed. You couldn't hurry him up anyway.

'So what you got?'

'It's not that simple,' Henry said.

'What isn't?'

'When Reagan goes to the UK. He flies into Heathrow, but then he disappears.'

I frowned. 'What do you mean?'

'George Reagan goes through formalities at the airport, and then he's gone. No more George Reagan.'

'Come on, Henry! I haven't got time for this.'

'Tut, tut! Well, that's it.'

I grimaced, and just had to hope he wasn't in a huff. I still needed him.

'Another thing,' he said, to my relief. 'I did some checking. Some of the Reagan family are in prison, as you know.'

'Yeah. For little offences like murder.'

'Are you being sarcastic, Frank?'

'Who, me?'

'Fuck you!'

'I'll add a little something to what I pay you, to compensate for my ill humour. What you got, Henry?'

'Well, they're not all in prison. And they're not all murderers, either.'

'No, I didn't suppose they were,' I admitted, rolling my eyes skywards. *Come on, Henry. For God's sake!*

'Some of those in Tenerife are legally *persona non grata* in the UK. In fact, some of them are fighting extradition proceedings. That includes two brothers, Ray and Barry Reagan, both nephews of George.'

I was slightly interested now, but only slightly.

'That right, Henry?'

'It is. I've been searching the passenger lists for people flying into Newcastle Airport lately from Tenerife.'

'Oh?'

'And guess what?'

This sounded promising.

'What, Henry?'

'Those brothers? They were on a flight that came in not long ago, travelling under the name of Wentworth.'

'Ah!'

I was staggered. The implications were immediately enormous.

'How do you know that's them, Henry? And how did you get all that?' I demanded.

'What? You want me to reveal my sources?' he said indignantly, his voice rising.

'No, of course not,' I said hastily. 'I don't want to interfere with your business arrangements and contacts. Forget I said that.'

'Well . . . what I can assure you,' Henry said, calming down, 'is that the info is true and reliable.'

'Right.'

'Would it help if I emailed you a couple of photos of the brothers?'

'Very much! That would be wonderful. Thanks a lot, Henry.'

* * *

What it meant, of course, was that Henry might have given me some leverage to use against the Tenerifes. I say might guardedly, because it depended on where these two brothers were and what they were doing. My hope, and guess, was that they were in Northumberland, in Alwinton, or at the farm even, keeping a look out for Jason. Why else would they have flown into Newcastle Airport?

All I needed to do now was find out if I was right.

CHAPTER FIFTY-THREE

I found the car park easily enough. It was just outside the village, on a wooded site overlooking the River Coquet. I was there early. So was Emma. She arrived just after two-thirty, ten minutes after me. The car park was empty. She drew up in a BMW SUV and parked alongside me. I got out and watched her extricate herself.

She looked just the same as I remembered from the other year. Tall, slim, athletic build, short-cropped hair and a lean, weathered face. Nobody would dare call her pretty, but she was a good-looking woman who would attract attention in any crowded room. The only change from when I first met her was that this time, she wore a smile. I flattered myself that she had learned the hard way to trust and even like me. A little bit, anyway.

'Good to see you, Emma.'

'Likewise, Frank.'

We closed together and hugged each other. It truly was good to see her again, and I sensed and knew the feeling was mutual. For a time, we had been much more than close, and I didn't think that would have faded away entirely. If she hadn't been even more of a loner than I am, we might have stayed together.

'Where have you come from, Frank?'

'Middlesbrough. It was a fast travel. How was your journey?'

'Quicker than I expected. Trucks and wagons on the A69 were a lot fewer than usual.'

'Good.' I nodded with satisfaction. 'Right. I want to get up to the farm in daylight. So let's get started. We'll take both vehicles up to Alwinton, about ten miles from here. Then we can take your car up to the farm and leave mine in the village for Jason.'

She turned and looked at my vehicle with a studied eye. 'You've had an upgrade, Frank. Have you come into money?'

I laughed. 'Not really. My vehicle got pretty beat up and is in dock now for some TLC. This is Jason's new Land Rover, but the Tenerifes don't know about it, and I'd like to keep it that way. So we'll leave it in Alwinton for him.'

'It must have cost a lot of money,' Emma said thoughtfully. 'I haven't seen one like this since I was last in Saudi.'

'You're right there. It was ridiculously expensive. But we needed a replacement vehicle urgently, and this was all my supplier could offer. I cringed at the price, but . . .' I shrugged. 'Well, Jason has come into a lot of money, as I told you, and he wanted to spend some of it. They call it the Beast, by the way.'

Emma studied things a moment or two longer before saying, 'The Beast, eh? Yes, I can see why. He's got good taste, has Jason. Already I can say that for him.'

We got going in our two-vehicle convoy. The temperature had fallen and the sky was clear now, which meant the light was good. I hoped it stayed that way. It would give us every chance of reaching the farm before darkness fell.

* * *

We reached Alwinton soon after three. I parked the Beast where it had stood before, making it easy for Jason to find. Then I spent a few minutes bringing Emma up to speed.

'Nice country,' she said approvingly, looking around.

'Not a bit bleak?'

'I like bleak,' she told me, straight-faced. 'It goes with my personality.'

'Keep it up,' I told her with a grin, 'and I might rediscover my sense of humour.'

We waited until Henry's email with the photos came through. After studying them for a few moments, we got moving and headed in Emma's car for the farm.

'Think you'll recognize them, if you see them?' I asked.

'Oh, yes.' Emma nodded. 'They're a pair of beauties, aren't they?'

'They are that. Let's hope they're easier to frighten than they look.'

CHAPTER FIFTY-FOUR

We drove up close to the farmhouse and parked behind a barn. Then we had a last-minute discussion about how to handle things before we set off to make for the house. On the way, we passed a big Mercedes that would have looked more in context in a city centre than out here. We split up, as arranged, and I made my way alone to the front door.

A man came to the door before I reached it. He wasn't one of the men I'd seen in the photo Henry sent me.

'Can I help you?' he asked, for all the world as if it were his own house and he was a social host welcoming visitors.

'You certainly can. I want you and the Reagan brothers out of here in the next couple of minutes.'

His expression changed. 'Who the fuck do you think . . .'

I grabbed him by the throat and squeezed hard. He squawked a little bit and his face changed colour.

'Do I make myself clear? Yes or no?'

He managed to nod. I released my grip and spun him round, his hands clasped around his injured throat. 'Now get inside!' I snapped.

I recognized the brothers as soon as I saw them sitting at the farmhouse table in the kitchen. They were relaxed and eating their meal, as if they were at home after a hard day's work chasing sheep around the hills. But they stopped eating and looked astonished and shocked when I sent their buddy hurtling through the doorway.

'Sid! What the hell . . . ?' Barry Reagan shouted.

He started to get up from his chair when he saw me. I pushed him back down, picked up the plate of what looked like stew and rammed it in his face.

'Don't!' I heard Emma shout.

She had come in through the back door and was clearly in control when I glanced her way. Her shotgun was pressed against the face of Ray Reagan, her finger tight on the trigger.

'Drop it,' she ordered him.

The steak knife he was wielding clattered to the floor, instead of into me, as no doubt intended.

'You're in big fucking trouble, mister,' Barry Reagan said, as he wiped the stew from his face.

'Not as much as you and your brother, and possibly your mate here, when I call the cops and tell them I've caught two members of the Reagan family who they're wanting to extradite from Tenerife. I'll be saving them a lot of time and expense.'

'What are you talking about? That's not us,' Ray said defiantly. 'You've got the wrong guys. What are you anyway — bounty hunters?'

'You could say that. And we're good at what we do. Before we go any further, let me tell you that we know the name you flew into Newcastle under, and it doesn't make any difference. We know exactly who you are. So no more lying about it. You shouldn't be in this house, and you shouldn't be in this country.'

'So what do you want?' Tom said, giving me an ugly, sullen look, but mindful of the shotgun in his face.

'Here's the deal. We want you out of here in the next few minutes, like I told your mate Sid. We also want you to forget about helping Junior any more, and go home while you still can. That's not too much to ask, is it?'

There followed a stricken silence, broken after a short pause by me. 'For good measure,' I added, 'in a way, you have my sympathy. You should never have returned to the UK.'

'We had no choice,' Barry said bitterly, rubbing his face with his sleeve to remove the last of the stew.

'I realize that,' I told him. 'Junior shouldn't have ordered you to come.'

'We don't take orders from Junior,' Ray snarled.

'No? Well, whoever told you to come here was in the wrong. They knew the risk you would be running. Now look where you are!

'As well as what's on your extradition rap, you're soon going to be looking at being part of a gang that took part in abduction, attempted murder and, quite possibly, even actual murder. Add in your career criminal backgrounds and you'll be lucky ever to see the Great Outdoors again.'

'Fuck you!' Ray said.

But it was an automatic riposte. There was no anger in it. Only resignation. He knew that what I'd laid out for them was pretty much right and true. They were in deep. They should never have come. Anywhere in Spain or its territories, they would still have had a fighting chance. Here they had none at all.

'So what else are you saying?' Ray added, staring at me. 'That can't be all of it.'

'Agree to do what we want, and I won't tell the cops you're here, or even in this country.'

'What? Just leave and go home, without telling Junior?'

Understandably, he looked and sounded very suspicious.

I nodded. 'Home, or wherever else you prefer. I don't much mind.'

'What's in it for you?'

'The owner of the farm doesn't want any of you Reagans here. He's asked us to see to it, because he thinks the police won't be very interested and will take their time. They have enough to do without chasing around after trespassers.'

'He'll pay you?'

'Yes.'

Ray nodded, as if he understood now. We probably didn't look much different to them, so far as he was concerned. And he knew full well what they themselves were capable of doing if they had the upper hand, as we had right now.

'Junior will kill us,' Barry said suddenly, seeing the way his brother's thoughts were going.

'He may have done that already,' Ray said heavily. 'This bloke's right. We should never have come here. This situation's nothing to do with us.'

After a pause for further thought, he nodded at me and said, 'OK. We'll do it. Deal.'

'There's just one more thing,' I said. 'I don't want Junior knowing we're here, or that you've seen us. If he or his mates turn up, I'll know you haven't kept your side of the bargain. Then I won't keep mine either. You won't get out of the country. OK? Understand?'

He nodded and said, 'How do we know you won't call the cops anyway?'

'There would be nothing in that for us. We're going to let you walk out of here, get in your vehicle and take off without hindrance. Then you'll just have to trust me, like I'll have to trust you.

'Remember, though, you have a lot more to lose than we have. We don't want the police involved, because it would just complicate things, and hold us up. And I don't have the time or the patience for it. But you can't afford to have them involved if you ever want to see dear old Tenerife again.

'Anyway, that's the deal. Take it or leave it. But if you decide to leave it, we'll call the police right now and sit here with you three at gunpoint until they arrive.'

'We'll take it,' Ray said, gently pushing his chair back and slowly getting to his feet, still acutely aware of Emma's shotgun. 'Come on, Barry! And you, Sid. Let's go.'

'You've got someone in the village, as well, haven't you?' I asked.

Ray shook his head. 'Sid was there, but he came up here. He got bored down there on his own.'

Sid agreed. 'There was supposed to be two of us there, but the other lad never turned up.'

How sensible of him, I couldn't help thinking. 'Come on, then. Let's get you all out of here.'

CHAPTER FIFTY-FIVE

On the way back south, Emma driving, I called Jason to tell him and Lydia that both the farmhouse and the cottage in Alwinton were clear of intruders. It would be safe to go back there.

'How did you manage that?' he asked.

'It's a long story, and it will have to wait till later. I just wanted to let you know that you don't have to stay in the hut any longer. You can move to Lydia's cottage, or start clearing up in the farmhouse, whenever you like.'

'Excellent! Well done, Frank. So what are you going to do now?'

'Some follow-up. I want to see what more we can do about the Reagans before you're due in Morpeth.

'The Beast is back in Alwinton, where you and I first left it, by the way. Undamaged, I might add. But don't go far in it. Just stay put until I get back to you.'

'Do you want me to help you?'

'No thanks, Jason. You're the target, remember. I want you to stay safe for now. I'll let you know when I want you to join me.'

'Or not?' Emma said, with a sideways glance, after I'd ended the call.

'Or not,' I agreed.

'Jason is a true innocent, isn't he?'

'Yeah, he is. He's a decent guy, but he's not cut out for what we have to do now. He would be at risk, and he'd be a hindrance.'

Emma nodded and said fervently, 'Lord save us from amateurs! It was a bit of luck that the men they'd sent to the farm weren't up to much, wasn't it?'

'You're right. They were just petty criminals. If they'd been wanted for murder, or something else serious, we couldn't have just let them go. And then we'd have been involved with the cops, which would have lost us a lot of time and convenience.'

'We could have just shot them?'

'Yeah, right.'

I glanced at her. She was smiling. But you never can tell with Emma.

There followed a period of silence as we started thinking about what lay ahead of us. Then I got on my phone again and started looking for holiday lets around Rosedale.

My assumption was that when the Tenerifes lifted Jimmy and Amy they took them back to their base, which had to be somewhere in the Rosedale area. There wouldn't have been any need to look for somewhere else.

Another assumption was that their base was close, but outside the village. Somewhere isolated, where they could avoid attracting attention. That pretty well ruled out a hotel or guesthouse, or anywhere else with owner or staff in residence. The likelihood was that they had rented a remote, self-contained property at short notice, which wouldn't have been difficult at this time of year. And that would be where they had stashed Jimmy and Amy. So what I was doing now was compiling a list of potential sites for us to visit.

'Finding much?' Emma asked eventually.

'A few.' I looked up from the screen. 'Where are we?'

'On the A697. We came through Rothbury five minutes ago. Heading for Morpeth now.'

'Ah! Better give Morpeth a miss.'

She nodded. 'Easy to do. We'll be on the bypass around it in a few minutes.'

'You must have been here before?'

'Oh, yes. Many times. Did you not know I was a northern lass?'

I chuckled. 'All I really knew was that you were not a townie.'

'Well, you got that right. Anyway, what about your searching?'

'I reckon they'll be holed up in an isolated holiday let. Something like that. If I'm right — and let's hope I am — there aren't that many eligible properties close to the village. So far as I can see, there are only three or four suitable places within five miles of Rosedale Abbey that are currently open for business.'

'What are they? Cottages?'

'Yes. They're all on farms. Two are isolated cottages. The others are groups of several cottages. Probably converted farm buildings.'

Emma didn't bother saying she hoped I was right. If I wasn't, we were in trouble, and poor Jimmy and Amy were in even worse trouble.

CHAPTER FIFTY-SIX

My phone buzzed when we were approaching Teesside. Amy again, I thought with a wince when I saw the caller's number. But it wasn't.

'Doy?'

Uh, uh!

'Who's this?'

'The old man and his niece are with us. So you know who this is.'

The accent was what I think of as Essex, estuarine any-way, and the tone full of self-confidence. I knew who it was, all right.

Obviously, Junior had got hold of Amy's mobile, and identified me and got my phone number from it. That was a pity, but there wasn't anything I could do about it. I just had to hope Amy and Jimmy were still OK.

'I've looked you up, Doy. I know who you are, and what you do. Impressive CV, by the way. Is it all true, or is all that stuff online just a marketing tool?'

'Depends what you've read, and who wrote it.'

I wondered if he'd noticed that I don't have a website. I've never felt the need to tout for business or write about myself. If others want to write about events involving me, and there's been plenty of them, there's nothing I can do to stop them. But I safeguard what's left of my privacy and anonymity. It's a personal preference, and it makes my life more comfortable.

'From what I've read, you seem to be a sensible, intelligent guy, one who knows a good deal when he sees one. So here's the deal I'm offering you.'

He paused, as if waiting for me to comment. Perhaps he was hoping to hear an expression of outrage. Something, anyway. I didn't give him the pleasure.

'Just get on with it, Junior.'

'Mr Reagan to you, Doy! I want you to remember that.'

Was that vanity revealed? It sounded like it.

'I don't know where you and the Mack kid are right now. I admit that. But get him here to talk to me, and his sister and uncle will be released unharmed.'

'You just want to talk to him?' I said, with a grim smile to myself.

'Yes. I want to tell him about an excellent investment opportunity for him on Tenerife. Got that?'

'I'll tell him. Where do you want to meet?'

'His house in Rosedale Abbey. I'll be there, waiting for him. When he agrees to take up the investment opportunity I'm offering him, I'll take him to pick up his relatives.'

'That's good of you! Just give us a couple of hours to get there, Junior.'

I ended the call.

* * *

'Did you get all that?' I asked, glancing at Emma.

She nodded. 'Sounds like they're still in Rosedale, as you thought.'

'Mmm. They must have taken Jimmy and Amy back there. Too risky for them to stay at Risky Point. Someone might have called in to see me or Jimmy.'

'So what's the plan now?'

'I'm working on it. Now shut up for a minute, and let me think.'

'Nice!' she said, flashing me a grin.

* * *

A couple of obvious things were running through my mind. One was the priority need to rescue Jimmy and Amy. Another was the need to keep Jason out of it, and well hidden from Junior. There was also the continued need to resolve Jason's problem long term, and avoid a revenge killing, or whatever. All that was going to require a balancing act, one that might be hard to maintain. But at least we'd made a start, and freed the farm from Reagan clutches.

As well as Junior, of course, there was also his old man to think about. The one was right here, on the ground, and the other was on that little island off Africa. They would both have to be satisfied, or somehow dealt with and neutralized. Not easy to do, if it could be done at all. More thought needed.

Then I recalled what Henry had told me about dissent within the family, and began to wonder if the interests of Junior and George were identical. There might be something there to explore. Worth thinking about. I wondered if George and his son saw things in the same light. Probably they did, being father and son, chairman of the family business and deputy, but not necessarily.

The trouble was, we didn't have time ourselves to do any digging. I'd have to try Henry again. He might know more than he'd told me so far.

'OK, Emma,' I said, turning back to my chauffeur. 'Here's the plan. First, we find where Junior's holding Jimmy and Amy. Then we rescue them. After that . . . We'll think of something else to do.'

'Sounds like a plan,' Emma said, nodding judiciously.

CHAPTER FIFTY-SEVEN

My phone buzzed not long after that, and I didn't need to call Henry again.

'I've worked out what he does,' Henry said without preamble.

'Who does what, Henry?'

'Reagan. He drops out of sight when he comes to the UK.'

'You said.'

'Changes his identity.'

'Go on.'

'Takes a taxi from Heathrow to King's Cross, and then buys a train ticket to Edinburgh for John McCall.'

'And that's himself?'

'Right.'

'Edinburgh, eh?'

'Yeah. He doesn't stop in London, and misses out Essex as well.'

'Branching out? Doesn't want his old gang to know?'

'Could be. I'm not sure, though. I'll have to work on it some more.'

'Might be worthwhile. There might be something there we could use. But, Henry, how do you know all this? Where's the info come from?'

'Well, it's taken some dogged, patient research and moments of inspiration as well as luck.'

'Of course. For which you will be well remunerated. But even so?'

'It started with a current account he has, and regular payments to a John McCall. Then it was a matter of checking passenger lists for Edinburgh trains, and putting the two together.'

I shook my head in awe. What this man could do!

'Keep after him, Henry. You're doing a great job.'

'That other business you were on about, by the way. It's interesting, and I can see now where you were coming from.'

'Oh?'

'That young feller you're helping, Jimmy Mack's nephew? I don't think he was ever married.'

'What?'

'I've been doing some checking. Tenerife is part of Spain. It's not a colony, or anything like that. It's simply an overseas part of Spain.'

'Like the Channel Islands and the isle of Man with the UK?'

'No. They have their own legal systems — and their own governments, come to that. But Tenerife and the other Canary Islands have the same legal and government systems as the Spanish mainland.'

'I didn't know that, Henry. But what's it got to do with Jason?'

'It means he's never been married. Under Spanish law, for a marriage to be legally recognized, it has to satisfy several conditions.

'For a civil marriage, which this one seems to have been, one partner must have been resident in Spain for at least two years. Obviously, Jason wasn't, but the Reagan woman might have been. So that's probably OK.

'The clincher, though, is that a marriage is only recognized legally if the wedding ceremony took place in a church or another building approved for marriages. A beach wedding doesn't qualify.

'What Jason probably had was a blessing ceremony, which isn't the same thing. People have that when they don't qualify for actual marriage. Before or after the blessing ceremony, which can be on the beach or anywhere else, some people get legally married in Gibraltar, or back in their own country.

'From what you've told me, though, Jason and the Reagan girl didn't do that. They just had the beach thing. After that they had a booze-up and then they all went home, or back to where they were staying.'

'Yes, I think that's more or less what happened.'

'So he wasn't married then, and he isn't married now either. QED, as the mathematicians say.'

'Quite.'

I tried not to sound too excited, but what it obviously meant in practical terms was that if Jason died, Francine wouldn't be his widow. And that meant she wouldn't inherit his money or other assets. Nor, probably, was she entitled to a wife's share of any of it now either, not least because she had walked out on him without cause.

So Henry's analysis was a game changer. Unless he was wrong, which not for one minute did I believe he was.

'Just before you go, Henry, there's something else I want to ask you. What have you picked up about the Reagans' management structure? How does Junior fit in, for example, and what's his relationship with his father?'

'That's very interesting, as well. Like I said before, Junior is his dad's deputy. He's the approved second in command who is expected to take over the running of the family business in due course.'

'So he gets on well with his old man, then? That's disappointing.'

'I'm not so sure about that, Frank. From what I hear, Junior is not only up and coming, he's also ambitious and impatient. He believes he should be in charge right now, never mind eventually.'

'You're giving me some hope, Henry! Go on.'

'I take it you want to hear about family discord?'

'It would be nice.'

'Well, I haven't heard too much of that nature, but it wouldn't be a surprise. George is a tough bugger, and from all accounts, Junior is a chip off the old block. Then there's George's brother, Oscar. He's not keen on the hotel and casino complex that George sees as his legacy. Thinks it's going to ruin them financially. That's about all I know so far. I'll see if I can dig anything else up.'

'If you would, Henry. If you would. One other thing. Can you see if you can get me a number, a personal number, for George Reagan?'

'Shouldn't be hard to do. Have you given up the idea of visiting him?'

'Not at all. But it would be good manners to phone first, and let him know.'

'That you're coming?'

'Yes. That's right. I want to give him fair warning. It wouldn't be very polite not to tell him what might happen if he doesn't see sense.'

'Oh, I see!'

I could almost hear his look of anguish.

'Well, good luck with that, Frank.'

'Thank you, Henry.'

'But don't say I haven't warned you.'

'As if I ever would!'

* * *

'What are you thinking?' Emma asked, with a sideways glance at me, after the call ended.

'Not much, I'm afraid. Just grasping at straws, really. But I'm wondering if there's any possibility of stirring up trouble in the heart of the Reagan family.'

'That would be nice.'

'Wouldn't it?'

Keeping Jason safe for now, and rescuing Jimmy and Amy, wouldn't count for much if it couldn't be made permanent. Somehow an end had to be put to this entire sorry saga. The Reagans had to be chased off for good, and made to see the sense of abandoning their designs on Jason's money. In the hope of achieving that, I was prepared to look at anything. No holds barred.

CHAPTER FIFTY-EIGHT

We reached Rosedale shortly before midnight and headed for the first of the cottages that had come up online. It was free-standing and on a lane on the west side of the valley. We drove slowly past, went on a couple of hundred yards and then turned round and came back again.

'Looks empty,' Emma said.

I nodded.

There were no lights showing, which wasn't too sur-prising at that time of a winter's night. Nor were there any vehicles standing around outside.

'I want to check anyway, just to make sure,' I said.

'I'll come with you.'

We circled the cottage and soon decided first impres-sions were justified. The place hadn't been used for a long time, possibly since late summer, judging by a couple of flyers stuffed in the letter box.

We moved on.

Moved on, and hit gold with our second shot. It was a farm a couple of miles out of Rosedale Abbey, a farm with several cottages that had been converted from outbuildings that were no longer needed. As soon as we spotted three high-end cars parked outside the most distant cottage, we knew this was it.

Emma reversed her car quietly back on to the road and drove a short distance away before parking in a gateway leading to a field. She switched off the engine and looked at me.

I nodded and said, 'Looks like we found them.'

'Let's hope so. We'd better get ready.'

I glanced at my watch. One o'clock now. Well into the night, but still early if you were used to casinos and nightclubs. There were lights on in the cottage, but until we took a look, there was no way of knowing what that meant.

'Maybe they're scared of the dark,' Emma suggested with a grin.

'Well, let's go and give them good reason to be.'

* * *

Only the one cottage appeared to be occupied. There were no cars outside any of the others, and no lights in them either. The cottage that we targeted was pretty big and had plenty of lights. First, though, we had to be sure it was the right one. To do that, we split up. Emma set off one way to make a circuit of the building, and I went the other way. We met on the far side, at the halfway point, and withdrew to a safe distance for a discussion.

'What did you see?' I asked. 'Anything? All I saw was closed curtains.'

'Four men sprawled across settees, drinking from cans of beer and watching TV.'

'It could be anyone,' I said with a frown. 'Doesn't have to be them. No sign of Amy and Jimmy?'

'No. It doesn't mean they're not there, though.'

'We're going to have to get inside and find out for sure. But first let's go back to the window where you saw those guys watching TV. I've got an idea.'

When we were in position, I took out my phone and called Amy's number. One of the men inside got up after a few moments and collected a phone from a nearby table. I gave Emma a thumbs-up and walked away a short distance.

'Yeah?' I heard.

'Junior?'

'No. It's Martin. Junior's . . . Who is this?'

'George Reagan's mother. Now get me Junior!'

There was a stunned silence. Then: 'He's not here, like I said.'

'Where is he?'

'I don't know. He didn't say where he was going. But he's with Joey and Seamus.'

'OK. Well, don't bother telling him I called. I'll tell him myself.'

I ended the call.

'Junior's not there, unfortunately,' I told Emma, who had come over to join me.

'We going in?' she demanded.

I nodded. 'Looks like the right place. Let's go!'

CHAPTER FIFTY-NINE

Emma took her shotgun. I took the tyre lever I keep in the car. Guns can be more trouble than they're worth, in my experience.

'Still got that, I see,' Emma said.

'Always. It's a good weapon.'

'Good to know. I'll just take the shotgun.'

'One gun's enough.'

'Let's hope so,' she said with a chuckle.

* * *

We went in via the front door, which was unlocked. Once inside, we moved swiftly along to the room where the noise was coming from, the TV room. There were the four of them there, still engrossed in watching a film that involved lots of shouting and banging. Gangsters watching a gangster movie avidly, relating it to their own experience no doubt, eager to give a running commentary.

I stepped into the room first. Emma followed and immediately moved to one side, covering the men with the shotgun. They were shocked. Even more so when I reached down to pull the plug and shut off the TV.

'Sit down!' I ordered, to stop the mass rising. 'Stay in your seats.'

Two did. Two didn't.

Emma fired a shot into the ceiling, bringing down on them a shower of plaster and bits of wood. The shotgun motioned them to get down. They got down.

'Do as you're told,' I said, 'and stay safe. If you don't, you'll be shot.'

'With heavy duty slugs,' Emma added. 'I'm not firing bird shot.'

The hole in the ceiling underlined her point.

'What the hell do you think you're doing?' a thickset guy demanded in a truculent tone. 'Do you have any idea who we are? Who you're messing with?'

'We know exactly who you are. And we've come for the hostages you're holding.'

'What hostages?' he said with a sneer.

'Stand up,' I told him, pointing. 'And move over to that wall over there.'

As he'd been the first to speak, I assumed he was the leader of the group. I needed to deal with him first. He stayed where he was and looked me in the eye, full of contempt.

I tapped him on the head with the tyre lever. 'Move!'

He did then, with waves of anger and pain flowing from him.

When he was against the wall, I told him to empty his pockets and dump the contents on a nearby table.

'You're all going to be doing this,' I said over my shoulder to the group. 'So make sure you understand what's required.'

Keys went on the table, followed by a phone.

'Now your wallet,' I told him.

That followed.

'Anything else?'

He shook his head.

'Take off your jacket.'

I didn't believe he'd brought out everything, and this was the moment I knew he would have been waiting for.

One arm came out of his jacket. Then, as he turned to shrug out of the other sleeve, he whirled round, bringing up a pistol that had been concealed somewhere on his person.

I had been expecting it, or something, and hit the gun arm hard with the tyre lever, breaking it. He screamed and sagged back against the wall. I grabbed him by the shirt collar and marched him back to the chair he had been using, his leadership qualities in rags.

'I want the rest of you over here, one at a time, emptying your pockets. Starting with you!' I added, pointing at the young guy who had answered the phone when I called.

They were no problem once their leader had been dealt with. None of them seemed to fancy being a hero. Soon we had a pile of stuff on the table. Some of it I didn't bother with, but I stuffed phones, wallets and a couple of handguns and knives into a big plastic bag I'd brought with me. It was partly self-defence, but somewhere amongst that lot there might be something we could use.

That done, I turned to the young guy again and said, 'Where are the hostages?'

'Martin!' one of the others said, in a warning tone.

He shrugged and looked away from me despairingly.

'If you've killed them,' I told him, 'none of you four will leave this room alive. Even if you've only injured them, none . . .'

'The cellar!' he said quickly. 'They're in the cellar.'

'Martin!'

'Show me,' I told him.

He got up. 'We can't do anything else,' he told the others.

I glanced at Emma before leaving with the kid. She just nodded. Things were cool with her.

Martin led the way to the kitchen, where he pointed to a trapdoor in the floor.

'Open it,' I told him.

He did.

'They'll kill me for this,' he said.

'They'll thank you,' I assured him. 'You're saving their lives.'

He switched a light on for the cellar and stood back. I looked down at a flight of sturdy timber stairs and grimaced. It didn't feel good.

'Amy?' I called. 'Jimmy? Can you hear me? It's Frank.'

After a moment, there came an answering call from Amy. 'Frank? Is that you, Frank?'

'Yes. Can you make your own way up, or do you need help?'

'I can. Uncle Jimmy needs help, though.'

I turned to the kid. 'Go down and help him up.'

Amy came up first, followed by Jimmy Mack and the young guy.

'Thank God you're here!' Amy said, wrapping her arms around me for a moment.

Jimmy Mack was spitting blood and fury. I gave him a hug too, and sat him on a kitchen chair.

'Did he beat you up?' I asked him, pointing to the kid.

Jimmy shook his head. 'Not him, no.'

I hadn't thought it would be. Turning to the kid, I said, 'You're in the clear. You can get back down there. The others will be joining you in a minute.'

'I'm staying with them!' he said.

'Get!' I said, prodding him with the tyre lever.

He went.

I called to Emma to bring the other three through to the kitchen.

'What about him?' I said to Jimmy, pointing to one of the men.

He shook his head.

'Down there,' I told the man.

Protesting, down he went.

'Him?' I asked Jimmy, pointing to the next one.

'Not him, no.'

That left the one with the broken arm.

'That's him!' Jimmy cried, as soon as he saw him. 'What's wrong with him?'

'He broke his arm, I think.'

'Oh, good!'

The man swore at Jimmy and said, 'No way, am I going down them fucking steps! Not with this arm.'

'You are,' I told him, giving him a push to get him started.

Then Jimmy stuck out a leg and tripped him, and he went head-first down the stairs, bellowing and screaming with pain as he went.

'You shouldn't have done that,' I told Jimmy. 'He's got a bad arm.'

'No,' Jimmy admitted. 'I should have shot him with Emma's gun first. He's a mean, evil bastard!'

CHAPTER SIXTY

I closed the trapdoor and secured it with the heavy iron bolt provided for the purpose.

'That should do it,' I announced, stepping back. 'It will give them opportunity to reflect on their miserable lives, and give us time to get clear.'

'Maybe they won't suffocate,' Amy said uncertainly. 'There was some ventilation down there.'

'Wouldn't matter if they did,' Jimmy chimed in spiritedly, 'the thieving, murderous bastards . . .'

'Uncle Jimmy!' Amy wailed.

'Sorry, pet. But I mean it.'

'No, you don't.'

With a smile, I moved out of the way. Family disputes, as I said earlier, are not my province.

* * *

While Emma went for her car, I disabled the three Tenerife cars. Nothing fancy about it. I just opened them up, using the keys I'd taken off the men inside, opened the bonnets and ripped out handfuls of wires and cables. They all went in the boot of Emma's car, when she came back with it, along with the keys.

'Right, Jim. You and Amy can climb in. We're ready to go now.'

'Not Risky Point, I hope?' Amy said as she ducked her head to get in.

'Of course it is!' Jimmy said. 'We're going home, lass.'

'No, Jim,' I told him as I climbed inside myself and slammed the door shut. 'That would be too risky — for all of us.'

Emma looked at me and I nodded. 'Let's go,' I told her.

As we left the farm site, I turned to speak to our passengers in the back seat. 'We're going to Whitby,' I told them. 'To your sister's, Jim. Your aunt's, Amy. It will be safer there for you.'

'Not going home?' Jimmy said plaintively, obviously massively disappointed.

'That's the first place they'll look for us, Jim, if we can't sort it out. You'll be all right in Whitby, won't you?'

I had thought about it in advance and come to the conclusion that it would make good sense. Jimmy's younger sister had a guesthouse there and he went there from time to time for a spot of R & R, or even just for a change of scene. From what I gathered, it was a four-storey terraced house up on the West Cliff, with loads of rooms going spare, except in July and August. Besides, she was family.

'Do you know your aunt, Amy?'

'Very well. I'm sure she'll take us in.'

'Good. Just be careful what you tell her. I don't want her running to the police because she fears gangsters will be smashing down her front door. Just say there's been some pressure because of Jason winning money on the Lottery. And you need to get away from it all for a while.'

'What will you and this lady be doing? I'm sorry,' Amy added, speaking to Emma. 'I don't know your name. But thank you for helping us.'

'I'm Emma.'

'Of course she is!' Jimmy said indignantly. 'She's a grand lass, Emma.'

'So you two know each other?' Amy asked with surprise.

'Why, aye!' Jimmy said proudly.

'I help Frank out from time to time, in his business,' Emma confided.

'Oh, I see,' Amy said, sounding highly dubious.

I came to her rescue. 'Don't worry, Amy love. Emma is an invaluable colleague, someone I'm happy to work with occasionally. She's a highly competent, professional close protection officer. We're both in the industry.

'As for what we'll be doing, we're going back to helping and supporting Jason for a little longer. We only came here to rescue you and your uncle. Now we have to get back to the main business.'

'Well, thank you both so much,' Amy said, sounding somewhat reassured now.

* * *

Henry called.

'I'm getting there,' he said.

'Good. Where's that?'

'George Reagan.'

'Oh! What you got, Henry?'

'It's not business.'

'In Edinburgh, you mean?'

'It's not business, and it's not in Edinburgh either. Arbroath is where it is.'

'Where the hell's that?'

'On the coast.'

'So it's holiday time?'

'You could say that, I suppose.'

Henry went on to tell me a whole lot more, and I was suitably astonished.

'Thanks, Henry,' I told him, when he eventually shut up. 'I can use that.'

CHAPTER SIXTY-ONE

We had to hang around Whitby for a couple of hours before we could offload our passengers. I hadn't rung the Macks' Aunt Elizabeth in advance, because it didn't seem likely that she would appreciate being woken up by the phone at three or four o'clock in the morning.

'Give it till six,' Jimmy said. 'She'll be up by then. She's an early riser.'

So that was what we did. Amy phoned her just after six and explained the situation. It was a brief call. The poor woman couldn't have understood very much about it, but she told Amy that she and Jimmy would be very welcome to stay with her. She would love to see them both.

'She's a good woman, Betty,' Jim said, when Amy gave Emma the nod to take them there. 'She always was.'

* * *

We dropped them off, leaving it to them to explain further some of what had been happening. I promised to keep in touch and let them know what was happening with Jason and ourselves. Then we left them to it.

221

We drove round the corner at the end of the street, and then Emma said, 'Where now?'

'Risky Point.'

'Really?'

'It's not far. And we need to get some sleep. Then we'll work out what we're going to do next. We're doing pretty well so far,' I added with a grin.

'You haven't let me shoot anyone yet, though,' she said with a pout.

'Don't worry about that. This thing is a long way from being over. You might still get a chance.'

At Risky Point, we parked a little distance from the cottage, in a fold of the land that meant the car wouldn't be immediately visible to anyone coming along the track. I didn't know how Emma was feeling, but after I don't know how many hours, days and nights even without much sleep, I really did need to get my head down. You can only run so long on adrenaline. After that, you need either stimulants or sleep to keep you going.

Between us, we carried Emma's shotgun and various bags to a point just short of the two cottages, mine and Jimmy Mack's. Then we paused to study the situation.

'It looks all right,' Emma said, after a few moments of staring through the misty, early morning light.

I agreed. It did. But you never can be sure. Had someone got inside, and now was lying in wait? Junior even? Or was he still at Jason's house in Rosedale, waiting for me to turn up?

'I'll do a circuit round the back,' Emma suggested. 'You approach from the front, as normal.'

It made sense.

'OK. Let's go,' I said. 'You first. I'll give you a couple of minutes' start.'

Emma dropped the bags she was carrying but kept the shotgun when she slipped away. It wouldn't be the only gun she had with her, but it had always seemed to be her favourite weapon, and she never went far without it when she was working. There had been times when I'd been glad of that.

I was also grateful for her expertise with firearms in a more general sense, thanks to her time in special forces with the Army. I was a rank amateur when it came to guns; she was a professional, through and through.

No Tenerifes, or anybody else, showed up. The cottage was as I had left it the night I drove to Rosedale, although by now it was pretty cold. I lit the wood-burning stove to warm the place up a bit, using wood from the store of driftwood collected from the beach, and then we went to bed. Emma started off in the guest bedroom, but cold was the unconvincing reason she gave me when I woke to find her nestled against me. I didn't object or chuck her out. We'd always been good together in bed. But I did go back to sleep. I'd been up a lot longer than Emma had been. We remedied my initial lack of attention when we were both fully awake in the late afternoon.

'You've reminded me how much I've missed you,' she said, nuzzling into my neck. 'We're still good together, aren't we?'

I smiled and turned to kiss her. There were no words just then for how I felt about her, and being with her, but she wasn't wrong, and her feelings were reciprocated. Had things been different . . . The road not taken, and all that. The clichés that I didn't want to fall back on.

'I've missed you, too,' I assured her finally. 'We shouldn't have left it as long as this.'

'No, we shouldn't.'

'Good,' she said then, with evident satisfaction. 'I'm glad we've got that sorted. Now how about making me a cup of coffee?'

'Ever the romantic, eh?'

I chuckled. But even then I knew, and knew that Emma knew too, that we really did have something special together. Whatever happened between us, and to us, that wouldn't change.

When we finally got up, I phoned Jason and Lydia, while Emma pulled together a meal for us from the meagre contents of my fridge, freezer and cupboards. Jason answered.

'Hi Jason! It's Frank.'

'Frank! We were just wondering how things were with you.'

'OK, thanks. Where are you?'

'Still at the hut. We thought we'd go over to the farmhouse tomorrow.'

'If you can, maybe you should delay that just a little bit longer. Wait until things are more settled. Although we did clear it yesterday, or whenever it was — I've lost track of time! — it's still possible that Francine's brother, Junior, might turn up there. I don't know where he is at present. But he's around somewhere.'

'You think it would be safer to wait?'

'I do, unfortunately. Just as a precaution, not because there's an actual threat.'

'We can do that. It's not a problem. We've got plenty to do here.'

Like what? I couldn't help wondering *Chasing creepie-crawlies?*

'Anyway, the good news, Jason, is that we've rescued Amy and your Uncle Jimmy. Junior's men had abducted them, to hold as hostages, but we released them last night. We've taken them to your Aunt Elizabeth's place in Whitby.'

'The Reagans had got them?' Jason said slowly, sounding devastated.

'Yes. Before they got back to Risky Point. But they're OK. And they're safe. There's nothing for you to worry about now.'

'Well, thanks for what you've done, Frank. You're certainly earning your money! But what happens now?'

'For you, nothing until signing day next Friday. Just stay put until you hear more from me. Amy and your uncle need to stay where they are, too. As of now, the Reagans have no idea where you all are. So you're all safe. Let's keep it that way.

'What I'm going to do next is talk to the Reagans, and persuade them to see sense. I want them to call it all off and go home — or else!'

'Fat chance!'

'I'm not so sure about that, Jason. You see, I've discovered something significant that you don't know.'

224

'What's that?'

'You're not married. You and Francine were never married.'

'I don't understand. What on earth do you mean?'

'The ceremony on the beach that you both went through was not a legal marriage according to Spanish law. Marriages are only legal anywhere in Spanish territory if they take place in an approved building, and that rules out the beach.'

There was a stunned silence. Then Jason said, 'Are you sure about this, Frank?'

'Very. Henry researched it for me, and I'd bet my house on what he says.'

'So I'm not married?'

'No. And never have been.'

'Yippee!'

'Now just hold on a moment, Jason. You're not out of the woods yet. That doesn't mean the Reagans will no longer want your money, or will stop trying to kill you. So stay safe. And I'll try to get them to see sense.'

* * *

'What's this?' I asked, as Emma slid a plate before me.

'An omelette. It's a dish made with eggs and –"

'I do know what am omelette is. I just wondered what was in it.'

'Everything. Everything I could find.'

I smiled, tasted it and said, 'Mmm. Lovely. Especially the anchovies. I've never had them in an omelette before, but they give it a real tang, don't they? What a good idea!'

'And this is red wine,' she said, pushing a full glass across the table towards me. 'It says so on the label on the bottle. See? "Red Wine", it says. What good taste you have, Frank!'

CHAPTER SIXTY-TWO

Over our meal, Emma asked, 'What's next?'

'I'm going to call Henry again. I need more information from him.'

'Like what?'

'For a start, I want to see if he's managed to get me a phone number for George Reagan.'

'Oh? Are you going to call him?'

I nodded. 'We need to shift up a gear. Like I said, I don't want to just wait around to see what the Reagans do next, and then run like mad again. I want to find a way of attacking them.'

'You told me that before. You've got some ideas, I take it?'

'Some. But first, I want to talk to Henry.'

'While you're doing that, do you mind if I go down to the beach? I'd like to get some fresh air.'

'Be my guest.'

'Is it still there? Still in the same place?'

'Last time I looked, it was. Enjoy yourself.'

* * *

'Hi, Henry. It's me again.'

'I guessed. What do you want now?'

'Just following up. Have you managed to get a phone number for the big Reagan yet?'

'Yeah. I can give you a couple. At least one of them should work.'

He read out a couple of numbers, which I wrote down.

'So you're going ahead with the plan, are you? You're going to make contact?'

'That's the idea. There's something else I wanted. Have you got anything more on dissent within the Reagan family?'

'Only that Oscar, George's younger brother, is dead set against the hotel complex. It's significant because he's the spokesperson for the opposition. Other family members agree with him, but they're keeping their heads down. Oscar is brave or stupid enough to say what he thinks.'

'Perhaps he believes his brother won't, or can't, touch him?'

'That's probably right, actually. George has to be careful, though. He can't risk splitting the family. Do that, and the whole pack of cards might collapse.'

'What does Oscar do? For a living, I mean. Do you know?'

'He has a bar in downtown Puerto de la Cruz. He just gets on with running that, so far as I know.'

'Does he own it?'

'I don't know. He might, but on the other hand, it might be family property and he just manages it.'

That seemed to be that. I thanked Henry and ended the call. Then I did some more thinking. I still didn't have much, but what I had was at least a start. I was starting to see a way to go.

First, I would call George Reagan, and put some simple facts to him, the obvious one being that his daughter was not married to Jason Mack, and never had been. See if that made any difference.

It might not, of course. If he was so desperate for ten million quid, Jason might still look like the best way of

227

getting it, even if it wouldn't be by legal means. To a man like him, thoughts of legality wouldn't exercise him very much. All that would matter was whether something was doable. So pressuring Jason might well still look like his best option, when it came to defending his legacy plan.

Something I couldn't afford to lose sight of was the friction within the family, the dissenting views. It existed, if Henry was right, and I might be able to do something with that. I had to, in fact. I didn't have much else to work with. My only other real option was giving up, now the Macks were safe, and handing the problem over to the authorities.

That wasn't an appealing thought for the simple reason that it wouldn't guarantee Jason's safety. It might lead to a crime against him being solved eventually, but it wouldn't stop one being committed long before that happened.

Preventing crime isn't really what modern policing is about in the UK. It is in New Zealand, I believe, but not here. In this country, we copy the American approach. The priority is getting squadrons of people in white overalls to look for clues on the ground in order to decide who done it.

Better career opportunities, I suppose, and more congenial work. No wonder my old mate DI Bill Peart feels aggrieved about his lack of advancement. He doesn't even possess a white overall.

I didn't want to see the Macks, any of them, going into the Witness Programme either. In that, you forfeited the life you had built, perhaps over many decades, in exchange for a security that could never be guaranteed, and that organized crime syndicates had proven able to penetrate without too much difficulty. We could do better than that, I still hoped.

* * *

The door opened.

'Got anything?'

I stood up, stretched and nodded as Emma came through the doorway. 'Henry gave me some of what I wanted. Sit down, and I'll tell you what I'm thinking.'

We kicked it around for a while, and Emma was in broad agreement with me.

'So the next step,' I concluded, 'is to call George Reagan.'

Emma nodded. 'Let's get it done,' she said briskly.

CHAPTER SIXTY-THREE

'Who's this?' a gruff voice demanded.

'Good evening, George! I'm a friend of Jason Mack. Remember him? Your daughter's so-called ex-husband?'

'I don't know what you're talking about. Who the hell are you? And what do you want?'

'Like I said, I'm a friend of Jason's. I just thought I'd let you know that you should stop chasing him for money. You're not going to get any. Your daughter, Francine, isn't either.'

'What the hell are you talking about?'

It was going well. He hadn't shut the phone down.

'George, Francine and Jason were never legally married. Not under Spanish law, or anybody else's. That means Francine isn't entitled to anything from him right now. And if Jason should die, she won't be his widow, and won't be entitled to anything then, either.

'Think about it, George — and tell Junior and his men to stop chasing Jason. It makes no sense.'

'Now, you listen to me, you dumb fuck! You need to stop spouting this nonsense. At the moment, I don't know who you are, but I will find you. And when I do, you'll wish you'd never been born. Do I make myself clear?'

'Perfectly. I admire your eloquence, George. It's making me smile with appreciation. What I suggest, though, is that you and I meet to discuss our differences. Then I can tell you in more detail why you should stop pursuing Jason.'

'That's not going happen.' After a brief pause, he added, 'Do you have any idea at all who I am?'

'Of course I do. That's why I've taken the trouble to phone you and offer my advice. I'm wondering now, though, if I've made a mistake. My understanding is that Junior is to take over the family business from you very soon. So it would probably be better to talk to him, or even to Oscar, now you're on the way out, as it were.

'I've already spoken to Junior, by the way,' I added. 'He knows who I am, and seems a sensible lad.'

'Keep away from Junior. And don't call this number again!' Reagan snapped, before ending the call.

'So, the hare is off and running!' I said, winking at Emma.

CHAPTER SIXTY-FOUR

We kicked it around some more for a while. Then I decided to call Junior. It was the obvious next step to take if we were to create more of a flurry within the family.

Looking at it from their side, they had lost track of Jason, lost control of the farm and lost their two hostages. Also, some of their men had dispersed and disappeared from Northumberland, and others were locked up in a cellar in Rosedale. Also, time was almost up on their due date, Monday, for repaying ten million quid that they owed. It was close to a disaster. And now I was hoping to add to the friction and unrest within the family. Not a bad scenario from our point of view, after just a few days' work.

But it was no time to be resting on our laurels. It was time to be pushing and probing further. So I called Amy's number, hoping Junior would still have her phone.

He did.

'Junior?'

'You again!' he snapped. 'I told you before what my name is.'

'So you did, but somehow I can't get my tongue around "Mr Reagan" when I think of you. You're not old enough. I'll just stick with "Junior".

'You and Mack were supposed to meet me, Doy. You never turned up. You looking to get the kid killed, or what?'

'I was worried about a reception party. Anyway, there's something I overlooked telling you when we last spoke.'

'What?'

'Your sister, Francine, and Jason Mack were never married, not legally. Did you know that?'

There was a snort of incredulous, disbelieving laughter. 'Is that the best you could come up with, Doy? Don't waste my time!'

'It's true. Ask your dad. He knows.'

'What the fuck are you talking about? What do you know about my old man?'

'Quite a lot, actually. I know where he lives, and I've spoken to him. A nice old chap, I thought. I told him Francine wasn't married, not legally, and to lay off Jason.'

'You shouldn't have done that, Doy.'

'No? Why not?'

'He has a lot on his plate.'

'You're telling me! A failing family business, a helluva lot of mouths to feed, a hotel to finish building, a philandering, manipulative daughter, a son and heir he can't trust to get things done . . . Need I go on?'

'You've said too much already. You're in a hole, Doy. You'd better stop digging.'

'Not like the hole you're in, Junior. I wouldn't want to be in your shoes. Your father is not a man to offend, intentionally or otherwise. If that's what's happened, your best hope is that he runs into the same sort of accident that poor old Ed Davey did.'

'What are you talking about?' he snarled.

'The family accountant. Terrible what happened to him, wasn't it? But you're right. I've said too much already.'

'The only thing I would add is just to repeat that your old man knows Francine isn't married, and never was. He must have known that anyway. He told me it doesn't make any difference.'

'That's what he said?'

'That's what he said.'

I winked at Emma and continued. 'He told me that what I'd said made no difference, and that as far as he was concerned, Jason is a dead man walking — and now I'm on the list, as well.'

'Yeah, well. He got that part right.'

'The other thing you could do, Junior, is ask Francine herself about the so-called marriage. She knows better than anybody about it.'

The absence of another foul-mouthed explosion suggested Junior was giving what I'd said some consideration. After all, he wouldn't be stupid. He would have seen the implications of what I'd told him immediately, just as I had myself when Henry informed me. But he would be wondering if it was true. He wouldn't be able to help it.

'What Francine and Jason had on the beach in Tenerife was a blessing ceremony,' I said, pressing on, 'not a wedding. Under Spanish law, that doesn't count legally. To make their relationship a proper marriage, they would have had to follow up with a legal wedding somewhere. And they didn't do that.

'Think about what it all means,' I added, before ending the call.

* * *

My advice to Junior was what I did next myself. I thought some more about it. Whatever else he was, including being a nasty piece of work capable of torturing and killing people, Junior was probably a reasonably intelligent man. He would have to be, to have got where he was in the family business. Well, maybe not so intelligent in the sense decent people mean. More like clever and cunning, as well as tough and streetwise, which in the end is a combination that can outweigh simple intelligence in the world of organized crime, and perhaps business and politics as well.

'Think it's going to work?' Emma asked.

I shrugged. 'Hard to say. But I've given him, as well as his father, something to think about.'

* * *

Next, I called Henry again.

'Can you give me a phone number for Oscar now, George's brother?'

'Not a personal number, not at the moment. But I can give you a number for his place of work.'

'Place of work? Oh, you mean his bar?'

'Yeah. Bar, restaurant or whatever it is. Do you want it?'

'Yes. That would help.'

'You going to call him, as well?'

'I think so. What's his place called, by the way?'

'Oscar's.'

'Yes, of course. What's it called?'

'I've just told you.'

'No, you haven't . . . Oh! Oscar's? That's what it's called?'

'Yeah. Like Rick's.'

'Rick's?'

'In *Casablanca*, or wherever the fuck it was.'

I shook my head and laughed. Without trying, Henry sometimes made me feel slow and stupid. Sometimes I feared I probably was.

'Just text me the number, Henry,' I said with a sigh.

CHAPTER SIXTY-FIVE

It was a disaster. His hostages gone. Francine's ex in hiding somewhere, and out of reach. The men he'd brought with him reduced, scattered and demoralized, apart from Seamus and Joey. No money obtained. All because of this Doy character, and his interfering in something that didn't concern him. And now all this stuff about Francine! What the hell was he going to tell the old man?

Junior brooded for a moment on his father's likely reaction. Rage? There would certainly be rage. Probably a towering, black inferno of a rage that would tear anyone in range to pieces and threaten to launch open war against his enemies, real and imagined. Family and allies, as well, if it suited him.

Well, it would just have to be weathered once again, he thought with a sigh. He could do that. He was used to it. Sick of it, but he'd been in this game long enough to know what to expect. After all, he'd had it all his life. The old man was never any different. He wouldn't change.

And if Doy really had talked to him, which seemed likely, the rage might be worse than usual. It might be something to behold! Better, perhaps, to be here, not in Puerto. He grinned reluctantly and shook his head.

Then he wondered if Doy was lying, or actually telling the truth. Could he find that out without actually asking George? Probably not, he thought reluctantly. The need to know was outweighed by thought of how his father might react if questioned on the subject. And did it matter anyway? They needed the money, however they got it — if they could get it.

God, he hated the current situation! The old man was obsessed by his bloody hotel, and its fucking casino. Nothing else mattered to him. The family business had been struggling for a year or two, mostly because of the pandemic, and the worse the financial situation got, the more that George wanted to hear about nothing but that bloody hotel!

Well, things were going to change in future. They would have to. He would just have to hope that when the old man finally stepped aside, and Junior took over the business himself, there would be something left for him to run.

If there was, it would be run as a proper business. That was something he'd been thinking about for a long time. He would set up a management team, have meetings, discuss things, hear people out. He'd read books and listened to experts and advisers, and he knew that was how it should be these days. Maybe they would still do some of the same things, but they would do them differently.

Except for the bloody hotel! That wasn't going to be kept, whatever happened in the next few days. He would get rid of it as soon as he could. Consign it to history, along with George.

He couldn't wait for that day to come, but would it? Would the old man ever just step aside? It was hard to believe.

Dissatisfied, fed up, he wondered, not for the first time, if he ought to stop waiting and just quit. Go and build a new life for himself, separately from the family business. That was a recurring fantasy, but running through it again didn't make it any more likely to happen.

A minute or two more of self-indulgence, and then he snapped out of it. At least there was something he could do right now. He could talk to his stupid sister and find out if what Doy had said was true.

CHAPTER SIXTY-SIX

It was getting late, but I decided to try George again. You never knew. He might have had a change of heart, unlikely though that seemed.

He hadn't.

'Frank Doy again, George. Now that you've had the chance to think about what I told you about your daughter not being legally married to Jason Mack, I really do think it would be sensible for us to talk. We can do that either on the phone or in person. Which do you prefer?'

'I know who and what you are now, Doy. Forget about talking. And know this: we're coming for you! That's all I've got to say to you.'

With that melodramatic line, to my amusement, he ended the call. He seemed to think he was still calling the shots.

* * *

'He won't talk to you?'

I shook my head.

'So?'

'So now it's Plan B. We go to Tenerife and persuade him to talk.'

'Oh, goodie! And if he still won't talk? Do we do something else?'

'Definitely.'

'Kill him?'

'Well . . . Let's just wait and see, shall we?'

'I hate bad guys.'

'You're not alone, dear friend. The ones that have their minions chasing around the country trying to kill me are a particular dislike of mine.'

CHAPTER SIXTY-SEVEN

Junior picked up his phone again, checked the number he had for his sister and began to punch in the numbers. At least they had server coverage up here in the cottage, not like in the rest of this godforsaken hole.

Holiday cottage? Why anyone would ever come here for a holiday he couldn't imagine. It defied understanding when they could go to somewhere like Tenerife for less money.

No wonder the boys seemed to have left, and taken the hostages with them. They shouldn't have. But he could almost understand it. It wouldn't have suited them very much here. At least George hadn't set up the family business in a dump like this. That was something to be eternally grateful for.

Not that any of that was going to save the crew who were supposed to be here when he caught up with them, he thought grimly, changing tune. There was going to be a reckoning for this desertion and dereliction of duty. Had to be. Fur was going to fly and heads get broken, as well as wages docked. Discipline had to be maintained. All the same, he did wonder where the hell they were, and why no one had called to tell him.

Surely the old man and the woman hadn't just overpowered them and escaped? He smiled at the thought. The lads that were supposed to be here were a tough crew, excepting the youngster, Martin.

Then, just as Francine's phone came to life, he thought of Doy, and wondered if that bastard had had anything to do with it.

' George? Is that really you?'

He smiled. At least Francine used his proper name. He hated the "Junior" label the old man had given him long ago, but there was nothing he could do about it. Not yet, at least. That was something else that was going to change.

'Hi, Fran! How are you? Just thought I'd give you a call, to see how you're getting on over there.'

'I'm so glad you did, Gerry. I was actually about to call you. Sometime soon, anyway. Gerry, I'm so happy.'

'Good. Glad to hear it. So you're enjoying yourself?'

'I am! You'll never guess where I am right now.'

'I don't suppose I will. But I can't hear waves breaking. So I'm guessing you're not on the beach?'

'No. I'm in Las Vegas! And it's seriously wonderful.'

'Huh? Vegas?' Junior wasn't sure how he felt about that. 'For crissakes, don't go near the tables, Fran. And if you go anywhere near the slots, only have the money on you that you can afford to lose. Serious people own and run Vegas, Fran. You can't afford to make mistakes.'

'Don't be silly! I know all that. I'm not here for the gambling anyway. I came to get married — to Tony, a lovely man I met in LA not long ago. The wedding was last night, and it was truly beautiful. Gerry, I'm so happy, more happy than I can begin tell you.'

'Married, Fran?' Junior clutched on to a chair to stop himself collapsing. 'Fran, you are married. You're married already. Remember?'

'What are you saying, Gerry?'

'You got married three years ago to that English guy you met in Tenerife. Jason, or something, wasn't it?'

'Jason? Oh, no! Don't be silly. I never married Jason. Not really. We just had a nice, hippie ceremony on the beach. But this thing with Tony is the real thing! Tony is a super guy, and he really loves me.'

'You didn't marry Jason?'

'No, of course not.'

Junior swallowed hard and struggled to get his thoughts in order.

'This Tony guy, Fran. Does he know who you are? Have you told him about the family business?'

'Oh, no! Nothing like that. He wouldn't be interested anyway. He's mega-rich himself.'

'But we're moving heaven and earth back here to get you your share of Jason's lottery winnings.'

'Oh, I don't care about that now. Jason can keep his measly lottery winnings. Tony will never let me go wanting.'

'That right? Fran, does Dad know what happened with you and Jason?'

For Junior, at least, that had become the key issue, that and the fact that he'd bought his sister a very expensive wedding gift when she did her thing with the Mack kid.

'Of course he does! He's my dad, isn't he?'

'So he knows you were never married?'

'Don't be silly! He knows everything.'

Junior nodded to himself.

'Gerry!' his sister wailed. 'You haven't even congratulated me yet.'

It took him a moment to get the words out, but out they came eventually.

'Congratulations, you stupid bitch!' he said, banging the phone down hard on the kitchen counter top.

CHAPTER SIXTY-EIGHT

Junior took a deep breath to help him calm down. It didn't work. He called George anyway.

'Got it all sorted, Junior?' his old man asked.

Junior winced. 'Not exactly. I have to tell you, George, things have got a bit out of control here.'

'How? What's happened?'

For once, Junior thought, it was hard to tell how angry George was. No raging — yet. But it would come. He was sure of that.

Still furious himself, after the talk with his sister, he decided to get it all out in one go. To hell with it!

'First, I don't know where Mack is. He seems to have teamed up with this Doy character, who has stashed him away somewhere. In short, we've lost him.

'Second, the hostages I told you about have got away. That's probably something to do with Doy, as well. I left some of our men with them, and now the whole lot have gone, just disappeared. I can't contact any of them.

'Lastly, I can't contact the men I posted to keep watch at the farm either. That may be something to do with server coverage up there in Northumberland, but the plain fact is that all our guys here are out of touch. I can't reach them.'

After a moment's silence, possibly because he was simply stunned, George said, 'That's a whole lot of negativity, Junior. Is there anything else? If there is, you'd better spit it out now. I don't think I would be able to stand any additions later.'

Junior grimaced. He recognized that way of talking, the tone and the seemingly gentle, innocent introduction. It would lead, he knew, to enough rage and invective to make the roof fall in. Before that happened, though, he wanted to make another point.

'I'm planning now to stop Mack next Friday, when he's due to see the solicitor and pay the money over for the farm. It doesn't really matter where he is now. We know where he'll be next Friday.

'I appreciate Monday is our due date, but there it is. We'll still be in the game after that, one way or another. But I'm hoping we can find Mack before then.'

'Get it done, Junior. Otherwise, I'll be looking for a new deputy.'

'Point taken. George, there's something else I want to talk to you about. I've just got off the phone with Francine, and . . .'

'Yeah? How is she?'

'Good. Pretty good, it sounded like. She's in Vegas.'

'Vegas?'

'She told me she's just got married there.'

'Has she now?'

Amazingly, the old man was chuckling. Junior couldn't believe it.

'George, she already was married, wasn't she? To the Mack kid.'

'Of course she wasn't. She never married him, not really, not legally.'

'You knew that?'

'Of course I bloody did! I'm her father, aren't I?'

Full-throated laughter now from the old man. Junior felt his own anger growing in response. Was he the only one who had been left out of the picture?

'What about my mother? Did she know?'

'She arranged it all — whatever it was, down there on the beach.'

'So I needn't have bought Francine that diamond necklace as a wedding present?'

'I guess not, Junior.'

He couldn't stand his father laughing at him.

'OK, George. Well, here's something else to think about. If Francine wasn't married to the Mack kid, killing him won't make her a widow, will it? So you can't get his money that way.'

'True, Junior. Perfectly true. Well, up to a point. Inheritance wouldn't be automatic certainly, but we could argue it was a common law marriage, and hope to get something eventually that way.

'But the best way has always been to persuade him to invest in the hotel project. That needs to be done before Monday. Get it done, Junior.'

'You lied to me,' Junior said, not far from rage himself now. 'And you know what, George? You can go fuck yourself!'

CHAPTER SIXTY-NINE

We flew from Newcastle very early the next morning, along with a couple of hundred people eager to see some winter sun. It wasn't the most convenient time, or departure airport either, but it was what we could get.

To make the flight, we had to pack quickly, forget about another night's sleep and get on the road not long after midnight. But we were lucky to be able to get flights at all at such short notice. And it was a relief that the airline no longer required us to wear face masks. I hate those damn things.

'I had to fly to Shanghai not long ago,' Emma confided. 'It was face masks all the way, there as well as back again.'

'You didn't think of shooting yourself?'

'If I'd been using my legal passport, it wouldn't have been necessary for me to do that. Someone would probably have done it for me.'

'Hmm.'

With just under four hours to go, I suggested we try to get some rest. We were going to be busy when we disembarked.

Emma agreed and soon indulged herself, no doubt aided by her Army experience. Grab sleep when you can, when on active service. I knew sleep wouldn't come into it for me, but once again, rest was the next best thing and I grabbed it readily. For the moment, thankfully, there was nothing more to be done.

* * *

We landed in Tenerife at a time before I usually have breakfast. It was still dark, still the night. I wondered what the sun-seekers from northern Europe thought of it. Probably disappointed the day was no longer here than at home, despite the temperature.

Half an hour later, with no suitcases to wait for, we emerged from the airport on the southern coast and looked for a taxi to take us to Puerto de la Cruz on the northern coast. That was where the Reagans were based, according to Henry.

Their town was in the gentile, tranquil and less sunny region north of Mount Teide, where frequent cloudy conditions take the edge off the African sun. I felt pretty sure, though, that a lot of the Reagans' business would be done on the hotter, more raucous south coast, where so many resorts have been built in modern times to accommodate sun-seekers, and the young in general.

Puerto de la Cruz is different. For one thing, it's an old town, with a botanic garden established nearly two hundred and fifty years ago. For another, it's in an area that sees a lot of cloud, if not rain. Nowhere on the island is supposed to experience actual rain.

All that said, I was still a little surprised that the hotel casino complex that the Reagans were building was in Puerto rather than on the south coast. But perhaps they just didn't like living over the shop, or else were intent on moving upmarket and targeting a more mature, and wealthier, clientele.

The day was breaking as we left the airport, revealing a landscape that could only be described as desert. It was all rock, gravel and sand, with scarcely a green leaf or frond of any description. As Emma spoke fluent Spanish, I left her to engage with the driver as we raced along the motorway to Santa Cruz, before turning north on to a smaller road that required the driver to reduce his speed, if only slightly. I used the time to search on my phone for a hotel, and soon found one in the old town, close to the sea front, that would accept us.

It was early morning, but here they would be used to people arriving at all times of day and night. The Canary Islands are like that, all year round. Their resorts are not places that close down for the winter, as so many do in the Med. They have no need. They don't really know what winter is in the Canaries, on the very edge of Africa. It just means less daylight. The temperature scarcely changes throughout the year, and there isn't even a wet season.

It took us a little under an hour to reach the hotel, improbably named Blue Lagoon, which was an old, ornate building on a cobbled street. Then it took us most of another hour to get into our room. First, the old guy on Reception, seemingly the only member of staff on duty, was struggling to find the mental energy to deal with registering incoming guests, as well as trying to placate an outgoing couple who were determined to argue long and hard about their bill, especially the part concerning their mini bar. *Memo to self: leave the mini bar alone. It's not worth the hassle.*

We reached the door to our room, but the plastic key card didn't work, and we couldn't get inside. I had to go back to Reception for another one, leaving Emma to guard our bags. It wasn't the most modern, efficient kind of hotel. Finally, though, we did get into the room.

'Great choice of hotel, Frank,' Emma said with a grin.

'Yeah, well. I didn't think we needed the biggest, newest, swankiest, most expensive place in town.'

'And you didn't get it,' she pointed out, glancing around a room that had seen better days, like the rest of the hotel. 'I thought you promised me the lap of luxury?'

'Did I? Oh, I forgot about that. Maybe it will look better in the morning.'

'It is morning already, and it doesn't.'

I just grinned. I wasn't really in the mood.

'Let's get some sleep,' I suggested. 'It's been a long day, even if it has only just started.'

We did manage to sleep for a while, but then one thing led to another, and that put an end to sleeping. Sleep would just have to be fitted in along the way, as usual.

CHAPTER SEVENTY

The hotel looked better in the afternoon. Even if it was siesta time, somehow, it seemed less tired and more alive. The sunshine streaming through every window helped. Then there was the main reason I had chosen it. The hotel was in the centre of Puerto de la Cruz, which was where we needed to be.

Thankfully, the dining room offered a buffet spread that nobody could have found wanting, and we took full advantage of it. There hadn't been an opportunity for a proper meal since Emma and I had hooked up again, and I'd been living on scraps for several days before that.

'This is good,' I said, digging into our magnificent paella for two.

'Not a little too traditional?' Emma queried with a smile.

'After the self-heating meal packs that Jason and I were living on before you showed up, this is wonderful!'

'That what you were doing — living on field rations?'

I nodded. 'It was lucky I had them in the back of the Land Rover. Jason and I had to get out of Rosedale in a mad scramble. No time or thought for anything but survival.'

'Been there, done that,' Emma said.

'Afghanistan, Iraq?'

'As well as elsewhere. Field rations are very welcome, when you need them.'

Emma had spent years in Army Intelligence, working as a field officer in special operations, before a bomb disposal that went wrong had brought her time in that role to an end.

After she recovered her mental and physical health, she didn't do what I would have done, and stayed away from the Middle East and North Africa. She began offering her services, freelance, as a close protection officer, mostly for rich men who wanted their womenfolk looked after by a woman rather than a man, and one who knew what she was doing with firearms. One way or another, I didn't doubt for a moment that she had seen a lot of field rations in her time.

'Back to the room for a discussion?' Emma asked, when we had cleared our plates and finished our coffee.

'Yes. Let's get on.'

We hadn't discussed our business. Not in a public space. Sound can carry in a dining room, and some people have extraordinarily acute hearing, even without the electronic aids available these days. Here, we were presenting ourselves as just another holidaying couple. Best to keep it that way, and hold business conversations somewhere private.

* * *

'How do you want to play this?' Emma said, when we were back in our room.

'First, we'll do it the civilized way. George has refused to speak to me, but we'll give him another opportunity.'

'Then?'

'Then you come into it. We may need to put the fear of God into him, and give him no alternative but to speak to me.'

Emma nodded and said thoughtfully, 'I'll need a little time to pull together what I need.'

Weapons, in other words.

'Will you be able to get it?'

'I think so. I'm connected here. I know where to go, and who to talk to. The price for guns has probably gone up since I was last here, though.'

'That won't be a problem. Jason will cover our expenses.'

'Jason sounds like my kind of guy,' Emma said with a smile. 'The best sort of client.'

'Oh, he's a nice lad.'

'Not what I meant, Frank.'

'But money isn't everything, is it?' I said, grinning.

'Hmm,' she mused. 'I'll have to think about that.'

* * *

I phoned George Reagan again.

'Frank Doy, George. We really need to talk.'

'Don't ever call me again, Doy. Be warned!'

'There are things to discuss, in your interests as well as Jason Mack's. I suggest you and I meet to consider them. Where . . .'

'There will be no talks, and no meeting,' George snapped before ending the call, and quite possibly throwing the phone at a nearby wall.

I caught Emma's eye and shrugged.

'Do we kill him now?' she asked.

'No, not yet. But you know what we are going to do, don't you?'

'What's that?'

'Play dirty!'

'Oh, good.'

CHAPTER SEVENTY-ONE

Emma went off to collect what she needed. And I got on my phone. First, I called Jason again. Lydia answered, not surprisingly. It was her phone I'd called. Jason hadn't managed to get himself a new one yet.

'It's Frank, just checking how things are with you two, and where you are.'

'Hi, Frank. Everything's OK here. And we're at the farm.'

'No trouble?'

'No. I've got a few friends from Alwinton here to help with cleaning up the house. It's a terrible mess.'

That sounded a good idea. I wasn't expecting any more invasions at the farmhouse but, just in case, there was safety in numbers.

'That's good. So you've got plenty to do?'

'Oh, yes. We're going to be busy all this week, and beyond. I don't like seeing the old place like this. What are you doing, Frank?'

'I'm in Tenerife.'

'Tenerife?'

'Negotiating with Francine's family. At least, that's the plan.'

'Oh, my God!'

'I'll be in touch again before next Friday. Meanwhile, stay where you are — and keep away from Morpeth until I get back.'

'Good luck, Frank!'

* * *

Next in line for a call from me was Junior.

'You again!' he said, sounding disgusted.

'Yep. Have you spoken to your sister or your father yet?'

'What's it to you if I have?'

'Plenty. If you've spoken to Francine, you'll know that, as I said, she isn't married to Jason Mack. That means she will inherit nothing if he dies. So there's no point trying to kill him, is there?

'And there's no point to this vendetta against him, either. He's not going to give up the money he won voluntarily, and you can't force him to take part in your investment project, because you don't even know where he is.'

'Got it all figured out, haven't you, Doy? Think you have, anyway.'

'Pretty much, Junior. I know you're desperate for ten million quid by Monday, but it's not going to come from Jason. You need to think again.'

He didn't say anything. So I pressed on a little further.

'It's the hotel, isn't it? That's the problem.'

'You don't know what you're talking about.'

'Oh, I do! The entire family business is in jeopardy, all because of George's mania about building a hotel casino complex as his legacy. I don't know if you share his obsession, but I do know plenty of others in the family don't. Your Uncle Oscar, for one.'

'You know nothing!' Junior scoffed.

'No? Well, how about this. Without the hotel project, there would be no need for this mad chasing around trying to borrow or steal ten million quid. It's all down to one man — your old man.'

'Persuade George to give up or move aside, and walk away from the hotel, and there'll still be a family business for you to inherit when the day comes. Continue supporting him, and you run the risk of ending up with nothing. And some of you will be facing all sorts of charges, including abduction and murder, for what you're doing in the UK to Jason and his relatives.

'Of course,' I added, 'what would be really nice from your point of view would be if George had an accident, like poor old Ed Davey, your accountant.'

'What the hell are you talking about?' he demanded, in a strangulated voice.

'An accident in his malfunctioning Bentley? Nice one! If I were you, Junior, I'd be thinking about that a lot.'

I ended the call, without giving him the chance to say anything more. My interest was not in what he said, but in trying to persuade him to do something. Assuming he wasn't totally stupid, I'd given him plenty to think about while he tried to find his scattered attack force in Cleveland and Northumberland.

* * *

There was one more call I wanted to make before I had a rest and waited for Emma.

'Is that you, Oscar?'

'Who is this?'

'My name is Frank Doy. You don't know me, but I've been giving George and Junior a lot of trouble the past few days. I'm trying to help Jason Mack avoid assassination by your mad brother's attack team.'

'I don't know what you're talking about. Your name's Doy, you say?'

'Yes. And I'd like to meet you to talk about how I can help you, and you can help me.'

There followed a long pause. Then he said, 'Phone me again in two hours,' and broke the connection.

I nodded to myself with satisfaction. It had been a good afternoon's work.

CHAPTER SEVENTY-TWO

'Did you get what you wanted?'

Emma held up the case she was carrying for my inspection. 'No problem.'

'How did you pay for it?'

'You don't need to know that, Frank. It's a trade secret,' she added with a grin.

'Fair enough. But keep the receipt, if you got one. We need to make sure you're fully reimbursed by Jason at the end of all this.'

'Don't worry. I will.'

'A receipt, though,' she added after a moment's thought. 'What would that look like?'

I had to laugh. 'Right,' I said, 'I've got one or two things to do. Can you check the rifle over while I'm doing that?'

She nodded. 'Are we still on for tonight?'

'We are.'

I left her to it. The success of the sniper depends on small, often infinitesimal, margins. She needed to make sure she was comfortable with what she had bought.

* * *

Later, I brought her up to speed with what I'd been doing. The phone calls, in other words.

She nodded thoughtfully as she took it all in.

'There's obviously concern in some family quarters about the hotel, from what Henry told you. I wonder how likely a palace revolution is?'

'Hard to say. Working on George may still be a better option. Still, it's good to have a couple of things running. Taking the initiative and going into attack mode is a very welcome change, so far as I'm concerned. I'm sick of being on the defensive all the time.'

'You're not used to it, are you?' she said with a smile. 'Probably because you were never in the British Army. That seemed to be all we ever did, defend ourselves. We rarely got the chance to attack anything, because of political considerations. I sometimes used to feel I'd been born a few decades too late.'

'I can understand that. You'd have been in your element in the Western Desert, hunting Rommel, wouldn't you?'

'You bet!' she said with a grin.

* * *

I phoned Oscar Reagan back after a couple of hours.

'What do you want with me, Doy?'

That was straightforward enough.

'I want to find out if there's any chance of you helping me get Jason Mack out of the kill zone your brother has put him in.'

Oscar chuckled. 'I know who you are now, Doy. I've done some checking. So you're trying to interfere in my brother's business affairs, are you?'

At least it wasn't an immediate cold shoulder. That was worth something. A lot more than I'd got from George, anyway.

'His and Junior's, actually. I've spent the past week keeping the lad away from them. I'm assuming you know what's going on?'

'Carry on.'

'What you also need to know is that George has got things all wrong. He's not going to get the ten million quid he needs by Monday from Jason Mack. Jason will not give up the money voluntarily, and now Junior no longer holds the hostages that were abducted to try to force him to invest in the hotel that George is building.

'Another thing to consider is that Jason was never legally married to George's daughter, Francine. What that means is that even if they do manage to kill him, which they've been trying to do, Francine will not inherit any money from him. OK, so far?'

'That it? That's all you wanted to tell me?'

'No, it's not actually. I've told George all this and asked for a meeting to discuss it. But he won't talk.'

'George never was much for meetings and discussion. He likes to take decisions and give out orders.'

Oscar sounded as if he was quite amused by my predicament. I took that as a sign that I could continue.

'As I understand it, the trouble Jason has run into is all because George has run into financial difficulties as a result of his obsession with building a legacy for himself, the hotel casino complex. He's run out of people he can borrow money from, and he doesn't know where else to turn.

'What that means is that the hotel is effectively endangering the entire family business. Reagan Enterprises, I believe it's called. Unless he can be persuaded to see sense, and let the hotel go, you're all going to suffer. I wondered if you might be the man to see that he does see sense.

'I know Junior is deputy company chairman, or whatever it's called, the heir apparent, but I've tried talking to him and found it's a waste of time. He doesn't have a thought in his head unless George put it there. So if George doesn't run the family business down himself, I reckon Junior will when he takes it over.'

Oscar chuckled, seemingly highly amused. Then he said, 'This is all very interesting, Mr Doy. You've obviously put a lot of time into it. But you know what? It doesn't matter a damn to me. You're a clown if you think I'm going to do anything about it. I don't run the family business. My brother does. Good day to you, sir!'

* * *

I'd had the call on the speaker for Emma's benefit. Now I looked at her with a wry smile and said, 'Did you get all that?'

'I think so. The ducks are all in a row now, and we need to nudge them along a bit, as per Plan B?'

'Exactly. Let's get something to eat, and then we can make our preparations.'

'Good idea.'

'And I wouldn't mind getting outside for a spell. Here we are, mid-winter in sunny Tenerife, and I've been indoors all day.'

'Poor you! I should warn you, though, that it might be too hot for you, coming from Risky Point.'

'And then Northumberland! I haven't told you what it was like there yet, have I?'

CHAPTER SEVENTY-THREE

Junior was perplexed. He was also angry, raging mad, in fact. Mulling things over, he didn't know what the hell he was going to do.

He knew now that much of what Doy had told him was true. Francine wasn't married to Mack, and never had been. And George had confirmed that he'd known that all along. He'd even laughed about it, as if it was the funniest thing he'd ever heard.

That changed things. Doy was right. Francine wasn't entitled to any of Mack's money, and killing the kid wouldn't mean the family inherited it. Also, so far, they hadn't been able to persuade him to give it up voluntarily. He hadn't been interested in the investment opportunity they had offered him, and now they no longer had the hostages to force him to change his mind. And they were running out of time, rapidly.

Doy was right about something else, as well. He'd lost control of the situation. He didn't even know where his own men were right now, never mind Mack. The lads who were supposed to be guarding the hostages had disappeared, along with the hostages. And those keeping an eye on the damned farm had vanished as well.

That brought him up hard against the cause of all his troubles. George, and his bloody hotel! Doy was right about all that, as well, damn him. If it wasn't for the hotel project they wouldn't be in this situation. He swore savagely under his breath. Then he swore again, out loud, in a long, rollicking tirade.

When he got his breath back, he decided the old man must be losing his marbles. He just couldn't see what his obsession was doing to the business. And they were doing all this, and putting themselves in trouble in the UK, just because George couldn't or wouldn't see sense. It was stupid. No other word for it. By the time George stepped aside, leaving him to run the business, there wouldn't be much of it left to run. Maybe nothing.

He'd been here before, but now he began to think the once unthinkable. He began to wonder if Doy was also right about it being time for him to take some action. Maybe he should tell George to quit and move aside, or else . . .

Or else what, though? He grimaced. Realistically, what could he do? Threaten to quit himself, and leave Tenerife and the Family? Or arrange an accident for George, like Doy had suggested? Promise Joey he would get his dad out of Belmarsh, and tell him to have a look at George's car, with that in mind?

An accident wouldn't have to be terminal, like Ed Davey's had been. But it needed to be enough to require George to take a long convalescence, and get him used to retirement.

He sighed dispiritedly. No, he didn't really think that would do it. The old man was a lion. A few bangs and scrapes wouldn't set him back much. As for something more permanent, well, that wouldn't go down well with the Family. They would know what had happened, and they wouldn't like it.

All the same, like him, they had to think about the future of the business, and their own futures. That would have to come into it. So who could really tell what they would think if something happened to George?

Then there was Oscar, of course. Whose side would Oscar be on if he moved against George? Would he bury the hatchet with his brother and work to settle things down, or would he be happy to help the Family turn on to a new page?

Junior gave a rueful smile. Once you identified the question, you didn't need to be a genius, or wait long for the answer. You already knew what it would be. Oscar would move to take over Reagan Enterprises himself.

It didn't help when Eddie, his main man in Rosedale, called to say they were all OK, and he shouldn't worry about them. As if he would!

'What do you mean, OK? You're supposed to be here, and you're not. What's going on?'

'That fucking Doy. That's what's going on! He got the jump on us and took the hostages.'

'How could one man take on the four of you?'

'He wasn't on his own.'

'How many of them were there?'

After a pause, Eddie said, 'Two. Him and a woman.'

'Two? And one a woman?'

'She had a shotgun.'

'A shotgun?' Junior rolled his eyes in disbelief. 'And you couldn't do anything about it — like shoot her?'

'Like I said, they got the jump on us. They locked us in the cellar and it took us all night to break our way out.'

It was getting worse and worse. Junior closed his eyes and took a couple of deep breaths before he allowed himself to speak again.

'So what now? Where the fuck are you? The cars are still here!'

'Doy took the keys and ripped the wires out of the cars. We couldn't fix them. Not straight away. And we had to get out of there fast. So we're on the A19 now, I think, heading for Essex.'

'Essex? What for?'

'To get help. We'll see Martin's dad there. We've got nothing. Doy took everything we had — passports, wallets, phones — the whole lot.'

'So you're walking down the A19, are you? That what you're doing?'

'No. We've nicked a couple of cars along the way. This one has a phone in it, which is how I'm able to call you to let you know what we're doing.'

'You're not doing that,' Junior snapped. 'No way are you going to Essex. You're going to turn that car round and get yourselves back here — now!'

'We can't . . .'

'Do it!'

'Reception's real bad now, Junior. I can't hear a thing you're saying hardly. I'll call again when we're in a better area.'

'Don't bother!' Junior said under his breath after the call was ended. *'And don't ever go back to Tenerife again, either!'*

But suddenly, things slotted into place. He knew exactly what he had to do.

'Right, you two,' he said, turning to Joey and Seamus. 'Get your stuff together. We're going back to Puerto.'

'Now?' Joey said.

'Right now. We're done here.'

'Good! Hear that, Seamus?'

'I heard. And I'm ready to go already.'

'When we get there,' Junior added, 'There's going to be some changes. I've had enough of following orders.'

Joey looked speculatively at him. 'Does that mean . . . ?'

'It means what I said, Joey. And when we get there, there's a special job I want you to do.'

'What's that, Junior?'

'There's no time to go into it now. But it's nothing you've not done before, using all your skills. I'll tell you about it on the way there. Now, let's go!'

CHAPTER SEVENTY-FOUR

It was actually very pleasant outdoors. Warm and dry. Definitely not hot or wet. And with a refreshing, gentle breeze, rather than the raging wind I could still recall from my night on the Cheviot Hills. The only downside was that it was dark now. Night comes early everywhere in November.

Emma led the way across a cobbled square, past a huge, handsome church and into a succession of narrow streets with small shops and little commercial premises.

'You've been here before,' I suggested.

'Oh, yes.' Emma smiled. 'I wasn't on holiday either. But it was still a fun place to be for a time.'

Something to do with the wars against drugs, illegal immigration or terrorism, I guessed, but I wasn't going to ask. I had enough to think and worry about.

'How far to go?' I asked as we reached and turned onto a palm-lined, illuminated *avenida*.

'Ten minutes. Think you can manage that?'

'Just about.'

It was a beautiful place. No doubt about it. The sea hissed and rumbled somewhere behind us. Off to our left, lights from buildings showed high up on towering cliffs. A gentle breeze shivered the palm trees we walked beneath. There were stone planters containing cacti and festooned with exotic tropical creepers at intervals along the walkway. I saw them, but had too much on my mind to pay them much attention. A lot depended on what we could accomplish in the here and now. Perhaps everything, so far as Jason Mack was concerned.

* * *

George Reagan lived in a house on the steep slope of a wooded ravine inside the city. He had built it when business was booming, and it had cost him over twenty million euros. For that much money, he could have built his house on a cliff top overlooking the ocean, as his late accountant had done, but for one thing. George didn't really like the ocean.

He never had done. Oceans and seas were inconveniences that separated pieces of land. Just looking at the Atlantic made him feel seasick. So he chose to live slightly inland, and was more than happy to do so. From his house, he could keep an eye on the city and hear and feel its pulse, as well as watch progress on the construction of his new hotel. There was nothing to bother him, let alone make him feel seasick.

He didn't even mind having neighbours. If they wanted to watch and envy him and his guests, that was up to them. And when he got tired of them, or didn't want people watching any more, all he had to do was go indoors and press the button that darkened the armoured glass in the windows, glass that could ultimately make the windows absolutely impermeable to light as well as to bullets. Sometimes, a man just wanted a little privacy.

The house had air con, of course, like all modern houses, but George didn't like overusing it. The reason had nothing at all to do with saving the planet. It had everything to do with the fact that air conditioning tended to give him a sore throat. So usually he preferred to open windows and have a natural current of air blowing through the house. The air con he reserved for times when he, or Tenerife, was insufferably hot.

So that was why on this particular evening George was standing by the open patio door leading on to the balcony of the top floor of his six-storey house, savouring a cold beer, admiring the view and listening to the comfortable sound of light traffic on the streets below. Absolute perfection, he thought with an appreciative smile. There was nowhere on earth where he would rather be.

It was just such a pity that Linda didn't fancy it, he thought with a sigh. But he couldn't blame her. And there was absolutely nothing he could do about it.

Just then his phone buzzed.

'Enjoying your beer, George? You might as well, while it lasts. How about we meet and talk about . . . ?'

Angrily, George glanced at the number, switched the phone off and rammed it back into his pocket. That bloody Doy! What the hell was Junior doing? He should have shut his mouth by now.

He picked up his glass of beer again, ready to savour its cool compensation, and then gave a yelp of astonishment as it shattered before his eyes. Shards of glass sparkled in the light from the terrace lanterns and beer cascaded over his hand and wrist, and washed down his lower arm. George dropped the base of the glass, which was all that was left of it, turned and scurried off the balcony and back into the safety of the house.

* * *

'Nice one, Emma!' I purred with satisfaction.

'A couple more shots, perhaps?' she asked wistfully.

'Why not? Might as well.'

I watched as she changed to heavier gauge ammo in order to cope with what was probably armoured glass.

'Not armoured enough,' I said, with even more satisfaction, as we studied the aftermath of a few more shots from Emma's rifle.

They had brought down a number of very big windows in George's house in sheets of fractured glass. Minutes later, we could still hear the tinkle of falling glass fragments.

'I'm happy with that,' Emma said with satisfaction. 'It's something for him to think about.'

I nodded and gave her a grin.

'Come on!' I said. 'Let's get out of here before he works out what happened.'

CHAPTER SEVENTY-FIVE

'Have you spoken to your sister yet?'

'None of your business.'

So he had. I winked at Emma.

'What did she say?'

'Unless you've got something significant to tell me, Doy, why don't you just fuck off?'

'Come on, Junior! I'm trying to help you out here. I take it Francine confirmed what I told you?'

I heard, or imagined, a big sigh. It was followed by: 'What difference does it make?'

'A lot. Murdering Jason Mack really would make no sense now, would it, now we've established that fact? Yet George still wants you to go ahead and do it — and take the blame for it!'

'What do you mean by that?' he asked, bristling.

'A lot of people know by now that you are in the country hunting Jason, and they also know what you've been doing to try to accomplish it. Once some of us tell the cops what we know, how easy do you think it's going to be for you to avoid their attention? You won't even be able to get out of the UK, let alone get back into Tenerife!'

'You don't know what you're talking about.'

'Don't I? I think you know by now that I do. But OK. Let's move on. Have you talked to George since you and I last spoke?'

'None of your damned business.'

Meaning that he had.

'Has anything changed?'

'Only that you're in even worse trouble, Doy.'

'I really don't think so, Junior. George is, though. Did he tell you what happened at his house?'

'What are you talking about now?'

'Talk to him again, Junior. Ask him how many bullet-proof windows his house has lost. And think about this. He lost a glass of beer, but it could just as easily have been his head. And it might come to that, if things don't change. George is in big trouble. If I were you, Junior, I would put him in the expendable category.

'However, unlike you, I'm not interested in protecting the family business. In fact, I'm enjoying seeing George set out to ruin it. I wish him every success.'

'Fuck you, Doy!'

* * *

'That seems to have got him wound up nicely,' I said with satisfaction. 'Guess who he's going to call next?'

'His dad, I reckon.'

'So do I.'

'It would be nice to be a fly on the wall,' Emma said wistfully.

CHAPTER SEVENTY-SIX

Notwithstanding the brush-off he'd given me the previous time we'd spoken, I called Oscar again, and he agreed to meet me at his place, Oscar's, the day after Emma had hit George's house. Perhaps he'd had second thoughts. Either that or he admired my perseverance. Something. Anyway, we met the next day, the Sunday, in the early evening.

Oscar Reagan was a very suave looking man, well-dressed in expensive casual clothes. He looked like what he was, the owner of a chic, upmarket restaurant in the centre of a prosperous Spanish town. Oscar's was definitely not a bar, whatever Henry believed it to be.

I glanced admiringly around at the ornate mahogany panelling and the wonderfully intricate ceramic flooring, all done in a traditional style that would be hard to get now without paying an awful lot of money.

'Nice place,' I said.

'Thank you,' Oscar said with a polite smile, inclining his head.

"Gangster smug" was how he struck me.

'You wished to see me,' he said. 'What can I do for you, Mr Doy?'

The bonhomie was fading fast, but I wasn't sorry to get down to business. Nor was I inclined to go easy on him.

'I want you to help me prevent my client being murdered.'

He stared at me for a moment, and then said, 'You do realize you might have taken your own life in your hands coming here? We Reagans are a tough lot. Always have been.'

'I believe I'm safe enough,' I said with a smile. 'I'm not alone, despite appearances. Besides, you're a smart man, and this is a smart restaurant.'

He looked around ostentatiously for my back-up team, failing to notice the young woman dining alone not far from where we were seated.

We were meeting in the actual restaurant rather than the private office he had first suggested. There was no way I would have met any of the Reagans anywhere but a public space.

'Will you have a drink?' he asked.

'A beer, please.'

He signalled a waiter and ordered a couple of beers. They came swiftly, and when they did I exchanged glasses — just in case.

Oscar smiled. 'You're a cautious man, Mr Doy.'

I nodded. 'Like you, Mr Reagan. You wouldn't have survived this long in opposition to your brother if you were not.'

The fencing continued a little longer. I sensed that he was quite enjoying our meeting, perhaps because he was intrigued and curious to hear what I knew, as well as what I wanted.

'My brother is upset,' he said, bringing the sparring to an end. 'Apparently, somebody shot out the windows in his house the other night, and very nearly did for him as well.'

'Oh dear. Perhaps he was too complacent about things, and thought the unpleasantness he visits on other people could never come to his door. Could that be it, do you think?'

'Perhaps you're right, but I don't really know. He and I don't have much to do with one another these days. This place is my business, and I stick to it. George looks after his business.'

'The Family business?'

He nodded. Staring hard at me now, he said, 'I don't have any influence over my brother. You're wasting your time, coming to see me about your problem. Young Mr Mack's problem, that is.'

I shook my head. 'I hope not. I've got nowhere with George, and nowhere with Junior, either. But there has to be someone in the Reagan family who can see sense. As I've already said, I'm hoping it might be you.'

'You've approached Junior?'

'We've had several conversations. He seems intent on carrying out his orders, however little sense they make. As I've already told you, Jason and Francine were never married. So there's no point killing him. Francine won't inherit anything if they do.

'Also, the hostages that were supposed to give Junior leverage with Jason have been rescued and, like him, taken to a place of safety. And the men holding the hostages have themselves been taken prisoner, while those stationed at the farm Jason intends buying have been scattered.

'So, all in all, Junior's execution of George's plan has been a disaster, and now Junior is a general in the field without an army. It's time to call it a day, and bring them back here to get on with their lives.

'Then, I would suggest, Reagan Enterprises should just walk away from the hotel project. It's threatening the entire family business. Actually, if they wait until midday tomorrow, they won't need to do anything. The project will be forfeit anyway. Do I make sense?'

'Indeed you do. I couldn't agree more.'

'Good.'

I was beginning to warm to Oscar, and to think I might be able to do business with him. Compared with the other Reagans I'd met and spoken to, he seemed like a rational human being. It made a change.

'But there is still the question I asked at the start,' Oscar said. 'What do you think I can possibly do about all this?'

I sidestepped the question. It was too blunt. At least, the answer would be.

'As I understand it,' I said briskly, 'Junior is the heir apparent when it comes to the family business. He's supposed to take over when old George decides he's had enough, pops his clogs or when the rest of the family decide they're tired of him. Is that right?'

'Pretty much. I have to say, though, that old George, as you referred to him, is in excellent health and still tall in the saddle. It would take a brave man to challenge him.'

'Maybe. But ill health and accidents can happen to the best of us, can't they? From what I hear, George was pretty lucky to survive last night's attack. And there but for the grace of . . .'

Oscar studied me a little more intently.

'Do you mean to say,' he began, 'that . . .'

'Oh, no! Of course not. But things do happen, don't they?'

'Indeed they do.'

'And while we're being frank and honest with one another, Oscar, I'll tell you this much. Young Junior might well be a fine, upstanding member of the Reagan family, but he's no George. If he does take over the family business, I shudder to think what will happen to it. Bankruptcy and devastation, probably.'

'Well, that's not likely to happen any time soon, is it?'

'I wouldn't be so sure of that. What I hear is that Junior is pretty much fed up with his dad's obsession about the hotel project. He's got sense enough to know it's ruining things for the whole family, and he's considering what can be done about it.

'My guess — and that's all it is — is that Junior is set to oust George and take over himself before very much longer.'

'Really? How interesting.'

'Perhaps in the next few days,' I added. 'Unless, that is, someone else has ideas, and ambitions, of his own.'

Oscar seemed amused. 'Well, that wouldn't be me, if that's where you're going with this. My brother can continue managing the Family business forevermore, so far as I'm concerned. Or Junior can, for that matter.

'I don't envy them at all. The only thing of George's that I have ever coveted,' he added with a chuckle, 'is his Ferrari. That, I have to say, is all that makes me jealous of my brother.'

'Buy one just like it?' I suggested.

He shook his head and looked at me sorrowfully, as if he was disappointed I didn't understand. 'That, Mr Doy, would be akin to cheating.'

I shrugged. Gangster ethics and philosophy didn't amount to much for me.

'That aside, Mr Doy, let me say you seem to know a great deal about our family business. But what makes you believe Junior is gathering himself to make a play now?'

'He's been given an unplayable hand. He has to find ten million in sterling for George by tomorrow, and he's not going to be able to do it. That means George's debtors will move in to take over the hotel project.'

'The Italians?'

'Right. And at that point, he believes George will go bananas and launch a street war to try to prevent the take-over. Junior doesn't want any part of that. Perhaps with a heavy heart, he'll tell George his time is up, and he has to go for the sake of the family.'

'And if George just tells him to fuck off?'

'Well, accidents do happen, don't they? Just consider what happened to poor old Ed Davey, the family accountant of many years standing, when he felt it necessary to tell George facts that he didn't like.'

I left it there. We talked a little longer, and Oscar said he would think things through and get back to me at the hotel. Then I made my excuses and departed. As I went, I exchanged glances with the solitary young woman diner, who was removing an ear bud and signalling for her bill. She hadn't been needed.

CHAPTER SEVENTY-SEVEN

Back at our hotel, we chewed over the meeting with Oscar, and what we had learned about him. I took a couple of little bottles of water from the mini bar. I would have preferred coffee, but, as usual in my experience of Spanish hotels, we had no means of making it.

'So,' Emma said as she twisted and removed the tops from the bottles, 'the impression you're giving me is that you want to throw in our lot with Oscar. Is that right?'

'Well, not in those words, perhaps. But, basically, yes I do. I think he's the best of a bad bunch.'

'And you'd like to see him take over and run the family business?'

I grimaced and said, 'If Reagan Enterprises still exists, then yes.'

'Why?'

Her questions were giving me the opportunity to put into words the thoughts and ideas that had been flashing through my mind since talking to Oscar. I welcomed that. It had to be done.

'First and foremost, he's had nothing to do with the vendetta against Jason, and may not approve of it. So, with him in charge, that would probably come to an end. That's why we came here, remember — to find a way of guaranteeing Jason's security in future?'

'True. What else?'

'With either George or Junior running the family business, Jason would remain at risk. Whether they continued to pursue him for the money or for reasons to do with ideas of family honour, or sheer spite, he would never be free of the threat.'

Emma considered that and eventually gave seemingly reluctant agreement.

'Something else in Oscar's favour is that he has nothing to do with his brother or with the running of the Family business. He appears to have stepped away from the inner circle of the family and got on with his own life, and with running his own business. That restaurant looks like a success story to me, and it's a legal and legitimate business.

'So I take my hat off to him. Probably he started off in the Family's criminal rackets, but he's come a long way since then, and I don't think he would go back to them.'

After a pause for reflection, Emma said, 'But can you really trust him?'

I smiled. 'The million-dollar question! I wish I could say yes without prevarication, but you know I can't. All I can really say for sure is that Oscar seems the best option we're likely to find for bringing this thing to a close and letting Jason get on with his life.'

'Fair enough. So now he's going to think it over and get back to you about what he can do?'

'Yes.'

'How's he going to make contact?'

'He has my number, and he knows we're staying here.'

'You told him?'

I nodded.

She grimaced, stared at me and said quietly, 'You shouldn't have done that, Frank.'

CHAPTER SEVENTY-EIGHT

I must have reached out for Emma in my sleep. She wasn't there, and that was what woke me up. I rolled on to my back, taut as a fully stretched spring and listened intently, relaxing only when I heard the gentle hiss of the toilet flushing behind the closed bathroom door.

I yawned with relief, relaxed and settled back down. For a moment.

Only for a moment because then there was a crash and the room was flooded with light. I jerked up. Three men were entering the room, all carrying guns.

'Gotcha!' one said with satisfaction.

That was Junior. I recognized the voice, even though it hadn't said much.

I swung round and put my feet on the floor, but made no attempt to stand up. It would have been pointless.

'What do you want?' I demanded.

Junior chuckled. 'As if you didn't know! I wanted to meet you face to face, Doy.'

'Yeah? Well, now you've done that. So you can get back out of here and let me get some sleep. Your father and uncle have just about worn me out. I don't envy you, having to deal with them every day.

'By the way, have you decided yet whether to make your play for George's job? You need to get a move on. Time's not on your side, not when Oscar's preparing a bid of his own.'

Anything! Talk about anything, I was thinking. *Just keep it going. Give yourself a chance to do something.*

Junior was at the foot of the bed, a pistol aimed at me. His men were stationed to each side of the bed, and were also carrying guns. I couldn't reach Junior, but I was weighing up my chances of reaching the guy on my side of the bed before he or Junior could pull the trigger. They weren't good.

They weren't good for Emma either. I just hoped she stayed where she was and kept quiet. They didn't know about her. There was a chance, a small one, that it might stay that way.

'Where's the kid?' Junior demanded.

'Who?'

'The Mack kid. Where is he?'

I shook my head. 'Somewhere in the UK. I don't know exactly where. I left him to it when I came to see your old man. Look, this has to stop, Junior. You know that, don't you?

'I've explained the situation to you. Nothing has changed, except tomorrow is nearly here. When it's over, the hotel will be gone. And so will George be, I hope. It will be your time, Junior. Or it could be, if you move.'

'Seamus,' Junior said, nodding at the guy on my side of the bed, who leaned over and tapped me hard with his gun.

'Damn! That hurt. What was that for?' I protested.

'Quit stalling,' Junior said. 'You know where the kid is, Doy. You'd better tell me before you really start to hurt.'

'No idea,' I said, shaking my head. 'You'll just have to look for him. How did you find me, by the way?'

'You shouldn't have gone to my uncle behind my back. Thought you were being clever, trying to set him up against me, eh?'

'Oscar told you?'

'We're working together now, Oscar and me. We both know George has to be stopped, or persuaded to retire, before he ruins things. You were right about that, at least.'

I grimaced. Colluding with Oscar, eh? I should have known better. Emma's instincts were better than mine.

'Well, good luck with that, Junior,' I said, trying to sound pleasant about it. 'What's the plan?'

'The plan is to get you to tell me where you've stashed the kid.'

'You're going to beat it out of me, are you? That the plan? Well, good luck with that, as well.'

Junior nodded at the man nearest to me again. He leaned forward. It was the moment I'd been waiting for. Now or never. If nothing else, I was determined to go down fighting.

I hurled myself forward, reaching for his gun arm with both hands. Someone yelled. I forced the gun towards the ceiling. He tried to knee me and use his body strength to weigh me down. I pulled him on top of me. There was a gunshot, and he went limp. I held him close, using his body as a shield, and pulled the gun out of his hand.

Junior's other man was in my line of sight and looking to get a shot at me. I shot him before he could. He staggered, flailing around with his arms. By then, though, Junior had moved sideways and had me cold. I knew it even as I started to swing round. It was too late.

But the bathroom door flew open and crashed against the wall. Junior automatically swung round to face it, reflexes overpowering reason. He must have caught a glimpse of Emma standing naked in the doorway, and perhaps that even slowed him down. But it cost him.

Emma fired twice. Then again. Junior went down.

I rolled the body of the first man off me and struggled to my feet. But it was over by then. Emma was the only other person still standing.

CHAPTER SEVENTY-NINE

We needed to talk, but even more, we needed to get out of there fast. I expected more of Junior's men arriving imminently.

Emma helped me drag a heavy bureau in front of the door to the room. It wouldn't stop anyone getting in, but it would slow them down for a while. We needed that.

Leaving the bodies where they had fallen, we pulled on clothes, grabbed our packs and headed for the window. This was an old hotel, and nothing like the streamlined, sleek, contemporary buildings erected for modern tourists. The external walls were festooned with ornate balconies, ledges, pipework, and little walkways for window cleaners and maintenance men. I knew we didn't have to worry about whether or not we could get down from the window. It was just a matter of which way to go.

Our room was on the second floor. By climbing down between the ends of balconies, using a variety of handholds and footholds, we made it to the pavement in three or four minutes. We found ourselves on a side street, well away from the entrance to the hotel, and there was no one about to see us slip away into the shadows.

After a few blocks of brisk walking, we entered a small park and sat on a wooden bench in early morning light to draw breath and talk about what had happened and what to do next. We were surrounded by cacti of all shapes and sizes, and shadowed by enormous palms that looked as if they had been there forever. On another day, at another time, we could have relaxed and enjoyed the moment of stillness and tranquillity.

'Bloody Oscar!' I said, anguished by my misjudgement, but not much bothered by the bodies left behind. Junior and his men had lived by the sword and died by it.

'I got him wrong, didn't I?'

Emma nodded.

'Thanks, by the way. Until you appeared, it looked like I was going down.'

'You were managing pretty well, I thought.'

I shook my head. 'Junior had a clear shot at me. He just wasn't quick enough to take it. I could see what was going to happen, but I couldn't do anything about it.'

'Maybe.'

'What was a gun doing in the bathroom, by the way?'

'It was there for emergencies.'

'Field experience, eh? Iraq?'

'And Afghanistan. You couldn't afford not to have a weapon with you when you went to the loo.'

'Some life you used to lead!' I said, with a grin. 'Nothing like now, was it?'

'Not much, no.'

No smile on her face or in her voice. So I didn't pursue it. Some things are better not laboured.

'What now?' I said, moving on. 'Part of me feels that we should head fast for the airport and hope to put Tenerife behind us as soon as we can.'

'But?'

'But we've got unfinished business here. Jason's still at risk, and either George or Oscar will still be running the

Reagan family business empire. I'm not leaving while it's like that.'

'Which one of them will it be, I wonder?' Emma asked. 'George still, or Oscar now?'

I shook my head. 'It's not going to be Junior, anyway. That's one thing we can be sure of.'

'Come on,' I added, getting to my feet. 'There's some traffic and a few people about. Let's see if we can find somewhere to get a cup of coffee.'

* * *

A steamy little café was doing a good trade with the early, very early, morning trade. The customers were definitely not holidaymakers at that pre-dawn hour. They looked like a mixture of people coming off their night shift in hotels and hospitals and the folks you get everywhere who start their work while most of us are still in bed, people who need strong coffee and sometimes something from a spirit bottle as well to set them up for the day and get them going.

I found a table and left Emma to order us something at the counter. Her Spanish was really good, and soon she was fast-talking locals in the queue, and even making them laugh. Of course she was, I thought with a smile. She had been a linguist once, originally, which was why the Army had drafted her into the special forces at a time when they didn't take women. I couldn't remember what she had said about her languages, apart from Arabic, but there had been quite a few in the list. She was pretty good with weapons, too, I thought wryly. A true Amazon!

She brought mugs of espresso and the Spanish equivalent of Belgian Buns back to the table. It wasn't a time for me to be eating a meal, but it was definitely time for us to be getting some nutrition into us. We'd had a hell of a night, and were not out of trouble yet.

Meanwhile, though, we were in a comfort zone. The espresso machine hissed. There was the buzz of lively conversation all around us. People eating and drinking. We were not in immediate danger. The coffee was good. And I was calming down, the adrenaline fading, my pulse rate nearing normal.

'What next?' Emma queried. 'I know we can't talk in here, but give me a clue.'

'Oscar,' I said. 'I'm going to call him. I must.'

CHAPTER EIGHTY

'I didn't expect to hear from you again, Mr Doy.'

'Why am I not surprised? I was mistaken about you, Oscar. You're just as bad as the rest of the Reagans. I had hoped I'd found some good in the family, but sadly, I hadn't.'

Laughter greeted that observation.

'You should leave here, Doy, while you still can.'

'Is that a threat?'

'No. Just a kindly suggestion. How is my nephew, by the way?'

'Who?'

'Junior, to you.'

'Oh, him! Well, sadly, I'm afraid you won't be hearing from him again. Nobody will.'

'Why's that?'

'He passed away.'

After a pause, I heard: 'Like that, is it?'

'Indeed it is. And it's down to you, Oscar. You should never have sent a boy to do a man's work. I shall make that point to George when I see him.'

'And the men with Junior?'

I didn't bother replying.

'My best advice now, Doy, is that you should leave here as fast as you possibly can — if you can. Plenty of people will be very upset.'

'Well-meant advice, I'm sure,' I said, before ending the call.

'That went well,' I said to Emma, feeling uplifted and satisfied. 'Now for George.'

* * *

It went better than I had expected. Mind you, I didn't tell him that his son had expired while trying to kill me. That might have made a difference.

'Ah, yes! Frank Doy,' he said. 'I'm glad you've called. I've been meaning to contact you.'

But probably hadn't had the time, I thought, what with dealing with glaziers, the Mafia people come to take over his new hotel and trying to keep the lid on an incipient palace revolution. Who'd be a crime boss, eh?

'You've reconsidered?' I asked.

'Yes. I have. I would like us to meet. We have several mutual interests, I believe. Perhaps you could come over to my home and join me in the garden for a drink? I have to say the flowers are looking at their best, and I'm sure that as a winter visitor from the UK, you'll appreciate them even more than I do myself.'

'I would be happy to do that, George. What time today would be convenient?'

'Early afternoon? Two o'clock, say?'

'Perfect.'

* * *

I grinned at Emma. 'Which public school would you think he attended, or has he taken elocution lessons?'

'Certainly a different conversation to your previous attempts, wasn't it?'

I nodded. 'There must be something he wants, very badly.'

'You, perhaps?'

'Could be.'

'What do you want from him?'

'First and foremost, I want to spell out the facts of life for him. All that stuff about his daughter never being married to Jason, and therefore entitled to nothing. Plus, I want to tell him that Jason is well out of Junior's sight, and anyway he's not prepared to hand over ten million quid either voluntarily or under duress. I might even tell him how and why Junior's mission in the UK has failed.'

'But not that Junior is no more?'

I grimaced. 'No. And I'm just going to have to hope he hasn't heard. How likely is that, do you think?'

'Hard to say.'

Indeed it was. But not very likely, probably.

'By now,' I added, 'the hotel will have brought in the police. But that doesn't mean they know yet who the bodies are.'

'The fact that they have been found — if they have — in a room that visiting holidaymakers were occupying might slow things down?' Emma suggested. 'The police will be trying to work out what they're dealing with. A drugs gang war, perhaps?'

I nodded. 'They'll also be looking for us. And possibly wondering if they're going to find us alive. All good reason for them to want to keep the information lid on for a bit longer.'

'So we need to see George, and then get the hell out before our departures from Tenerife are blocked?'

'I couldn't agree more, if it were not for one thing.'

'What's that?'

'I don't want to leave without bringing George and Oscar down. The rest of the Reagans don't seem to amount to much. But bring the leaders in the family down, and Reagan Enterprises will be as good as finished.'

Emma nodded. 'It's a big agenda. We'd better get going.'

Once again, all I could do was agree with her.

CHAPTER EIGHTY-ONE

We set off in good time to set Emma up in a position over-looking the garden of George's house. That wasn't easy. His garden, with its trees and shrubbery, was a lot harder a prop-osition than the upper storeys of the house had been. Some parts of it were actually not visible at all from any vantage point that we could find. Eventually, we had to compromise and settle high on the side of the ravine where the house was located for a view overlooking table and chairs on the patio beside the house.

Emma wasn't happy. 'It means we have to assume there isn't somewhere else he could take you that has a table and chairs. If there is, I can't cover you.'

'True. But I don't think he'll do that. He'll want to stay close to the house.'

'You hope!'

I grinned. 'Come on! This whole thing's a risk, and has been from the start. What's wrong with a bit more?'

She shrugged. 'I'll just have to do the best I can.'

'Which I am certain will be very good.'

'Flattery isn't going to cut it,' she snapped. Then she lightened up and added, 'But getting me a ride in that car might.'

She was pointing to the open-topped, red sports car standing in the parking area, next to a huge SUV.

'What is it?' I asked, peering hard. 'I only know Land Rovers. A Lamborghini?'

She shook her head. 'Ferrari. One of my clients in Dubai had that model. I used to get to drive it from time to time, because she wasn't allowed to.'

'Being a woman?'

'Being a woman.'

'So how did you qualify?'

'Oh, they didn't count me as a woman. I was just an alien. They weren't concerned about me.'

'Nice people.'

'They were, actually, apart from in that respect.'

'I can see why you left,' I said with a grin. 'Come on, let's go!'

* * *

I wondered why George had changed his tune. Shooting out his windows might well have brought home to him that he wasn't invulnerable, which had been the idea in the first place, but I couldn't afford to let myself think that that was all it was when it might not have bothered him very much at all. What else could it be? Hard to know, and not worth speculating about.

He might, by now, have learned about the death of Junior, which he hadn't known this morning when I called him, and be wanting to lure me close so he could exact revenge. That needed to be configured in, but how? I just had to shrug. Too many unknowns.

Emma hired a nifty little Fiat 500 for us to run about in, and after confirming our arrangements and dropping her off I drove up to George's house in it and parked outside on the street. Two men I took to be part of George's security team met me at the gate and led me to the house. With appropriate apologies, they patted me down looking for weapons before taking me to their boss, who was seated at the table on the patio.

So far, so good, I couldn't help thinking, but this was still very much a high-risk situation for me. Even Emma keeping vigil wasn't a guarantee that I would leave here alive. But, in the old way of looking at it, nothing risked, nothing gained. I was in too far now to be able to turn my back and walk away.

* * *

George played the genial host perfectly, and gave me an elaborate welcome to his home. If I hadn't known better, I could easily have been persuaded that he meant it. But I did know better. This was one evil man. I wasn't likely to forget that.

'What was it you wanted to talk to me about?' George asked casually when the preliminaries were done. 'Anything urgent?'

Perhaps shooting out his windows had made an impression, then, I couldn't help thinking. Not that I was going to mention it. I was very much aware of being at risk here, and I wanted to keep the conversation civilized. His two security guys were not far away on the other side of the patio, out of hearing range but not out of striking range.

'I want you to end the pursuit of Jason Mack, who I represent. I've been helping him fend off attacks from Junior and his people. Jason and your daughter were never married, and she's not entitled to any of the money he has won.

'Jason isn't prepared to invest his money in your hotel, either, and he can't be coerced into it. Junior doesn't even know where he is right now, and the hostages he took have been released and taken to a safe location. So continued pursuit of Jason would be absolutely futile. I hope you will accept that and bring it all to an end.'

George poured us both another coffee while he considered what I'd just said.

'What is your interest in this matter?' he asked, putting down the heavy silver coffee jug carefully.

'Jason retained me. Security work is what I do for a living, and Jason pays me my standard daily rate.'

'So the longer it goes on,' he said with a smile, 'the more money you make?'

I nodded. 'Put like that, the answer is yes. But I don't want this business to go on any longer, anyway. I've got plenty of other work to do, and my judgement is that I'm not the only one who's had enough of all this. Am I right?'

He cleared his throat and nodded. 'Speaking for myself, yes, you are right. The investment opportunity we offered Mr Mack is no longer available now, since noon today. And, as you say, my daughter is not legally entitled to anything from him, as they were never legally married. Besides, she is properly married now, to a man she met in California. Her husband is well able to provide for her.

'Also, a number of my men are scattered around the UK, it appears, thanks to you. I need them back here. So, yes, you can rest assured. Mr Mack is safe now. You can take that from me.'

It all sounded so good, but I didn't trust him at all. His word meant nothing to me. As things stood, there was no way I could hold him to anything he'd said.

So it was a good thing I had something to hold over him, although he didn't know it yet. Henry had given me what I believed and hoped would prove to be the trump card.

'Now, there's something I need from you,' he said.

Ah! Metaphorically, I sat up straighter. Was this why he was being so agreeable?

'What's that?'

'You seem to know a lot about the Reagan family business, and my role in it.'

'Well, let's just say I know something.'

He nodded. 'For some time, there's been dissent within the family about the wisdom of pursuing the hotel project that I regarded as a priority. I know that. And so, seemingly, do you.

'I would like to know what you can tell me about the opposition within the family, if we can call it that. It may make a difference to how I see my role and future. In particular, I would like to know what my brother, Oscar, and my son, Junior, are up to.

'Tell me what you know, Mr Doy, and you have my word that Jason Mack will no longer be at risk.'

Oh, boy! What a can of worms this meeting was turning out to be. It looked like time to play my trump card.

CHAPTER EIGHTY-TWO

'You've given me your word about Jason Mack,' I said. 'And I'll hold you to that. In return, I will make a promise to you. If you stick to your word, I will say nothing of the family you have somehow managed to keep secret from the world all these years.

'Their existence will only be revealed if anything untoward happens to me or to Jason Mack or any of his family. I have made appropriate legal arrangements for that to happen should it become necessary.'

George seemed absolutely flummoxed. He hadn't seen this coming, and now he stared hard at me with disbelief and anguish. He said nothing. He just waited for me to go on, perhaps dreading what else I would say.

'I'm not making it up,' I assured him. 'I do know about your other family, George. The woman and the two children in Arbroath that you have kept secret, in order to protect, for so long. Your secret will remain safe with me so long as no harm comes to the Mack family or myself. Is that clear?'

It took him a few moments, but then he nodded and said, 'Clear as a bell. And agreed.'

So there was no need for a protracted discussion on the subject. We each knew where we stood.

'So far as your query about Reagan family dissent goes,' I said, moving on, 'you are right. Sections of the family are up in arms about what they see as your legacy project, the hotel, which they believe is undermining the entire family business. Feelings are so strong that both Oscar and Junior have started moving against you.'

'They want me out, as head of Reagan Enterprises?'

This was a great opportunity for me to further stir the unrest, and I didn't hesitate.

'Yes, they do. Out, George. And they don't much mind whether that means your resignation or assassination.'

'It's that bad?'

I nodded. My sympathy was non-existent. So far as I was concerned, they were all as bad as each other.

'People have a lot to lose, and they believe the current financial crisis is likely to crash the whole business.'

'I'll have to do something, then,' he said, after a moment's reflection. 'The hotel project is finished now, anyway. It was taken over by an Italian company when we went into default at 12.00 p.m. today, and I've had to accept that. It's why the investment opportunity offered to your Mr Mack is no longer available.'

Investment opportunity indeed! What a nice way of putting it. Still, it was over, and that was good for Jason. The trump card I'd played was even more of a reassurance for his future.

'By the way,' he said, without his tone changing, 'who killed Junior?'

So he knew!

The question was a tough one to deal with and I hadn't been ready for it. I hadn't expected his composure, either. But I did have to answer him, and I decided to give it him straight.

'He was killed in a struggle in my hotel room, as were the two men he came with to attack me. Things were so hectic it's hard to say who shot whom, but I can tell you this much with certainty: I had no gun with me. I've long believed guns are more trouble than they're worth in the work I do.'

It wasn't a lie, but then again, it wasn't the whole truth either. I felt I deserved a bit of poetic licence.

'Did Oscar send them?'

'I don't know about that, but Junior and Oscar were certainly working together. Junior admitted it.'

'You were lucky,' he said, looking at me thoughtfully. 'Either that or I've underestimated you all along.'

'It didn't feel like luck at the time!' I assured him.

He nodded and added, 'He never was any damn good, Junior. He wouldn't have been up to running the business if he ever had taken it over. I realized that a long time ago.'

'But it suited you to still have him as heir apparent?'

'It did. It kept my dear brother at arm's length. But it should always have been Oscar who was next in line.'

'I have the feeling you didn't care for Junior?'

'No,' he said heavily. 'He wasn't up to much, and I never liked him. In fact, I was never sure he really was my son, even. But given the situation you seem to know about, it suited me not to raise the question with his mother.'

Humph. This was plainer speaking from him than I had anticipated.

'That's all very interesting,' said a new voice on the patio, 'but now it's my turn.'

Both our heads swung round with astonishment.

CHAPTER EIGHTY-THREE

'What the fuck do you want, Oscar?' demanded George, recovering fast. 'How did you get in anyway?'

'George, George, calm yourself! You don't rule the world, you know. You might think you do, but you don't. Not really.

'I came to tell you it's over. I'm tired of your insults and your inadequacy as the head of Reagan Enterprises. I'm taking over.'

'Oh, no you're not!' George bellowed, starting to rise from his chair.

That was when pandemonium, or mayhem, started. I've never been sure how best to use those terms.

A gun appeared in Oscar's hand and he shot his brother. George stopped rising from his chair and fell lifeless to the ground, scattering chair and table, and coffee pot, cups and glasses as he went. Oscar turned towards me with his gun, but in the second or two before that happened, another security guy, one who had come in with him, found himself in the line of fire. Before he could step aside, a rifle bullet whizzed past me and hit him. He sprawled helplessly towards Oscar.

Afterwards, I learned that the bullet that hit the security guy had been fired by Emma, who shot at Oscar to stop him firing at me. At the time, though, I didn't even think about it. Instinct and reflexes took me hurtling backwards to get out of Oscar's line of fire. I fell, and rolled and scrambled into the back porch of the house under the covering fire of rifle bullets thudding and screaming into brickwork and timber.

Once under a roof, I got to my knees, then my feet, and raced through the house, trying to reverse the route taken when I arrived. I had very little sense of what was happening behind me, and even less interest. My priority was to get out of the way as fast as possible.

Inevitably, I suppose, my memory was at fault and I took a wrong turning, ending up at a side entrance to the house instead of the front door. I didn't go back. I kept going and a couple of minutes later managed to reach the parking area at the front of the house.

I was just in time to see the Ferrari passing through the gate. As it turned onto the road outside, I realized that the face that glanced my way was Oscar's. It seemed that it wasn't only George's role as head of family that he'd taken over.

CHAPTER EIGHTY-FOUR

I climbed into the Fiat, got it started and drove away almost as fast as the Ferrari had been moving. No way was I going to hang around in a free-fire zone, especially as an unarmed civilian. My sole object was to get of there, and had been for the past several minutes.

I drove the short distance to the pick-up point agreed in advance with Emma. She wouldn't be there yet, I knew, but she would be safe. I was sure of that. She'd been nowhere near the patio when the bullets were flying. Indeed, most of them had been hers anyway.

While waiting, and keeping an anxious eye out, I tried to process what I had just experienced and what the outcome had been.

First, Oscar had obviously decided his time had come. The cards had fallen in his favour. There had been collusion between him and Junior; they had launched either a joint operation against George, or had agreed that one of them would support the other. My guess was that, however it had been engineered, Oscar would have ended up the sole part-ner. As it happened, he hadn't needed to lift a finger against Junior. We'd done it for him.

Then, once he had momentum, Oscar must have decided on the direct course of action he'd taken against his brother. It looked like George's security guards had either been prepped in advance, or had decided for themselves to go with Oscar when the time came. In any event, Oscar hadn't wasted any time or energy negotiating with his brother. He'd just put a summary end to a regime that wasn't working very well.

I knew now that if it hadn't been for Emma's vigilance, he would have put an end to me too. It was just bad luck for him that his own security guy had got in the way. Anyway, the outcome of his play was that Oscar was now the man. He had even commandeered the previous man's car.

I saw Emma coming and opened the door for her. She slung her stuff onto the back seat and got in.

'You OK?' she asked.

'Thanks to you,' I said, starting the car. 'Pity you couldn't get Oscar.'

'Yeah. He used the dead security guy as a shield and got away round the corner of the house. I don't know where he went after that.'

'I do. He took George's Ferrari and scarpered. I saw him driving off.'

'The cheeky devil! I wanted that car.'

I smiled and shook my head. Then I slowed down and observed the speed limit.

'So the business is all Oscar's now,' Emma said. 'George and Junior both gone.'

'That's how it looks. But there's still time. We haven't finished yet, have we?'

She shook her head. 'Oh, no! Not yet.'

* * *

We needed to slow down and assess things, and to do that we ended up in the little café we had visited very early that morning.

'Still busy,' I pointed out as we went in.

'Yeah. It's a really good business.'

It a was comfortable place to be. At least, I felt comfortable there, amongst people who worked hard and honestly for a living, and did the best they could. My kind of people, even if they did speak a different language.

'Something to eat?' I asked.

Emma shook her head. 'I don't want coffee either.'

'Beer?'

'That's more like it!'

So I got a couple of beers, and we sat in a quiet corner with them and tried to work out where things stood and what we should do about them. One thing on my mind was how Oscar had finally got his brother's car, the one he had had his eye on for some time. Not that I was holding a torch for George, but it seemed like affirmation that there was no justice in the world. Not their part of it, at least.

It just didn't seem right that Oscar had been able to take off like that, having murdered his brother, been instrumental in getting his nephew killed, tried to murder me, got at least one security guard shot dead, and . . . and then taken his late brother's pride and joy, as well.

Then something else I'd thought and said about cars, and the advice I'd freely dispensed, came to mind and I smiled ruefully. If only, I couldn't help thinking!

'What?' Emma said, seeing my expression.

'Oh, nothing. I was just thinking about something else. Let's talk about how we're going to take the fight to Oscar. I don't like the idea of him feeling on top of the world, which he undoubtedly is.'

'After the killings today, you mean?'

'Especially after them.'

'And I don't suppose you trust the local forces of law and order to catch up with him any more than I do?' Emma said with a shrug.

'Less than that, even.'

'I suppose we could hang around until I get a clear shot at him. Or would you consider that unethical?'

'I wouldn't say no in principle, not after all this, but I don't think we can afford to stay in Tenerife very long. The Reagans will have people in law and order on their payroll, like all organized crime syndicates do. We need to get of here for our own protection. I don't want to be shot while "resisting arrest", or whatever the local equivalent is.'

'That's a good point. So what, then?'

'I don't know. I'm working on it,' I said with a rueful smile.

'Ha!'

Just then, there was a sudden lull in the hubbub of conversation around us. The whole café had become quiet. People had stopped whatever they were doing, beer glasses halfway to their lips, card hands laid down, glass drying behind the bar on hold. All eyes and ears seemed to be focused on a little television in a distant corner of the room. A waiter went to it and turned up the volume as a man seated behind a desk appeared on the screen.

'What's happened?' I asked.

Emma shushed me with her finger across her lips and listened intently. I couldn't understand what was being said, even though the volume of the commentary had been turned up, but I could see the screen and I began to understand. A car seemed to have plunged off the road and into a deep ravine, where it had caught fire.

'Who was it?' I whispered.

Emma nodded but held up a finger again, wanting further silence.

A minute or two later people in the café began talking. Some were excited, others subdued.

'A well-known local businessman died today in Puerta de la Cruz, when the Ferrari sports car he was driving failed to slow down for a dangerous bend and leapt into space,' Emma said in a low, portentous voice. 'His name was . . .'

'Oscar Reagan?'

Emma nodded.

She stared at me for a moment. Then she grabbed my arm and squeezed it. 'You knew, didn't you? You expected it! That's why you weren't too bothered about him getting away.'

I shrugged. 'What do you want me to say?'

'What did you do to the car? And when?'

'It wasn't me that did it. That was Junior, or his ace mechanic. They knew what to do. After all, they'd done it once before.'

She considered for a moment and then said, 'But you put him up to it?'

'Let's just say I suggested that he could get rid of George, if he wanted to, the same way that George had had him get rid of the family's accountant.'

Emma laughed. 'What goes around comes around, doesn't it?'

'Indeed it does, sometimes.' I nodded and smiled. 'All three leaders down now,' I added with satisfaction. 'And Reagan Enterprises will be soon, as well. There's nobody to keep it afloat, and there's nothing to keep us here any longer either. Come on! Let's go home.'

We managed to get flights on an unfilled plane and left that same evening. Job done.

THE END

THE JOFFE BOOKS STORY

We began in 2014 when Jasper agreed to publish his mum's much-rejected romance novel and it became a bestseller.

Since then we've grown into the largest independent publisher in the UK. We're extremely proud to publish some of the very best writers in the world, including Joy Ellis, Faith Martin, Caro Ramsay, Helen Forrester, Simon Brett and Robert Goddard. Everyone at Joffe Books loves reading and we never forget that it all begins with the magic of an author telling a story.

We are proud to publish talented first-time authors, as well as established writers whose books we love introducing to a new generation of readers.

We have been shortlisted for Independent Publisher of the Year at the British Book Awards three times, in 2020, 2021 and 2022, and for the Diversity and Inclusivity Award at the Independent Publishing Awards in 2022.

We built this company with your help, and we love to hear from you, so please email us about absolutely anything bookish at feedback@joffebooks.com

If you want to receive free books every Friday and hear about all our new releases, join our mailing list: www.joffebooks.com/contact

And when you tell your friends about us, just remember: it's pronounced Joffe as in coffee or toffee!

ALSO BY DAN LATUS

www.ingramcontent.com/pod-product-compliance
Lightning Source LLC
Chambersburg PA
CBHW032152190626
46814CB00005BA/1965